Music Abbreviations

A Reverse Dictionary

Donald L. Hixon

The Scarecrow Press, Inc.
Lanham, Maryland • Toronto • Oxford
2005

SCARECROW PRESS, INC.

Published in the United States of America
by Scarecrow Press, Inc.
A wholly owned subsidiary of
The Rowman & Littlefield Publishing Group, Inc.
4501 Forbes Boulevard, Suite 200, Lanham, Maryland 20706
www.scarecrowpress.com

PO Box 317
Oxford
OX2 9RU, UK

British Library Cataloguing in Publication Information Available

Library of Congress Cataloging-in-Publication Data
Hixon, Donald L.
  Music abbreviations : a reverse dictionary / Donald L. Hixon.
      p. cm.
  ISBN 0-8108-4834-1 (pbk. : alk. paper)
  1. Music–Abbreviations–Dictionaries. 2. Abbreviations–
Dictionaries. I. Title.
ML100.H45 2005
780'.1'4–dc22   2004021561

CONTENTS

PREFACE

Included in this volume are abbreviations, acronyms, and initialisms for the following:

- musical terms
- monograph and serial titles
- academic degrees
- record labels
- music software and computer programs
- international, national, and regional organizations
- performing groups
- music facsimiles and manuscripts
- notation conventions
- chant designations

This volume focuses on "classical" music, although entries representing jazz and folk music have been included. The volume is divided into two parts. The *first part*, "The Dictionary," is arranged alphabetically by the abbreviation, acronym, or initialism. Following the abbreviation is the full form of the entry being abbreviated. In this volume, the abbreviated entries always begin with a capital letter, regardless of the capitalization conventions of the language involved. The *second part*, "The Reverse Dictionary," is arranged alphabetically by the full form of the entry, followed by the acronym, abbreviation, or initialism.

Because of limitations of space and a desire to avoid unnecessary duplication, the second part of this volume, i.e., "The Reverse Dictionary," includes more extensive information than that found in the "The Dictionary." For instance, associations, organizations, and performing groups identified simultaneously by different languages, *including English*, are entered in "The Dictionary" under the *English* form of name. "The Reverse Dictionary," however, provides entries under *all forms of names* in the variant languages. Similarly, those wishing detail concerning title histories of journals and former and subsequent names of organizations and performing groups are advised to consult "The Reverse Dictionary."

The impetus for this volume was provided by Ann P. Basart, former music reference librarian at the University of California, Berkeley, who graciously provided me with thousands of handwritten cards created during her few quiet moments at the reference desk. While I subsequently expanded upon her work, I wish to publicly extend to Ms. Basart the most heartfelt gratitude for her expertise, generosity, and kind counsel.

General Abbreviations

comp. lang.　computer language
ed.　editor, edition
F　French
Facsim.　facsimile
G　German
I　Italian
instr.　instrument(s)
jl.　journal
L　Latin
ms.　manuscript
nota.　notation
perc.　percussion
proc.　processing
publ.　publisher
rec. lab.　record label
Sp　Spanish

THE DICTIONARY

I tonic

1^{ma,},1mo, 1° *prima, primo*

2da, 2do, 2° *seconda, secondo*

II supertonic (Roman numeral)

III mediant

3° trio

IV subdominant (Roman numeral)

4^{tet}, 4^{tte} quartet

V dominant (Roman numeral)

5. *quinto, quintus* (part, voice)

5^a *quinta pars*

5^{tet}, 5^{tte} quintet

5-v, five voices or parts

VI submediant (Roman numeral)

6. *sesto*

6^a *sexta pars*

6^{tet} , 6^{tte} sextet, *sestet*

VII subtonic, leading tone (Roman numeral)

7. *settimo*

7^a *septima pars*

7^{tt} *septet*

8. *ottavo* (I=octave)

8^a, 8va *ottava* (I=octave)

8va alta *ottava alta*

8va bassa *ottava bassa*

8° *octavo* (L=eighth)

19th-c.M. *Nineteenth-Century Music* (jl.)

45s 45-rpm recordings

78s 78-rpm recordings

A aggregate (vertical combination of pitches); *alto*; *Antiphonale sacrosanctae romanae ecclesiae pro diurnis horis*; *arco* (I=bow)

A. *altus*

a 4 for 4 (voices)

A.a. *appena aperta* (I=[mouth] slightly open)

AA Authors' Agency of the Polish Music Publishers

AAA American Accordionists' Association; Associated Audio Archives

AACM Association for the Advancement of Creative Music

AACO Associate of the Canadian College of Organists

AAGO Associate, American Guild of Organists

AAM Association of Anglican Musicians; Austrian Association for Musicology

AAMOA Afro-American Music Opportunities Association

AAMS African-American Music Society; American Accordion Musicological Society

AAMT American Association for Music Therapy

AATS American Academy of Teachers of Singing

Ab *armonica a bocca* (I=harmonica)

AB bipartite form, binary form

ABA American Bandmasters Association; tripartite form

ABCBA arch form

ABF American Bach Foundation; American Banjo Fraternity;

American Boychoir Federation

ABM   Association for British Music

ABOF   American Berlin Opera Foundation

About   *About Time* (rec. lab.)

ABPT   Association of Blind Piano Tuners

ABS   American Beethoven Society

ABSM   Associate of the Birmingham School of Music (now,
   Birmingham Conservatoire, part of the University of Central
England
   in Birmingham)

Abt., Abth., Abtlg.   *Abtheilung* (G=part, section, division)

Ac   *Accent* (rec. lab.)

Ac.   acoustic(s) / *acoustique* (F) / *acustica* (I) / *acústica* (Sp)

A capp.   *a cappella*

AC   *Accent on Worship, Music, and the Arts* (jl.)

ACA   American Composers' Alliance

ACA-CFE   American Composers' Alliance. Composers' Facsimile
   Edition

ACB   Association of Concert Bands

ACBH   Association of Composers of Bosnia and Herzegovina

ACBM   *see*   CAML

Acc.   accompaniment, accompany; *accord* (F=chord), *accordo*
   (I=chord); accordion(s)

ACC   *Accent* (rec. lab.); *ad accendentes*; Association of Choral
   Conductors; Association of Croatian Composers

Accel., accel°.   *accelerando* (I=faster)

Accomp.   accompaniment

Accpt.   accompaniment

Accres.   *accresciuto* (I=increased)

ACDA   American Choral Directors' Association

ACEUM   Association canadienne des écoles universitaires de musique

ACI   Association of Conductors and Instructors

ACIM   Association canadienne des industries de la musique / Music

Industries Association of Canada, MIAC

ACJI À Cœur Joie International

AcM *Acta musicologica* (jl.)

ACM American College of Musicians; *Anthology of Canadian Music* (rec. lab.)

ACMP Amateur Chamber Music Players

ACNMP Alliance for Canadian New-Music Projects

ACO Association of Canadian Orchestras

Acomp. *acompañamiento* (Sp=accompaniment)

Acoust. acoustic(s) / *acoustique* (F) / *acustica* (I) / *acústica* (Sp)

ACR *American Choral Review* (jl.)

ACS Austrian Choral Society

Act Mozart *Acta Mozartiana* (jl.)

Act Music *Acta musicologica* (jl.)

Acta *Acta musicologica* (jl.); Internationale Gesellschaft für Musikwissenschaft. *Mitteilungen* (jl.)

Acta mus *Acta musicologica* (jl.)

ActaMusicol *Acta musicologica* (jl.)

ACU Azerbaijan Composers' Union

ACWC Association of Canadian Women Composers

A/d analog to digital

Ad l., ad lib. *ad libitum* (L=at liberty)

ADAF Association pour la diffusion des accordéonistes

Adag., adg⁰, adgo *adagio*

Adc analog-digital converter

ADC Arbeitsgemeinschaft Deutscher Chorverband

ADCM Archbishop of Canterbury's Diploma in Church Music

Add. Additional manuscripts (British Museum)

Adel *Adelphi* (rec. lab.)

AdHM Adler, Guido. *Handbuch der Musikgeschichte*

ADJA American Disc Jockey Association

AdlerH, AdlerHdb, AdlerHMG Adler, Guido. *Handbuch der Musikgeschichte*

Adlung Mus. mech. org. Adlung, Jacob. *Musica mechanica organoedi*

ADMH Association for Dutch Music History Administrators

ADMV Allgemeiner Deutscher Musikverein

Adº, ado *adagio*

Adr analog-to-digital recorder

Adv *Advance* (rec. lab.)

AE *American Ensemble* (Chamber Music America) (jl.)

AEC Association européenne des conservatoires

AEDBCS Association européenne des directeurs de bureaux de concerts et spectacles

AEF Association européenne des festivals

Aeuia alleluia

AFBC Association for the Furtherment of Bel Canto

Affettº *affettuoso*

Affrettº *affrettando*

AFJS American Federation of Jazz Societies

Aflg. aflevering

AFM American Federation of Musicians of the United States and Canada

AfMf *Archiv für Musikforschung* (jl.)

AFMM American Festival of Microtonal Music

AFMS Association of Finnish Music Schools

AfMW *Archiv für Musikwissenschaft* (jl.)

AFNA Accordion Federation of North America

AF of M American Federation of Musicians of the United States and Canada

AFPC American Federation of Pueri Cantores

AfricanM *African Music* (jl.)

AFSO Association of Finnish Symphony Orchestras

AFVBM American Federation of Violin and Bow Makers

Ag *Agnus Dei*

AGAC American Guild of Authors and Composers

AGEHR American Guild of English Handbell Ringers

AGM   American Guild of Music

AGMA   American Guild of Musical Artists

AGO, A.G.O.   American Guild of Organists

Ag⁰   *agitato*

AGS   American Guitar Society

AGSM   Associate of the Guildhall School of Music and Drama

AH   *Analecta hymnica medii aevi* (jl.)

AHS   American Harp Society

AHu, Ahu   Angles, Higinio. *El Códex musical de Las Huelgas*

AICE   Association de l'industrie canadienne de l'enregistrement

AICP   Association of Independent Composers and Performers

AIM   American Institute of Musicology

AIMA   American Industrial Music Association

AIBM   Association Internationale des Bibliothéque, Archives etCentres de Documentation Musicaux

AIDO   Association internationale des directeurs d'opéra

AIMS   American Institute of Musical Studies; Association of Irish Musical Societies

AIO   American Institute of Organbuilders

AIOF   American Israel Opera Foundation

Air.   *Aircheck* (rec. lab.)

AIVS   American Institute for Verdi Studies

AJ   *Arthur Jordan Choral Series*

Ak.   *Akkord* (G=chord); *Akustik* (G=acoustic(s)), *akustisch*

Akk.   *Akkordeon* (G=accordion)

Akust.   *Akustik* (G=acoustic(s)), *akustisch*

AL   Abr. Lundquist AB (publ.)

Al.   alleluia

Al seg.   *al segno*

ALAM   Associate of the London Academy of Music and Drama

Alap   as loud as possible

ALCM   Associate of the London College of Music (now, London College of Music and Media, within Thames Valley University)

Algord Algord Music (publ.)

All. alleluia

ALL *alleluiatici* (chant)

All E. *All Ears* (rec. lab.)

All' ot, all' ott., all' 8va *all'ottava*

Allgtto., allgtt° *allegretto*

Alli. *Alligator* (rec. lab.)

All° *allegro*

ALMA American Lithuanian Musicians Alliance; Association for Latin-American Music & Art

Almgl. *Almglocke(n)* (G=herd bells)

ALS American Liszt Society

Alt. *alto*

Alv alleluia verse

AM *Acta musicologica* (jl.); *Allgemeine Musikzeitung* (jl.); *Année musicale* (jl.); *Antiphonale monasticum pro diurnis horis*; Associated Music Publishers (publ.); *Ave Maria*; Internationale Gesellschaft für Musikwissenschaft. *Mitteilungen* (jl.)

AMA American Matthay Association; Australian Musical Association

Ambient S. *Ambient Sound* (rec. lab.)

AMC American Music Center; American Music Center. *Newsletter* (jl.); American Music Conference; Anthologie de la musique canadienne (rec. lab.); Association de Musicothérapie du Canada; Association of Macedonian Composers

Am Choral R *American Choral Review* (jl.)

Ame *Algemene muziekencyclopedie*

AME American Music Editions

Am Ens *American Ensemble* (Chamber Music America) (jl.)

AmerChoralR *American Choral Review* (jl.)

AmerRecorder *American Recorder* (jl.)

AMes *Algemene muziekencyclopedie: Supplement*

Amf *Archiv für Musikforschung* (jl.)

AMFA American Music Festival Association

AMG   Algemeine Musikgesellschaft; Audio Manufacturers' Group

Am Harp J.   *American Harp Journal* (jl.)

AMI   *Arte musicale in Italia* (Luigi Torchi, ed.)

AMICA   Automatic Music Instrument Collectors' Association

AMII   Association of Musical Instrument Industries

AMIS   American Musical Instrument Society; *Antiquae musicae italicae scriptores* (jl.)

AMIS J   American Musical Instrument Society. *Journal* (jl.)

AMIS N   American Musical Instrument Society. *Newsletter* (jl.)

AML   *Acta musicologica* (jl.)

AMM   *Anthology of Medieval Music* (Richard H. Hoppin, ed.); *Antiphonale missarum juxta ritum Sanctae Ecclesiae Mediolanensis*

AMMM   *Archivium Musices Metropolitanum Mediolanense*

Am Mus Tcr   *American Music Teacher* (jl.)

Am Org   *American Organist* (jl.)

Amp.   *Amphion* (rec. lab.); amplified

AMP   *Antiquitates musicae in Polonia* (jl.); Associated Music Publishers (publ.)

Ampli.   amplified

AMRA   Australian Music Retailers Association

Am Rec G   *American Record Guide* (jl.)

Am Recorder   *American Recorder* (jl.)

AMRM   *Aspects of Medieval and Renaissance Music* (Jan LaRue, ed.)

AMS   American Musicological Society; Association des musiciens suisses

AMSA   American Music Scholarship Association

AMT   *American Music Teacher* (jl.)

AMTA   American Music Therapy Association; Australian Music Therapy Association

Amu   *Annales musicologiques* (jl.)

AMU   American Musicians' Union

A Mus   Associate in Music

AMusLCM Associate in Music of the London College of Music (now, London College of Music and Media, within Thames Valley University)

A Mus TCL Associate in Music, Trinity College of Music, London (earlier, Associate of Trinity College, London, ATCL)

AMUTA *American Music Teacher* (jl.)

Amw *Archiv für Musikwissenschaft* (jl.)

AMZ, Amz *Leipziger Allgemeine Musikzeitung* (jl.)

An. Antiphon

Anacom analog computer

Anal. analysis

Anal. hymn. *Analecta hymnica medii aevi* (jl.)

AnalectaMusicol *Analecta musicologica* (jl.)

AnChopin *Rocznik Chopinowski* (jl.) / *Annales Chopin* (jl.)

Ancia d. *ancia doppia* (I=double reed); *strumenti ad ancia doppia* (I=double reed instruments)

And. *andante*

Andno, and^{no} *andantino*

Andr. *Andrew's Music* (rec. lab.)

Andte *andante*

Ang-Can Anglo-Canadian Music Publishers' Association

Anhalt. *anhaltisch* (G=continuous)

Anim. *animato*

AnM *Anuario musical* (jl.)

AnMc *Analecta musicologica* (jl.)

Ann. mus. *Annales musicologiques* (jl.)

AnnM *Annales musicologiques* (jl.)

AnnMl *Annales musicologiques* (jl.)

Annu. *Annuit Coeptis* (rec. lab.)

ANSCR Alpha-Numeric System for the Classification of Records

ANT antiphons

Ant. *Antilles* (rec. lab.); Antiphon

Ant. cym. antique cymbals

Ant M   *Antiphonale monasticum pro diurnis horis*

Ant MI   *Antiquae musicae italicae* (jl.)

Ant R   *Antiphonale sacrosanctae romanae ecclesiae pro diurnis horis*

AntP   *Antiphonarium ad usum sacri et canonici ordinis Praemonstratensis*

Ant. Vat.   *Antiphonale missarum juxta ritum Sanctae Ecclesiae Mediolanensis*

AnthM   Fellerer, Karl, ed. *Anthology of Music*

Anu Mus   *Anuario musical* (jl.)

Anuario M, Anuario Mus.   *Anuario musical* (jl.)

Anv   antiphon verse

ANZ   Algemeen Nederlands Zangverbond

Ao   *Codex Aosta* (15th cent. ms.)

AOAI   Amateur Organists and Keyboard Association International

AOC   Association des orchestres canadiens

A of D   *Ace of Diamonds* (rec. lab.)

AOSA   American Orff-Schulwerk Association

APA   American Pianists Association

A.p.a.   *a parte ante* (nota.)

APCC   Antique Phonograph Collectors Club

APCT   Association of Piano Class Teachers

Apel Anth, ApelAnth   *Historical Anthology of Music* (Archibald T. Davison)

ApelG, ApelGC   Apel, Willi. *Gregorian Chant*

ApelMK   Apel, Willi. *Masters of the Keyboard*

ApelN   Apel, Willi. *Notation der polyphonen Musik, 900-1600*; Apel, Willi. *Notation of Polyphonic Music, 900-1600*

APEM   Associação Portuguesa de Educação Musical

ApF   Apel, Willi. *French Secular Music of the Late Fourteenth Century*

APMT   Association of Professional Music Therapists

ApMZ   Apel, Willi. *Musik aus früher Zeit für Klavier*

ApN   Apel, Willi. *Notation of Polyphonic Music, 900-1600*

ApNPM   Apel, Willi. *Notation of Polyphonic Music, 900-1600*

APOBA   Associated Pipe Organ Builders of America

Apoc.   *Apocrypha*

Apogee   Apogee Press (publ.)

A.p.p.   *a parte post* (nota.)

APRA   Australasian Performing Rights Association

APRA Journal   Australasian Performing Rights Association. *APRA Journal*

APVE   Association of Professional Vocal Ensembles

Ar   *arco* (I=bow), *arpa* (I=harp)

AR   *American Recorder* (jl.); *Antiphonale sacrosanctae romanae ecclesiae pro diurnis horis*

Ara.   *Arabesque* (rec. lab.)

ARAM   Associate of the Royal Academy of Music

Arb.   *Arbeit, -en* (G=work, works)

ARC   Archive of Recorder Consorts

Arc.   *arcato, coll' arco* (I=with the bow, bowed)

Arc. Folk   *Archive of Folk & Jazz Music* (rec. lab.)

Arc. Piano   *Archive of Piano Music* (rec. lab.)

ARCCO   Associate of the Royal Canadian College of Organists

ARCE   Archives and Research Centre for Ethnomusicology

Arch.   archets

Arch Mus, Arch Musik   *Archiv für Musikwissenschaft* (jl.)

Arch. mus. lat.   *Archivio musicale lateranense*

Archambault   Archambault Musique (publ.)

Archi   *strumenti ad arco* (I=bowed stringed instruments)

Archiv fMF   *Archiv für Musikforschung* (jl.)

Archiv fMW   *Archiv für Musikwissenschaft* (jl.)

ARCM   Associate of the Royal College of Music

ARCO   Associate of the Royal College of Organists

Ard⁰   *ardito*

ARG   *American Record Guide* (jl.)

Arhoo   *Arhoolie* (rec. lab.)

Ari.   *Arista* (rec. lab.)

Ari./Free. *Arista/Freedom* (rec. lab.)

Ari/GRP *Arista/GRP* (rec. lab.)

AriNo *Arista/Novus* (rec. lab.)

Arm. *armonia* (I=harmony), *armonio* (I, Sp=harmonium)

ARMCM Associate of the Royal Manchester College of Music (merged with the Northern School of Music, now Royal Northern College of Music)

Arp., arpio. *arpeggio*

Arr. arranged, arrangement, *arrangiert* (G)

ARS American Recorder Society; American Recorder Society Editions; Association for Recorded Sound Collections

ArsA Paris. Bibliothèque de l'Arsenal, ms. 135

ARSC Association for Recorded Sound Collections

ARSCM Associate of the Royal School of Church Music

Art/Dir *Artist-Direct* (rec. lab.)

ARTA American Recorder Teachers Association

Arti mus *Arti musices* (jl.)

Artists *Artists House* (rec. lab.)

AS Alkan Society; *American String Teacher* (jl.); *Antiphoniale Sarisburiense* (jl.)

A.S.A. Acoustical Society of America

ASA Accordion Society of Australia

ASAI American Society of Ancient Instruments

Asap as soft as possible, as soon as possible

ASBDA American School Band Directors' Association

Asc *ascendens, ascendentes*

ASCAP American Society of Composers, Authors, and Publishers

ASCT Association of String Class Teachers

Ashb *Ashbourne* (rec. lab.)

AsianM, Asian Mus *Asian Music* (jl.)

ASIJB *Asian Musician* (jl.)

ASJ *American Suzuki Journal* (jl.)

ASJM American Society for Jewish Music

ASM *Asian Music* (jl.)

ASMAC American Society of Music Arrangers and Composers

ASMC American Society of Music Copyists

ASME Australian Society for Music Education

ASO Adelaide Symphony Orchestra

ASOL American Symphony Orchestra League

ASSO Association of Swedish Symphony Orchestras

Assoc Recor Association for Recorded Sound Collections. *Journal*

AST *American String Teacher* (jl.)

ASTA American String Teachers' Association

ASUC American Society of University Composers

ASVBM *adsit scribendi Virgo Beata mihi*

Asy *Asylum* (rec. lab.)

A.t. *a tempo*

At *Atlantic* (rec. lab.)

ATCL Associate of Trinity College, London (now, Associate in Music, Trinity College of Music, London, A Mus TCL)

A tem. *a tempo*

ATG Accordionists and Teachers Guild, International

ATMI Association for Technology in Music Instruction

ATOE American Theatre Organ Enthusiasts

ATOS American Theatre Organ Society

ATSC Associate of the Tonic Sol-fa College of Music

Au Augener (publ.)

AudioD *Audio Directions* (rec. lab.)

Audio Fi *Audio Fidelity* (rec. lab.)

Audiop *Audiophile* (rec. lab.)

Auff. *Aufführung* (G=performance)

Aufgef. *aufgeführt* (G=performed)

Aug. augment

Augm. augmented

Augsb *Augsburg* (rec. lab.)

Augsburg Augsburg Publishing House (publ.)

Aural *Aural Explorer* (rec. lab.)

Ausgew., auswg. *ausgewählte* (G=selected)

Australian J Mus Ed *Australian Journal of Music Education* (jl.)

Ausw. *auswahl* (G=selected)

Av *Avant-Garde* (rec. lab.)

AV *Anthologia vocalis* (jl.)

A. vla. *alto viola*

AVS American Viola Society

AW *ausgewählte Werke* (G=collected works)

AWA Anstalt zur Wahrung der Aufführungsrechte auf dem Gebiet der Musik

AWAPA Academy of Wind and Percussion Arts

AWC American Women Composers

AWT Association of Wind Teachers

B *bajo* (Sp=low; bass); bass / *basse* (F), *Bass* (G) / *basso* (I); brevis (nota.)

B. back; Brainard, Paul. *Le Sonate per violino di Giuseppe Tartini*; Bryant, Giles. *Healey Willan Catalogue*; Burghauser, Jarmil. *A. Dvorak: Thematic Catalogue of Works*

B & B, B&B Bote & Bock (publ.)

B&H Boosey & Hawkes (publ.)

B&VP Broekmans & Van Poppel (publ.)

B and P *Brass and Percussion* (jl.)

B. ch. *basse chiffrée* (F=figured bass) / *bocca chuisa* (I=mouth closed)

B. cif. *bajo cifrado* (Sp=figured bass)

B. guit. bass guitar

B.D. bass drum

B.f. *bouche fermée* (closed mouth)

B.G. Bach-Gesellschaft

B.V.K. Bärenreiter Verlag (publ.)

Ba Bamberg Codex, Ed. IV6

Bä Bärenreiter Verlag (publ.)

BA *Bach* (Riemenschneider Bach Institute) (jl.); Bands of America

BABS British Association of Barbershop Singers

BACA British Association of Concert Agents

Bach *Bach Guild* (rec. lab.)

BachJb *Bach-Jahrbuch* (jl.)

Bach, PDQ pen name of Peter Schickele

Bach Versuch Bach, Carl Philipp Emanuel. *Versuch über die wahre Art das Clavier zu spielen*

Back. *Backstreet* (rec. lab.)

Bain. *Bainbridge* (rec. lab.)

BalgarskaM *Balgarska muzyka* (jl.)

BAM Bachelor of Arts in Music

BAMS American Musicological Society. *Bulletin* (jl.)

Bar & Bar Barger & Barclay (publ.)

Bar *Baroque* (rec. lab.)

Bar. baritone / *Bariton* (G) / *barriton* (F) / *baritono* (I)

Barc. *barcinonense*

BarcA Barcelona. Biblioteca central, M. 853 (ms.)

BARD British Association of Record Dealers

Bari., bari. baritone / *Bariton* (G) / *barriton* (F) / *baritono* (I)

BARZREX Bartók Archives Z-Symbol Rhythm Extraction

BASBWE British Association of Symphonic Bands and Wind Ensembles

Basskl. *Bassklarinette* (G=bass clarinet)

BayerischeVolksm *Bayerische Volksmusik* (jl.)

BB *Billboard* (jl.); Bote & Bock (publ.); Broude Brothers (publ.)

BBAA Big Band Academy of America

BBB Bach, Beethoven & Brahms

BBC S.O. British Broadcasting Corporation. Symphony Orchestra

BBCSSO British Broadcasting Corporation. Scottish Symphony

Bc bass clarinet

B.c. *bocca chiusa* (I=mouth closed) / *basso continuo* (I) / *basse continue* (F) / *bajo continuo* (Sp)

BChN böhmische Choralnotation

BCM *British Catalogue of Music*

BCMA British & Continental Music Agencies

BCS *Bennington College Series of New Music*

Bd. clp. board clapper

BDAA Balalaika and Domra Association of America

BdMH National Association of German Musical Instrument Manufacturers / Bundesverband der Deutschen Musikinstrumenten Hersteller

Be *Benedictus*

Be JB *Beethoven-Jahrbuch* (jl.)

Bears. *Bearsville* (rec. lab.)

Bee *Bee Hive* (rec. lab.)

Begl. *Begleitung* (G=accompaniment)

Beih. IMG Internationale Musikgesellschaft. *Beihefte* (jl.)

Beisp. *Beispiel* (G=example)

Beitr. Musik *Beiträge zur Musikwissenschaft* (jl.)

Beitr. Mw *Beiträge zur Musikwissenschaft* (jl.)

Beiträge Österreichische Gesellschaft für Musik. *Beiträge* (jl.)

BeJB *Beethoven-Jahrbuch* (jl.)

Bel *Belfagor; Rassegna di varia umanità* (jl.)

Bell p., bell pl. bell plate(s)

Bem. *Bemerkung* (G=comment, note); *bémol* (F) / *Bemol* (G) / *bemolle* (I) (=flat)

BeMMR Besseler, Heinrich. *Die Musik des Mittelalters und der Renaissance*

Ber Berandol Music (publ.)

Bes. *Besetzung* (G=scoring, instrumentation)

Beserk *Beserk* (rec. lab.)

BeW Beethoven, Ludwig van. *Werke* (Guido Adler, ed.)

BFA Broadcasting Foundation of America

BFMF British Federation of Music Festivals

BG Bach, Johann Sebastian. *Werke* (ed. by the Bach Gesellschaft)

BhAfMW *Archiv für Musikwissenschaft. Beihefte* (jl.)

Bhr basset horn

Bibl. Laur. Florence. Biblioteca Mediceo-Laurenziana

Big *Big Tree* (rec. lab.)

BIJS British Institute of Jazz Studies

BILLA *Billboard* (jl.)

BIMG Internationale Musikgesellschaft. *Beihefte* (jl.)

BIN Billboard Information Network

Bio. *Biograph* (rec. lab.)

BIRS British Institute of Recorded Sound; British Institute of Recorded Sound. *Bulletin* (jl.)

Bisc. *Biscuit City* (rec. lab.)

BJ *Bach-Jahrbuch* (jl.)

BjB *Bach-Jahrbuch* (jl.)

BJMTD *British Journal of Music Therapy* (jl.)

Bjo. banjo

Bkl *Bassklarinette* (G=bass clarinet)

Bl ballo; *Black Perspective in Music* (jl.)

Bl. *Blasinstrumente* (G=wind instruments)

Black. *Blackbird* (rec. lab.)

Black per in music, Black Per M, BlackPerspectiveM *Black Perspective in Music* (jl.)

Bläqua *Bläserquartett* (G=woodwind quartet)

Bläqui *Bläserquintet* (G=woodwind quintet)

Blar. *Blarney Castle* (rec. lab.)

Blasinstru. *Blasinstrumente* (G=wind instruments)

Blechbl. *Blechblasinstrumente*

Blind *Blind Pig* (rec. lab.)

Blofl. *Blockflöte* (G=recorder)

Blue *Blue Note* (rec. lab.)

Blue G *Blue Goose* (rec. lab.)

Blue Th. *Blue Thumb* (rec. lab.)

Blueb. *Bluebird* (rec. lab.)

Bluegrass Bluegrass Unlimited

BM Bachelor of Music; Boston Music Co. (publ.)

BMA Black Music Association

BMB *Biblioteca musica Bononiensis*

BMC Boston Music Co. (publ.)

BME Bachelor of Music in Education

BMI *BMI: The Many Worlds of Music* (jl.); Broadcast Music, Inc.

BMIC BMI Canada

BMPS British Musicians' Pensions Society

BMR *Black Music Research Journal* (jl.)

BMS British Music Society

Bmus Bachelor of Music

BMus (PSM) Bachelor of Music in Public School Music

BMusEd Bachelor of Music in Education

Bmw *Beiträge zur Musikwissenschaft* (jl.)

Bn. bassoon(s) / *Fagott* (G) / *fagotto* (I) / *fagot* (Sp)

BNL *Banjo Newsletter* (jl.)

BNMT *Benedictiones* (chant, Mass)

BNOC British National Opera Company

BNS *Benedictiones* (chant, Mass)

Bo & Ha Boosey & Hawkes (publ.)

Bo&Bo Bote & Bock (publ.)

Bo&H Boosey & Hawkes (publ.)

BoHa Boosey & Hawkes (publ.)

Bol. Lat-Am. Mús. *Boletin latino-americano de música* (Bogotà)

BolInteramerM *Boletin interamericano de música* (jl.)

Boll. Bibl. Mus. *Bolletino bibliografico musicale* (jl.)

BollstStudVerdiana Istituto di Studi Verdiani. *Bollettino* (jl.)

Bons. bassoon(s) / *Fagott* (G) / *fagotto* (I) / *fagot* (Sp)

BordasD *Dictionnaire de la musique* (Bordas)

Boston I. *Boston International* (rec. lab.)

Boul. *Boulevard* (rec. lab.)

Bouwsteenen: JVNM *Bouwsteenen: Jaarboek der Vereniging voor muziekgeschiedenis* (jl.)

BPN Bohemian plainsong notation

BQ *Brass Quarterly* (jl.)

Br Bärenreiter Verlag (publ.); *breve, breves, brevis* (nota.)

Br. baritone / *Bariton* (G) / *barriton* (F) / *baritono* (I); brass instruments; *Bratsche* (G=viola)

BR *Bennington Review* (jl.)

Br. & H. Breitkopf & Härtel (publ.)

Br-a *brevis altera* (nota.)

Brahms-Stud *Brahms-Studien* (jl.)

Brake dr. brake drum(s)

Brass B *Brass Bulletin* (jl.)

BrassWoodwindQ *Brass and Woodwind Quarterly* (jl.)

Brev M *Breviarum monasticum*

Brev R *Breviarum romanum*

BRM Council for Research in Music Education. *Bulletin* (jl.)

BRMg *Beiträge zur Rheinischen Musikgeschichte* (jl.)

BrownI Brown, Howard Mayer. *Instrumental Music Printed Before 1600: A Bibliography*

BRS Bohemian Ragtime Society

Brus Museum Brussels. Museum of Musical Instruments. *Bulletin* (jl.)

BrusselsMuseumInstrumentsBul Brussels. Museum of Musical Instruments. *Bulletin* (jl.)

Bs bass / *basse* (F), *Bass* (G) / *basso* (I); *Benedictus*

BS Bantock Society; *Blätter der Sackpfeife*

Bs. cl. bass clarinet

BS Mu Bachelor of Sacred Music

BS Mus Bachelor of Sacred Music; Bachelor of School Music

BSA Bruckner Society of America

BSI British Suzuki Institute

BSIM *Mercure musical* (jl.); Société internationale de musique. *Bulletin français* (jl.)

BSM   Bachelor of Sacred Music; Bachelor of School Music; Belgian Society of Musicology; Birmingham School of Music (now, Birmingham Conservatoire, part of the University of Central England in Birmingham)

BSMu   Bachelor of Sacred Music

BSMus   Bachelor of Sacred Music; Bachelor of School Music

Bsn.   bassoon(s) / *Fagott* (G) / *fagotto* (I) / *fagot* (Sp)

BSO   Boston Symphony Orchestra; Bournemouth Symphony Orchestra

Bsp.   *Beispiel* (G=example)

Btb.   bass trombone

Bte.   *Benedicite*

BUC   *British Union-Catalogue of Early Music Printed Before the Year 1801* (Edith Schnapper, ed.)

BUCEM   *British Union-Catalogue of Early Music Printed Before the Year 1801* (Edith Schnapper, ed.)

BückenH, Bücken Hdb   Bücken, Ernst, ed. *Handbuch der Musikwissenschaft*

BüHM, BÜHM   Bücken, Ernst, ed. *Handbuch der Musikwissenschaft*

BuenosAiresM, Buenos Aires M   *Buenos Aires musical* (jl.)

Bulgar Muz   *Bulgarska Muzika* (jl.)

Bull.   Union musicologique. *Bulletin* (jl.)

BullSIM   Société internationale de musique. *Bulletin français* (jl.)

BulMusashinoAcademiaM   Musahino Academia Musicae. *Bulletin* (jl.)

BulSocBachBelgique   Société Johann Sebastian Bach de Belgique. *Bulletin* (jl.)

BulVieMBelge   *Bulletin de la vie musicale belge / Bulletin van het Belgisch Muziekleven* (jl.)

BUM   Union musicologique. *Bulletin* (jl.)

BuMBE   Bukofzer, Manfred. *Music in the Baroque Era*

BurneyH   Burney, Charles. *A General History of Music From the Earliest Ages to the Present*

BV   Bärenreiter Verlag (publ.)

BvO   Bond van Orkestdirigenten en Instructeurs

BW *Brass and Wind News* (jl.)

BWQ *Brass and Woodwind Quarterly* (jl.)

BWV Bach Werke-Verzeichnis

BzMw *Beiträge zur Musikwissenschaft* (jl.)

C *cantus*; center (of perc. instr.); Colmarer Handschrift (Cgm 4997) (medieval ms.)

C. *cordes* (F=strings); *cuerda*

C. 8va *coll'ottava* (doubled at the octave)

C. bn. *contrabassoon*

C. cym. crash cymbal(s)

C. fag. *Contrafagotto* (I=contrabassoon)

C.a. *cor anglais* (F=English horn)

C.b., c.B. *col basso* (I=with the bass); double bass (contrabass) / *contrebasse* (F) / *contrabasso* (I) / *contrabajo* (Sp); cowbell(s)

C.d. *colla destra*

CD compact disc

C.f. *cantus firmus*

C.l. *col legno*

C.s. *colla sinistra* (I=with the left hand); *con sordino* (I=with the mute)

C.S.O. Composers' Symphony Orchestra

Ca M, CaM *Catalogus musicus*

Ca. Cambrai. Bibliothéque Municipale. Ms. 1328 (1176)

CAA Concert Artists' Association

CAAA Composers, Authors, and Artists of America

Cab. cabaza (perc. instr.)

Cad. cadence

CAG Concert Artist Guild

CAGO Colleague of the American Guild of Organists

CahCanadiensM *Cahiers canadiens de musique*

CahDebussy *Cahiers Debussy* (jl.)

Cal. *calando* (I=gradually diminishing)

Cam *Camden* (rec. lab.)

CAM   Canadian Amateur Musicians / Musiciens amateurs du Canada, MAC

CAMEO   Creative Audio and Music Electronics Organization

CAML   Canadian Association of Music Libraries, Archives, and Documentation Centres / Association canadienne des bibliothèques, archives, et centres de documentation musicaux, ACBM (earlier, Canadian Music Library Association, CMLA / Association canadienne des bibliothèques musicaux, ACBM)

Camp.   *campana* (I, Sp=bell)

CAMT   Canadian Association for Music Therapy

Can   *Canticle* (jl.)

Can Composer   *Canadian Composer* (jl.) / *Le Compositeur Canadien*

Can Folk B   *Canada Folk Bulletin* (jl.)

Can Folk Mus   *Canadian Folk Music Journal* (jl.)

Can Mus   *Canadian Musician* (jl.)

Can Mus Bk   *Canada Music Book*

CanB   *Canadian Bandmaster* (jl.); *Canadian Bandsman* (jl.)

Canc.   *cancionero*

CanComp   *Canadian Composer* (jl.) / *Le Compositeur Canadien*

CanD   *Cantate Domino*

CanJM   *Canadian Journal of Music* (jl.)

Canna   *canna d'organo* (I=organ pipe)

Canna d. l.   *canna ad anima di legno* (I=flute pipe, wood) (organ)

Canna d. m.   *canna ad anima di metallo* (I=flute pipe, metal)

Cant.   cantata; *Cantate*; *cantique*; *canto* (I=high voice)

Cantab.   *cantabile* (I=singing)

Canto Greg   *Canto Gregoriano*

CAO   Composers' Autograph Publications

Cap.   *Capitol* (rec. lab.)

CAPAC   Composers, Authors, and Publishers Association of Canada / Association des compositeurs, auteurs et éditeurs du Canada, ACAEC

CAPEM   Certificat d'aptitude pédagogique à l'enseignement de la musique

Capp. *cappella*

CAPRA Composers' Autograph Publications Records Association

Carnet mus *Carnet musical* (jl.)

CAS Catgut Acoustical Society

CASA Contemporary A Cappella Society of America

CAUSM Canadian Association of University Schools of Music

CBA Canadian Band Association; Canadian Bandmasters' Association

CBAM Canadian Bureau for the Advancement of Music

CBCSO Canadian Broadcasting Corporation Symphony Orchestra

CBDA Canadian Band Directors' Association

CBDM Centre Belge de Documentation Musicale

CBDNA College Band Directors National Association

CBMT Certification Board for Music Therapists

CBSO City of Birmingam Symphony Orchestra

CCE Traditional Irish Singing and Dancing Society / Comhaltas Ceoltóiri Éireann

CCO, Canadian College of Organists / Collège Canadien des Organistes; Center for Contemporary Opera

CCS Composers' Cooperative Society

CCSCM *Cobbett's Cyclopedic Survey of Chamber Music*

CCTE Cumann Cheol Tire Eireann

CDAO Co-Operating Danish Amateur-Orchestras

CDCM Consortium to Distribute Computer Music

CDMI *Classici della musica italiana*

Ce collected edition(s)

CE *Central Opera Service Bulletin* (jl.)

CeBeDeM, Cebedem Centre Belge de Documentation Musicale

CEK, CEKM *Corpus of Early Keyboard Music*

Cel. *celeste / celesta* (I)

Celli *violoncelli*

CEM *Collection d'études musicologiques*

Cem. *Cembalo* (G=harpsichord)

CEMA Council for the Encouragement of Music and the Arts

Cemb. *Cembalo* (G=harpsichord)

CEMF *Corpus of Early Music in Facsimile*

Central Opera *Central Opera Service Bulletin* (jl.)

CercetariMuzicol Cercetări de muzicologie

CF Carl Fischer (publ.)

CFD Company of Fifers and Drummers

CFE Composers' Facsimile Edition

Cfg *Contrafagotto* (I=contrabassoon)

CFMA *Classiques français du moyen age*

CFMJ *Canadian Folk Music Journal* (jl.)

CFMS Canadian Folk Music Society

CFMTA Canadian Federation of Music Teachers' Association

CFP *ad confractiones panis*; Peters, C.F. (publ.)

CG Covent Garden (Royal Opera House)

CGGB Composers' Guild of Great Britain

CGI Creative Guitar International

CGL *Choristers' Guild Letters* (jl.)

Ch chamber music; chant; Chantilly. Musée Condé. Bibliothèque. Ms. 564 (olim 1047); chorus; J & W Chester (publ.)

CH *Connchord* (jl.)

Ch. pop. *chant populaire*

Chal. Chalumeau

Cham. chamber

Chans. *chanson* (F=song); *chansonnier*

Chap. Chappell & Co. (publ.)

Chb. *Chorbuch, -bücher* (G=choirbook(s))

Chdgt. *Chordirigent* (G=choir conductor)

ChDir choir director; *Chordirektor*

Chev Chevalier, Ulysse. *Repertorium hymnologicum*

CHF Český Hudební Fond

Chin. cym. Chinese cymbal

CHIS Czech Music Information Centre / Československé Hudební

Informačni Středisko

Chit. *chitarra* (I=guitar); *chitarrone* (Sp=Mexican bass guitar)

CHM Choirmaster's diploma of the Royal College of Organists; *Collectanea historiae musicae* (jl.)

Ch.M. Choirmaster's diploma of the American Guild of Organists; Choirmaster's diploma of the Royal Canadian College of Organists

Choeur d'enf. *choeur d'enfants* (F=children's chorus)

Choeur d'h. *choeur d'hommes* (F=men's chorus)

Choeur de f. *choeur de femmes* (F=women's chorus)

Choeur m. *choeur mixte* (F=mixed chorus)

Chor. chorus

Choral J. *Choral Journal* (jl.)

Chrom. chromatic; *Chromatik* (G=chromatic; noun); *chromatisch* (G=chromatic; adj.)

CHS Československý Hudebni Slovnik Osob a Instituci

Cht. chant

CHU *Church Music* (jl.)

Church Mus *Church Music* (jl.)

Chw. *Das Chorwerk*

Ci *corno inglese* (I=English horn)

CIA Confédération internationale des accordeonistes

CIC Conseil international des compositeurs

CIDEM Consejo interamericano de música; Inter-American Music Center

CIM Conseil international de la musique

Cimb. *cimbalom*

CIMCIM International Committee of Musical Instrument Museums and Collections / Comité international des musées et collections d'instruments de musique / Comité internacional de museos y colecciones de instrumentos musicales

CIRM Centre international de recherche musicale

CISAC Confédération internationale des sociétiés d'auteurs et compositeurs

CISM Confédération internationale des sociétes musicales

CISPM   Confédération internationale des sociétiés populaires de musique

CJ   *Choral Journal* (jl.)

CK   *Contemporary Keyboard* (jl.); *Keyboard* (jl.)

CL   *Clavier* (jl.)

Cl.   clarinet / *clarinette* (F) / *clarinete* (Sp) / *clarinetto* (I)

Cl. cb.   *clarinetto contrabasso* (I=contrabass clarinet)

Claro.   *clarino*

Clav   *clavicembalo* (I=harpsichord)

Clav.   *Clavier*

CLAVA   *Clavier* (jl.)

Clb, c.l.b.   *col legno battuto*; *clarinetto basso* (I=bass clarinet)

CLF   *Corpus des luthistes français*

CLGA   Composers' and Lyricists' Guild of America

CLM   *Clamores* (chant, Mass)

CLMO   *Clamores* (chant, Office)

Clno.   *clarino*

Clt, c.l.t.   *col legno tratto*

Clv., clvd.   *clavecin* (F) / *clavicembalo* (I), *clavecin* (Sp); clavichord

CM   *choeur des muses*; *Church Musician* (jl.); *Collegium musicum*; *Concentus musicus*; *Current Musicology* (jl.)

CMA   Chamber Music America; Church Music Association; Walther, Hans, ed. *Carmina medii aevi posterioris Latina I/I*

CMAA   Church Music Association of America

CMB   *Canada Music Book*

CMBA   Concert Music Broadcasters' Association

Cmc   *Current Musicology* (jl.)

CMC   Creative Musicians Coalition

CMF   Creative Music Foundation

CMI   *Classici musicali italiani*; *Creative Music Index*

CMLA   *see* CAML

CMLE   Classical Music Lovers' Exchange

CMM   *Corpus mensurabilis musical*

Cmp *campane* (I=bells)

CMP Consolidated Music Publishers; Contemporary Music Project

CMPA Canadian Music Publishers' Association; Church Music Publishers' Association

CMRRA Canadian Musical Reproduction Rights Agency

CMS, C.M.S. Canadian Music Sales Corp. (publ.); Clarion Music Society; College Music Society; *College Music Symposium* (jl.); Computer Music Society

CMSNA Chinese Music Society of North America

CMT Church Music Trust

CMTJ *Canadian Music Trades Journal* (jl.)

CMUEB Council for Research in Music Education. *Bulletin* (jl.)

CMUED *Contributions to Music Education*

Cmz Cercetări de muzicologie

CNC Consejo Nacional de Cultura, Havana

CNM Comité national de la musique

CNOS China Nationalities Orchestra

CNRS Centre national de la recherche scientifique

Cnto *cornetto* (I=horn)

CNV *Cum Notis Variorum* (jl.)

Co *Canto organo* (I=for voice and organ)

C° 1ᵐᵒ *canto primo*

Co. *corno* (I, Sp=horn)

Co. 1ᵐᵒ *come primo*

Co. so. *come sopra*

COC Canadian Opera Company

Cod. codex; codice

Coda *Coda: The Jazz Magazine* (jl.)

Col coloration (nota.); colored (nota.)

Col. c. *col canto*

Col. ottᵃ *coll'ottava* (doubled at the octave)

Col. *Columbia* (rec. lab.)

Col. vo. *colla voce*

Coll. *collana*

Coll Music, Coll. mus. *College Music Symposium* (jl.); *Collegium musicum*

College Msymposium *College Music Symposium* (jl.)

College Mus *College Music Symposium* (jl.)

COM *The Composer* (jl.)

Com. comique; *comodo*

COMA Canadian On-line Musicians' Association

Comp. composed (by, in); composition; *compositore* (I=composer)

Comp. ed. complete edition

Compl. *completorium* (compline; last of the canonical hours)

Compn. composition

Compr. composer

Comps. *composizione* (I=composition)

Comput Mus, Computer mus *Computer Music* (jl.)

Computer Mus J *Computer Music Journal* (jl.)

Con Concordia Publishing House (publ.)

Con esp. *con espressione* (I=with expression)

Con Mus Ed *Contributions to Music Education*

Conc. *concertante*; *concertato*; *concerto*

Conductor condr.

CONHAN Contextual Harmonic Analysis

ConnaissanceOrgue Connaissance de l'orgue

Cons. conservatory / *conservatoire* (F) / *conservatorio* (I)

Cont. *continuo*

Cont. Key., Cont. Keybd. *Contemporary Keyboard* (jl.)

Cop. *Cum opposita proprietate* (nota.)

Cor, Cor. *corno* (I, Sp=horn; *Coronet* (rec. lab.)

Cor angl. *cor anglais* (F=English horn)

Cor. i. *corno inglese* (I=English horn)

Corda *strumenti a corda* (I=stringed instruments)

Corr. corruption

COS Central Opera Service

Costr   *costruzione* (I=[instrument] making)

CouncilResearchMEducationBul   Council for Research in Music
   Education. *Bulletin* (jl.)

Cour Mus France   *Courrier musical de France* (jl.)

CourrierMFrance   *Courrier musical de France* (jl.)

Coussemaker Scr   Coussemaker, Charles Edmond Henri. *Scriptorum
   de musica medii aevi. Nova series*

CousseS   Coussemaker, Charles Edmond Henri. *Scriptorum de musica
   medii aevi. Nova series*

Cov   communion verse

Cowb.   cowbell(s)

Cp   *canto primo*; counterpoint / *contrappunto* (I) / *contrapunto* (Sp) /
   contrepoint (F); *cum perfectione* (nota.)

CP   *Capolavori polifonici del secolo XVI*

CPE   Composer-Performer Edition

CPPIM   Center for Preservation and Propagation of Iranian Music

Cpr   *cum proprietate* (nota.)

Cps   cycles per second

Cpt.   counterpoint / *contrappunto* (I) / *contrapunto* (Sp) / *contrepoint*
   (F)

CQR   Toronto. Conservatory of Music. *Quarterly Review* (jl.)

Cr, Cr.   Credo

CRC   Collectors Record Club

Cres, cresc.   *crescendo*; *Crescendo International* (jl.)

CRI   *Composers' Recordings, Inc.* (rec. lab.)

CRIA   Canadian Recording Industry Association

CRMA   *Canadian Review of Music and Art* (jl.)

CRME   Council for Research in Music Education; Council for
   Research in Music Education. *Bulletin* (jl.)

Crot.   crotale(s)

Crti   *cornetti* (I=horns)

Cs   countersubject

CS   Clarasch Society; Coussemaker, Charles Edmond Henri.

Scriptorum de musica medii. Nova series

CSA   Catch Society of America

CSFM   Canadian Society of Folk Music

CSHS   Československý Hudební Slovník

CSM   Conseil suisse de la musique; *Corpus scriptorum de musica*; Société des Concerts Symphoniques de Montréal

CSMT   Canadian Society for Musical Traditions

CSTA   Canadian String Teachers' Association

CT   Composers Theatre; *Corpus troporum*

Ct.   *chitarra* (I=guitar); countertenor / *contratenor* (I)

CTI   *Creed Taylor, Inc.* (rec. lab.)

CTL   *Canadian Talent Library* (rec. lab.)

Ct°   *concerto*

Cto.   contralto

Ctpt.   counterpoint / *contrappunto* (I) / *contrapuno* (Sp) / *contrepoint* (F)

Cu, CU   *Current Musicology* (jl.); Curwen, J., and Sons (publ.)

CUMS   Cambridge University Musical Society; Canadian University Music Society

Curr. Music   *Current Musicology* (jl.)

Current Musicol   *Current Musicology* (jl.)

CUS   *Composer/USA* (National Association of Composers) (jl.)

Cv   *clavicembalo* (I=harpsichord)

Cw, CW   *Das Chorwerk*

Cycl.   cyclic / *cyclique* (F)

Cym., cymb.   cymbals / *cymbales* (F)

Cym. tngs.   cymbal tongs

D   difficult; *discantus*; Oliver Ditson (publ.); dominant, V (i.e., five); *duplex longa* (nota.)

D.   *destra* (I=right); Deutsch, Erich Otto. *Franz Schubert: Thematisches Verzeichnis seiner Werke*; *Diskant / Diskantus / Diskantz / discantus*

DA   Davison, Archibald T. *Historical Anthology of Music*

Daff. *Daffodil* (rec. lab.)

Dal s. *dal segno* (I=go back to the sign and repeat)

DAM *Dansk aarbog for musikforskning* (jl.)

Dansk Mus *Dansk musiktidsskrift* (jl.)

DanskAarbogMf *Dansk aarbog for musikforskning* (jl.)

DARMS Digital Alternate Representation of Music Symbols (computer-based notational system)

DarmstädterBeitrNeuenM *Darmstädter Beiträge zur neuen Musik* (jl.)

DB *Down Beat* (jl.)

Db decibel

Dbl. bass double bass (contrabass) / *contrebasse* (F) / *contrabasso* (I) / *contrabajo* (Sp)

Dbn. double bassoon (contrabassoon)

DBP *Dicionário biográfico de musicos portuguezes*

DC, D.C. *da capo* (I=from the beginning)

DCHP Dějiny české hudby v přikladech

DCI Drum Corps International

DCM Vinton, John, ed. *Dictionary of Contemporary Music*

DCS Dead Composers Society

DdT, DDT *Denkmäler deutscher Tonkunst*

De cantu *De cantu et musica sacra* (Martin Gerbert)

Dec. *ad decimam*

Decic *delicatamente*

Decr. *decrescendo* (I=becoming softer)

Delius Delius Society. *Journal* (jl.)

DeM *Deus misuratur*

Der Derry Music Co. (publ.)

Desc *descendens, descendentes*

Dest. *destra* (I=right)

Deutsch Deutsch, Erich Otto. *Franz Schubert: Thematisches Verzeichnis seiner Werke*

Deutsches Jb. Volkskunde, DeutschesJbVolkskunde *Deutsches*

Jahrbuch für Volkskunde (jl.)

DeutschesJbMu   *Deutsches Jahrbuch der Musikwissenschaft* (jl.)

DG   *Deutsche Grammophon Gesellschaft* (rec. lab.)

DGG   *Deutsche Grammophon Gesellschaft* (rec. lab.)

Dgt.   *Dirigent* (G=conductor)

Di   duration series, inversion of a (nota.)

DI   *The Diapason* (jl.); inversion of a duration series

Diap   *The Diapason* (jl.)

Diap.   diapasons (organ pipes, stops)

DIC   inverted cancrizans of a duration series

Dim   *diminuendo* (I); *diminuieren* (G)

Dim.   diminution

DIME   Dialogue in Instrumental Music Education

Dimin.   *diminuendo* (I)

Dipl.   Diplomatic transcription (facsimiles traced or copied freehand)

Dipl. U.   *Diplomatische Umschrift* (G=diplomatic transcription; nota.)

Dir.   *dirección* (Sp) / *direzione* (I) / *direction* (F) / *dirigierend* (G) = conducting/conductor

Dirs.   directors

Disc   *Discographical Forum* (jl.)

Discoteca   *Discoteca alta fedeltà* (jl.)

Div.   *divertimento; divisi*

Divert.   *divertimento*

DJBFA   Danske Jazz, Beat og Folkemusik Autorer

DJbM   *Deutsches Jahrbuch der Musikwissenschaft* (jl.)

DJbMw   *Deutsches Jahrbuch der Musikwissenschaft* (jl.)

DLCM   *Drinker Library of Choral Music*

DM   *Die Musik* (jl.); *Documenta musicologica* (jl.)

D.M.A.   Doctor of Musical Arts

DMD   *Diletto musicale*, DM

DMG   Deutsche Mozart Gesellschaft; Deutsches Mozartfest der deutschen Mozart-Gesellschaft

DMK   *Deutsche Musikkultur* (jl.)

DMl   *Documenta musicologica* (jl.)

DMMZ   *Deutsche Militärmusikerzeitung* (jl.)

DMN   Deutsche Choral-Mensurale Mischnotation (G=German mixed plainsong and mensural notation)

DMS   Schuh, Willi, ed. *Dictionnaire des musiciens suisses*

DMT   *Dansk musiktidsskrift* (jl.)

DMV   Association of German Music Publishers / Deutscher Musikverlegerverband

Dob   Doblinger (publ.)

Doctor   *Doctor Jazz* (jl.)

Dod.   *dodecafonia* (I, Sp=12-tone music)

Dodekaph.   *Dodekaphonie* (noun), *dodekaphonisch* (adj.) (G=12-tone music)

Dol.   *dolce* (I=sweet, -ly)

Dolmetsch B   Dolmetsch Foundation. *Bulletin* (jl.)

Dom.   *Dominion* (rec. lab.)

DonSoc   Donizetti Society

Dopp. ped.   *doppio pedale*

Dor.   Dorian (mode)

Dot   dotted

Down Bt.   *Down Beat* (jl.)

Dpf.   *Dämpfer* (G=mute)

Dr.   drum

Dreist.   *dreistimmig* (G=three-part)

DRS   Django Reinhardt Society

Ds   duration series (nota.)

D.S.   *dal segno* (I=go back to the sign and repeat)

DS   Delius Society

DSG   Danish Songwriters Guild

DSJRFC   Danish Society for Jazz, Rock, and Folk Composers

DSM   Danish Musicological Society / Dansk Selskab for Musikforskning

DSS   Društvo Slovenskih Skladateljev

DTB *Denkmäler der Tonkunst in Bayern*

DTKV German Musicians' Association / Deutscher Ton-künstlerverband

DTÖ, DTOe *Denkmäler der Tonkunst in Österreich*

Du *duplum* (nota.)

DUT Det Unge Tonekunstnerselskab

DVfM, DVFM VEB Deutscher Verlag für Musik (publ.)

DVM VEB Deutscher Verlag für Musik (publ.)

E easy

E.Hr. English horn / *Englisch Horn* (G)

E.m. *edizione moderne* (I=modern edition)

E.M.D.E.S.A. Ediciones musicales Demetrio, S.A. (publ.)

E.s. *enforcer silencieusement* (F=depress the keys silently)

E-M easy to medium (difficulty)

EA *Ear Magazine* (jl.); *erst Aufführung, Erstaufführung* (G=first performance)

EAC European Association of Conservatoires

EAM Editorial Argentina de Música (publ.)

EAMF European Association of Music Festivals

EAMI Editorial Argentina de Música Internacional (publ.)

Earl Mus *Early Music* (jl.)

Early M *Early Music* (jl.)

Early Mus G *Early Music Gazette* (jl.)

EB Éditions françaises de musique (publ.)

Ebg. Eulenberg (publ.)

EBM *Early Bodleian Music*; Edward B. Marks (publ.)

EC Edizioni Curci (publ.); *Encyclopédie de la musique et dictionnaire du Conservatoire* (Albert Lavignac, ed.)

ECA *Edición culturales argentinas*; Federation of European Choral Associations / Arbeits Gemeinschaft Europäischer Chorverbände

ECIC Editorial Cooperativa Interamericana de Compositores

ECM *Ediciones cubanas de música*

ECo Edition Cotta'sche (publ.)

ECO English Chamber Orchestra

ECS E. C. Schirmer (publ.)

ECYO European Community Youth Orchestra

Éd. Arch. Palais Monaco *Éditions des Archives du Palais de Monaco*

Éd. compl. *éditions complètes* (F=complete editions)

Éd. fr. de mus. Éditions françaises de musique (publ.)

ED J *Jazz Educators' Journal* (jl.)

Éd. Transatl. Éditions Transatlantiques (publ.)

EDIMCE Editorial musical del centro (publ.)

EdM, EDM *Erbe deutsche Musik, Das* (jl.)

ÉducationM *L'Éducation musicale* (jl.)

Educazione M *L'Educazione musicale* (jl.)

EECM *Early English Church Music* (jl.)

EEH Wooldridge, Harry Ellis, ed. *Early English Harmony from the 10th to the 15th Century*

EF *Encyclopédie de la musique* (Fasquelle)

EFA European Festivals Association

EFDS English Folk Dance Society

EFDSS English Folk Dance and Song Society

EFL *English School of Lutenist Song Writers* (Edmund H. Fellowes, ed.)

EFMEditions J. Buyst Éditions françaises de musique (publ.)

EFYC European Federation of Young Choirs / Europäische Föderation Junger Chöre

EG *Études grégoriennes*

EGMIA Educational Group of the Music Industries Association

EGREM *Empresa de grabaciones y ediciones musicales*

EGS Emil Gilels Society

EGZ Editore G. Zanibon (publ.)

Eh English horn / *Englisch Horn* (G)

EiMB Einstein, Alfred. *Beispielsammlung zur Musikgeschichte*

Einl. *Einleitung* (G=introduction)

Einst. *einstimmig* (G=monodic)

Einstein Beisp. Einstein, Alfred. *Beispielsammlung zur älteren Musikgeschichte*; *Beispielsammlung zur Musikgeschichte*

Eitner S Eitner, Robert. *Bibliographie der Musiksammelwerke des XVI. und XVII. Jahrhunderts*

EitnerBg Eitner, Robert. *Bibliographie der Musiksammelwerke des XVI. und XVII. Jahrhunderts*

EitnerQ Eitner, Robert. *Biographisch-bibliographisches Quellenlexikon*

EKM *Early Keyboard Music* (jl.); *English Keyboard Music* (jl.)

EKS Early Keyboard Society

EL *English Lute-Songs*; *English School of Lutenist Song Writers* (Edmund H. Fellowes, ed.)

Elab. *elaborazione*

Elec. pno. electric piano

Ell Ellinwood, L., ed. *Landini, Francesco. Works*

EM *Early Music* (jl.); *English Madrigalists*; *Ethnomusicology* (jl.)

EMC Electronic Music Consortium; *Encyclopedia of Music in Canada / Encyclopédie de la musique au Canada*

EMCUSA Estonian Music Center, U.S.A.

EMDC *Encyclopédie de la musique et dictionnaire du Conservatoire* (Albert Lavignac, ed.)

EMFJ Europees Muziek voor de Jeugd

EMFY European Music Festival for the Youth

EMI Electrical and Musical Industries

EMN *Exempla musica neerlandica*

Emp. Empire State Publishers (publ.)

EMS *English Madrigal School* (Edmund H. Fellowes, ed.)

EMU Europäische Musikschul-Union

EMW *Early Musical Masterworks*

Eng Dance *English Dance and Song* (jl.)

Eng. hn. English horn / *Englisch Horn* (G)

Englh. English horn / *Englisch Horn* (G)

EnglishChurchM *English Church Music* (jl.)

EnglishDanceSong *English Dance and Song* (jl.)

EnglishMJ *English Music Journal* (jl.)

ENO English National Opera

Ens. ensemble

EOL *Éditions de L'Oiseau Lyre*

Ep *estremamente sul ponticello* (I=far up on the bridge)

EP Eitner, Robert. Gesellschaft für Musikforschung. *Publikationen älterer praktischer und theoretischer Musikwerke*; *Encyclopédie de la Pleiade: Histoire de la musique*

EPM *Études de philologie musicale*

EPTA European Piano Teachers Association

Eq equal (voices, parts)

ES E. C. Schirmer (publ.)

ESA European Suzuki Association

ESCOM European Society for the Cognitive Sciences of Music

ESCR Editura Societatii Compozitorilor Romini

Esec. *esecutore* (I=performer), *esecuzione* (I=performance)

ESLS *English School of Lutenist Song Writers* (Edmund H. Fellowes, ed.)

ESM Eastman School of Music

ESME Eastman School of Music. *Studies* (jl.)

Espr. *espressivo* (I=expessively)

ESTA English String Teachers' Association

Et *estremamente sul tasto* (I=far up on the fingerboard)

ET *Ethnomusicology* (jl.)

Ethmus., Ethnomus., Ethnomusic. *Ethnomusicology* (jl.)

Eul. Eulenberg-Verlag (publ.)

EUMS European Union of Music Schools

Ev *estremamente vibrato*

Exp. exposition

ExpertMMFR Expert, Henri, ed. *Les monuments de la musique française au temps de la Renaissance*

ExpertMMRF   Expert, Henri, ed. *Les maîtres musiciens de la renaissance française*

ExpertMonuments   Expert, Henri, ed. *Les monuments de la musique française au temps de la Renaissance*

Expn   exposition

Expos.   exposition

ExRP   Expert, Henri, ed. *Répertoire populaire de la musique de la Renaissance*

F   Florence. Biblioteca Mediceo-Laurenziana, ms. (plut.29.1) (medieval ms.); *choeur de femmes* (F=women's chorus); very fast; front (of a perc. instr.); *fusa* (nota.)

F.   *Falck Verzeichnis* (Martin Falck's cat. of W.F. Bach's works); Fanna, Antonio. *Antonio Vivaldi. Catalogo numerico-tematico delle opere strumentali*; *forte* (I=loud)

F. Chor   *Frauenchor* (G=women's chorus)

F. org.   full organ

F.o.   full organ, *organo pleno*

F.p.   first performance, first performed (in, by)

Fa.   Faenza. Biblitoeca Comunale. Cod. 117

Fag.   bassoon(s) / *Fagott* (G) / *fagotto* (I) / *fagot* (Sp)

FAGO   Fellow of the American Guild of Organists

FAM   *Fontes artis musicae* (jl.)

FAMA   Finnish Amateur Musicians' Association

Fanf.   fanfare

FasquelleE   *Encyclopédie de la musique* (Fasquelle)

Fb   fingerboard

FBC   Fellow of the Birmingham Conservatoire

FBSM   Fellow of the Birmingham School of Music

FCA   First Chair of America, Inc.

FCAPM   Fédération canadienne des professeurs de musique

FCCO   Fellow of the Canadian College of Organists

FCM   Fellowship of Christian Musicians

FCMF   Federation of Canadian Music Festivals

FCVR *Florilège du concert vocal de la renaissance*

FE Facsimile Editions

FétisB, FétisBS Fétis, François J. *Biographie universelle des musiciens*

Ff *fortissimo* (I)

Fff *fortississimo* (I)

Ffz *forzatissimo* (I)

Fg. bassoon(s) / *Fagott* (G) / *fagotto* (I) / *fagot* (Sp)

FGSM Fellow of the Guildhall School of Music

FH Frederick Harris Music Co. (publ.)

Fiati *strumenti a fiato* (I=wind instruments)

FICE Fédération internationale des choeurs d'enfants

FIGA Fretted Instrument Guild of America

FIH Fédération internationale de l'harmonica

FIJM International Federation of Jeunesses Musicales / Fédération internationale des jeunesses musicales; Festival Internationale de Jazz de Montréal

FIM Fédération internationale des musiciens

Fin. finale

Fing. cyms. finger cymbals

Fis *fisarmonica* (I=accordion)

Fischb. Fischbacher (publ.)

FJ *Flute Journal* (jl.)

Fl. fluttertongue

Fl. fls. flute(s) / *flauto* (I) / *flûte* (F) / *flauta* (Sp) / *Flöte* (G)

Fl. trav. *flûte traversière* (F=flute)

FLCM Fellow of the London College of Music

Fl.d. *flauto diritto* (I=recorder); *flûte droite* (F=recorder)

Fld *flauto dolce* (I=recorder)

Flex. Flexatone

Flhn. Flügelhorn(s)

Flo. Florence. Biblioteca Mediceo-Laurenziana, ms. (plut.29.1) (medieval ms.)

FM *Feuilles musicales*

FMCIM Fédération mondiale des concours internationaux de musique

Fmo. *fortissimo* (I)

FMOB Federation of Master Organ Builders

FMS Federal Music Society

FMSI Folk Music Society of Ireland

FNACEM National Federation of Cultural Associations for the Promotion of Music / Fédération nationale d'associations culturelles d'expansion musicale

FNMC French National Music Committee

Folk *Folkways* (rec. lab.)

Folk Harp J *Folk Harp Journal* (jl.)

Folk Mus J *Folk Music Journal* (jl.)

Folk Music *Folk Music* (jl.)

FoMRHI Fellowship of Makers and Researchers of Historical Instruments

Fon art mus *Fontes artis musicae* (jl.)

Fontes, Fontes artis m *Fontes artis musicae* (jl.)

FOPS Fair Organ Preservation Society

Forts. *Fortsetzer* (G); *Fortsetzung* (G=continuation)

ForumM *Forum musicum* (jl.)

Fp *fortepiano* (I)

FP Florence. Biblioteca nazionale centrale. Panciatichi 26 (ms)

Fps frames per second

FRAM Fellow of the Royal Academy of Music

Framm. *frammento* (I=fragment)

FRCCO Fellow of the Royal Canadian College of Organists

FrCh. *Frauenchor* (G=women's chorus)

FRCM Fellow of the Royal College of Music

FRCO Fellow of the Royal College of Organists

FRMCM Fellow of the Royal Manchester College of Music

FRMS Federation of Recorded Music Societies

FRSCM Fellow of the Royal School of Church Music

FSK Union of Lapp Composers / Foreningen Samiske Komponister

FSM French Society of Musicology

FSPM *Feuillets suisses de pédagogie musicale*

FST Föreningen Svenska Tonsättare

FTCL Fellow of Trinity College, London (now, Fellow of the Trinity College of Music, FTCM)

FTCM Fellow of the Trinity College of Music (earlier, Fellow of Trinity College, London, FTCL)

FTSC Fellow of the Tonic Sol-fa College of Music

Fu *fusa* (nota.)

FVB *Fitzwilliam Virginal Book*

Fz *forzato* (I)

G *Graduale sacrosanctae romanae ecclesiae de tempore et de sanctis*

G. *gauche* (F=left); Gérard, Yves. *Thematic, Bibliographical, and Critical Catalogue of the Works of Luigi Boccherini*; Giegling, Franz. *Giegling Verzeichnis* (Franz Giegling's cat. of Giuseppe Torelli's works)

G & S J *Gilbert & Sullivan Journal* (jl.)

G. org. great organ

G.o. *grand orgue, great organ*

G.p. *grand positif*

G.P. *Generalpause* (G=rest for entire ensemble)

G.r. *grand récitatif*

GA *Gesamtausgabe* (G=collected ed.)

GAkF Fribourg, Switz. Gregorianische Akademie. *Veröffentlichungen*

GAL Guild of American Luthiers

GALA Gay and Lesbian Association of Choruses

Galpin Soc *Galpin Society Journal* (jl.)

GalpinSJ *Galpin Society Journal* (jl.)

GalpinSocJ *Galpin Society Journal* (jl.)

GAM Groupe d'acoustique musicale; Groupe d'acoustique musicale. *Bulletin* (jl.)

GAMA Guitar and Accessories Marketing Association, Guitar and

Accessory Manufacturers' Association of America

Gav   *Gavotte* (rec. lab.)

Gb.   *Generalbass*

GB   Bénévent. Bibliothèque Capitulaire. Codex VI.34 *(Graduel de Bénévent avec prosaire et tropaire)*

GBSM   Graduate of the Birmingham School of Music

GChN   Gothic plainsong notation / *gothische Choralnotation*

GCNA   Guild of Carillonneurs in North America

GD   *Gesamtdauer* (G=total length); *Grove's Dictionary of Music and Musicians*

Gd.   grand

GdM   Wolf, Johannes. *Geschichte der Mensural-Notation von 1250-1460*

GDM   Gesamtverband Deutscher Musikfachgeschäfte; Association of German Music Dealers

GDSS   General Dutch Singing Society

Géhm, GéHM   Gérold, T. *Histoire de la musique des origins à la fin du XIVe siècle*

GEM   *Gemshorn* (jl.)

Gem.   *gemischt* (G=mixed)

Gem. Chor   *gemischter Chor* (G=mixed chorus)

GEMA   Gesellschaft für musikalische Aufführungs- und mechanische Vervielfältigungsrechte

GemCh   *gemischter Chor* (G=mixed chorus)

GeNeCo   Dutch Composers' Society / Genootschap van Nederlandse Componisten

GerberL   Gerber, Ernst Ludwig. *Historisch-biographisches Lexikon der Tonkünstler*

GerberN, GerberNL   Gerber, Ernst Ludwig. *Neues historisch-biographisches Lexikon der Tonkünstler*

Gerbert   Gerbert, Martin. *De cantu et musica sacra*

GerbertMon   Gerbert, Martin. *Monumenta liturgiae*

GerbertS   Gerbert, Martin. *Scriptores ecclesiastici de musica sacra potissimum*

Ges. *Gesang* (G=song)

Ges-Pädagogik *Gesangspädagogik* (G=teaching of singing)

Gest. *gestopft* (G=muted)

Gestr. *gestrichen* (G=bowed strings)

Get. *geteilt* (G=divided)

Gew. Notenschr. *gewöhnliche Notenschrift* (G=normal notation)

GF Gaudeamus Foundation

GFA Guitar Foundation of America

GfMKB Gesellschaft für Musikforschung Kongressbericht

Ggs. *Gegensatz* (G=contrasting theme)

G.G.S.M. Graduate of the Guildhall School of Music

Git. *Gitarre* (G=guitar)

GKV Georg Kallmeyer Verlag (publ.)

GL *Guitar & Lute* (jl.)

Gl. *Glockenspiel*; *Gloria*

Glar. *glareanus dodecachordon*

Gliss. *glissando* (I)

Glk. *Glockenspiel*

Glock. *Glockenspiel*

Glsp. *Glockenspiel*

Glsp. (Kbd.) keyboard glockenspiel

GM *Gopher Music Notes* (jl.); Schering, Arnold. *Geschichte der Musik in Beispielen*

GMA Gospel Music Association

GMB Schering, Arnold. *Geschichte der Musik in Bayern*

GMD *Generalmusikdirektor, General-Musik-Direktor*

GMS German Mozart Society

GMWA Gospel Music Workshop of America

Gottesd u Kir *Gottesdienst und Kirchenmusik* (jl.)

GottesdienstKm *Gottesdienst und Kirchenmusik* (jl.)

GP *Guitar Player* (jl.)

Gps groups

GPWM Guild for the Promotion of Welsh Music

GR *Graduale sacrosanctae romanae ecclesiae de tempore et de sanctis*

Gr. *gradual*; great organ; *gruppo*

Gr. Tr. *grosse Trommel*

Gra *Grackle, The: Improvised Music in Transition* (jl.)

Grad. *gradual, graduale*

Grad. Vat. *Graduale sacrosanctae romanae ecclesiae de tempore et de sanctis*

Grainger J *Grainger Journal* (jl.)

Gram. gramophone, *grammofono, gramófono* (I, Sp=phonograph)

Grat act *pro gratiarum actione*

Gray H. W. Gray Co. (publ.)

Grc *gran cassa, grancassa* (I=bass drum)

GrHWM Grout, Donald Jay. *History of Western Music*

GRM Groupe de recherches musicales

GRNCM Graduate of the Royal Northern College of Music

Grove *Grove's Dictionary of Music and Musicians*

GRSM Graduate of the Royal Schools of Music

Grv Gradual verse

GS British Museum. Library. Addl. 12194 (*Graduale Sarisburiense*) (ms.); G. Schirmer (publ.); Galpin Society; *Gegensatz* (G=contrasting theme); Gerbert, Martin. *Scriptores ecclesiastici de musica sacra potissimum*; Glazounov Society; *Graduale Sarisburiense: A Reproduction in Facsimile* (Walter Howard Frere, ed.)

GSCC German Society of Concert Choirs / Verband Deutscher Konzert-Chöre

GsgB. *Gesangbuch* (G=song book)

Gsge. *Gesänge* (G=songs), Gsge.

GSJ *Galpin Society Journal* (jl.)

GSM Guildhall School of Music and Drama; Society for Self-Playing Musical Instruments / Gesellschaft für Selbstspielende Musikinstrumente

Gsp. *Glockenspiel*

GSSME German Society of School Music Educators

Gt. grand organ

GU *Guitar Review* (jl.)

Gui guitar / *guitare* (F)

Guilmant-Pirro Guilmant, Alexandre, ed. *Archives des maîtres de l'orgue des XVIe, XVIIe, et XVIIIe siécles* (Alexandre Guilmant et André Pirro, ed.)

Guit. guitar / *guitare* (F)

Guitar *Guitar Player* (jl.)

GuitarR *Guitar Review* (jl.)

GVT Gordon V. Thompson (publ.)

GW *Gesammelte Werke* (G=collected works)

H *choeur d'hommes* (F=men's chorus); halfway (on perc. instr.); *Hauptstimme*; hymn, *hymnus*

H. *haut* (F=high); Helm, Eugene. *New Thematic Catalog of the Works of Carl Philipp Emanuel Bach*; high; Hoboken, Anthony van. *Joseph Haydn: Thematisches Werkverzeichnis*; hoch (G=high)

H & H Hawkes & Harris Music Co. (publ.)

H.c. *haute-contre* (F=alto)

H.G. Händelgesellschaft (G=Breitkopf & Härtel's ed. of Händel's works)

H.M.V. *His Master's Voice* (rec. lab.)

HACM Hellenic Association for Contemporary Music

HAM Davison, Archibald T. *Historical Anthology of Music*

Handb. handbell(s)

HändelJb *Händel-Jahrbuch* (jl.)

Har Hargail Music Press (publ.)

Harm. *harmonisch* (G=harmonic); harmonium

Harmon. *Harmonie* (G=harmony)

HarmonikaJb *Harmonika-Jahrbuch* (jl.)

Hauptw. *Hauptwerk* (G=great organ)

Hausm. *Hausmusik*

Haut. *hautbois* (F=oboe)

HäW   Chrysander, Friedrich, ed. *Händel, Georg Friedrich. Werke*

HawkinsH   Hawkins, John. *A General History of the Science and Practice of Music*

Haydn Stud   *Haydn Studien* (jl.)

Haydn Yb   *Haydn Yearbook* (jl.) / *Haydn Jahrbuch*

Hb.   *hautbois* (F=oboe)

HbMw   *Handbuch der Musikwissenschaft* (Ernst Bücken, ed.)

HBS   Historic Brass Society

HC   *Horn Call* (jl.)

HD   *Harpsichord* (jl.)

Hd.   *Händig* (G=handed)

HDM   Apel, Willi. *Harvard Dictionary of Music*

HdMw   Bücken, Ernst, ed. *Handbuch der Musikwissenschaft*

HdN   Wolf, Johannes. *Handbuch der Notationskunde*

Hdn.   *Händen* (G=hands)

Herd b.   herd bell(s)

HF   *High Fidelity/Musical America* (jl.)

HF/MA   *High Fidelity/Musical America* (jl.)

Hf.   *Harfe* (G=harp)

HFAA   Hardanger Fiddle Association of America

Hfe.   *Harfe* (G=harp)

HGZ   Croatian Music Institute / Hrvatski Glazbeni zavod

HHA   *Hallische Händel-Ausgabe*

Hi fi   high fidelity

Hi Fi/Mus Am   *High Fidelity/Musical America* (jl.)

HIFMA   *High Fidelity/Musical America* (jl.)

HindemithJb   *Hindemith Jahrbuch* (jl.) / *Annales Hindemith*

HJb   *Händel-Jahrbuch* (jl.)

Hk.   *Hauptwerk* (G=great organ)

Hm   harmonic mean

HM   *Hortus musicus*

HmT, HMT   Eggebricht, Hans Heinrich. *Handwörterbuch der musikalische Terminologie*

HMUB Hudební Matice Uniělecké Besedy (publ.)

HMw Bücken, Ernst, ed. *Handbuch der Musikwissenschaft*

HMwBüHM Bücken, Ernst, ed. *Handbuch der Musikwissenschaft*

HMY *Hinrichsen's Musical Year Book* (jl.)

HMYB *Hinrichsen's Musical Year Book* (jl.)

Hob. Hoboken, Anthony van. *Joseph Haydn: Thematisches Werkverzeichnis*

Holzbl *Holzblasinstrumente* (G=woodwind instr.)

Hpcd. harpsichord

HPD Croatian Singing Society / Hrvatsko pjevačko društvo

Hpd. harpsichord

HPM *Harvard Publications in Music*

Hpsd. harpsichord

Hptw. *Hauptwerk* (G=great organ)

HR *Hauptrhythmus* (G=principal rhythm); *Hudební revue* (jl.); *Hudební rozhledy* (jl.)

Hr. horn; *Hörner* (G=horns)

HRS Harp Renaissance Society

HS *Hauptsatz* (G=principal theme)

HSA Hymn Society of America

Htb. *hautbois* (F=oboe)

Hu *Codex Huelgas* (*Codex Burgos*)

Hud Roz *Hudební rozhledy* (jl.)

Hud veda, Hudveda Hudební věda

Hud Zivot Hudební život

HudNástroje Hudební nástroje

HudR *Hudební rozhledy* (jl.)

HÜHM Bücken, Ernst, ed. *Handbuch der Musikwissenschaft*

HV Hudební věda

HWML Henry Watson Music Library, Manchester Public Libraries

Hy hymn, *hymnus*

HY *The Hymn* (jl.)

Hymn hymns

Hymn S Hymn Society of Great Britain and Ireland. *Bulletin* (jl.)

Hymns A & M *Hymns Ancient and Modern*

Hz Hertz (cycles per second)

I undesignated instrument; inversion

I/O input/output (data proc.)

I. pr. NA in praktischer NeuausgabeA

I.A.M.I.C. International Association for Music Instrument Collections

IABS International Alban Berg Society

IACFM International Association of Concert and Festival Managers

IACM International Association of Concert Managers

IAEKM International Association of Electronic Keyboard Manufacturers

IAJE International Association of Jazz Educators

IAJRC International Association of Jazz Record Collectors; International Association of Jazz Record Collectors. *The IAJRC Journal* (jl.)

IAM Institute of the American Musical

IAMC Inter-American Music Council

IAML International Association of Music Libraries, Archives, and Documentation Centres

IAO Incorporated Association of Organists

IAOD International Association of Opera Directors

IAOJA International Association of Jazz Appreciation

IAOT(U) International Association of Organ Teachers USA

IAPBT International Association of Piano Builders and Technicians

IASA International Association of Sound Archives

IASPM International Association for the Study of Popular Music

IAWM International Alliance for Women in Music

IBG International Bruckner Gesellschaft

IBMR International Bureau of Mechanical Reproduction

IBS International Bach Society

ICA International Clarinet Association; International Confederation of

Accordionists

ICC   International Cello Centre; International Council of Composers

ICEM   International Confederation for Electroacoustic Music

ICGA   International Classic Guitar Association

ICMA   International Computer Music Association

ICME   International Contemporary Music Exchange

ICMP   International Confederation of Music Publishers

ICPMS   International Confederation of Popular Music Societies

ICS   International Clarinet Society

ICSAC   International Confederation of Societies of Authors and Composers

ICSM   International Confederation of Societies of Music

ICSOM   International Conference of Symphony and Opera Musicians

ICTM   International Council for Traditional Music

IDOCO   Internationale des organisations culturelles ouvrières

IDRS   International Double Reed Society

IEM   Instituto de extensión musical; Spain. Consejo Superior de Investigaciones Científicas. Instituto Español de musicologia

IFCC   International Federation of Children's Choirs

IFCM   International Federation for Choral Music

IFG   International Fasch Society / Internationale Fasch-Gesellschaft

IFLS   International Federation of "Little Singers"

IFM   International Federation of Musicians

IFMC   International Folk Music Centre; International Folk Music Council; International Folk Music Council. *Yearbook* (jl.)

IFPI   International Federation of the Phonographic Industry

IFR   International Federation of Ragtime

IGMG   International Gustav Mahler Society

IGMM   Internationale Gesellschaft für Musik in der Medizin; Internationale Gesellschaft für neue Musik

IGW   Internationale Gesellschaft für Musikwissenschaft

IHF   International Harmonica Foundation

IHS   International Horn Society

IHSG International Heinrich Schütz Society

IHWG International Hugo Wolf Society

IIM Bulgarska Akademiia na Naukite, Sofia. Institute za Institute za Musikozname. Izvestiia; Instituto Interamericano de Musicología

IISM Istituto italiano per la storia della musica

IITM International Institute for Traditional Music

IJS Institute of Jazz Studies

IKS International Kodály Society

ILWC International League of Women Composers

IM Instituta et monumenta; *International Musician* (jl.); Internationale Musikbibliothek (publ.)

Ima Instituta et monumenta

IMA Independent Music Association; International MIDI Association; International Music Association

IMAMI Istituzioni e monumenti dell'arte musicale italiana

IMC Intercollegiate Men's Chorus, an International Association of Male Choruses; Intercollegiate Musical Council; International Music Centre; International Music Council

IMF Israel Music Foundation

IMG *Internationale Musikgesellschaft* (jl.)

Imi Istituzioni e monumenti dell'arte musicale italiana

IMI Israel Music Institute

IMIC Iceland Music Information Centre

IMIT Institute of Musical Instrument Technology

IML Intermediary Musical Language (comp.lang)

IMM Institute of Medieval Music

IMP Israel Music Publications

IMPS International Manuel Poncé Society

IMS International Musicological Society

IMusSCR International Musical Society. *Congress Report* (jl.)

IMZ Internationales Musikzentrum

Inc *incipit*

Incip *incipit*

IncV   *Incipit-Verzeichnis* (G) / *index des incipit* (F) / *incipit index*

Indian MS   Indian Musicological Society. *Journal* (jl.)

IndianMJ   *Indian Music Journal* (jl.)

INS   *Instrumentalist* (jl.)

Inst.   instrument (E, F) / *Instrument* (G)

Instl.   instrumental (E, G)

Instr.   instrument (E, F) / *Instrument* (G); instrumental (E, G); instrumentation

Instrk.   *Instrumentenkunde* (G)

Instrument   *Instrumentalist* (jl.)

InstrumentenbauZ   *Instrumentenbau-Zeitschrift* (jl.)

Int Banjo   *International Banjo* (jl.)

Int Mus   *International Musician* (jl.)

Int Mus Ed   *International Music Educator* (jl.)

Int R Aesthetics & Soc   *International Review of the Aesthetics and Sociology of Music* (jl.)

Int Rev Aes   *International Review of the Aesthetics and Sociology of Music* (jl.)

Int.   introit / *introitus*

Int. Rev. of Music Aesth. & Sociol.   *International Review of the Aesthetics and Sociology of Music* (jl.)

Intab   intabulation, keyboard

Intam Mus R   *Inter-American Music Review* (jl.)

InterAmerMBul   *Inter-American Music Bulletin* (jl.)

Intr.   introit / *introitus*

IntRAestheticsSociologyM   *International Review of the Aesthetics and Sociology of Music* (jl.)

Intv   introit verse

Inv   *invitatorium* / invitatory (chant)

Invitat.   *invitatorium* / invitatory (chant)

IO   inverted 12-tone row that begins on the first pitch of the orig. row

IOFS   International Organ Festival Society

IPA   International Polka Association

IPEM   Institute for Psycho-Acoustics & Electronic Music

IPG   International Piano Guild

IPM   Suñol, Gregoire Marie. *Introduction à la paléographie musicale*

IPMA   International Planned Music Association

Ips   inches per second

IPS   Incorporated Phonographic Society

IPTA   International Piano Teachers Association

IPTF   International Piano Teachers Foundation

Ir   *tonus irregularis* (church mode)

IRASM   *International Review of the Aesthetics and Sociology of Music* (jl.)

IRCAM   Institut de recherche de coordination acoustique et musique

IrishFolkMStud   *Irish Folk Music Studies* (jl.)

IRMO   Ginzburg, S. L. *Istoriya russkoy muziki v notnikh obraztsakh*

IRMPM   International Record and Music Publishing Market / Marche international du disque et de l'édition musicale, MIDEM

IRMS   Imperial Russian Music Society

IRP   Tribune internationale des jeunes interprètes

IRSG   International Richard Strauss Society / Internationale Richard Strauss Gesellschaft

IRYP   International Rostrum of Young Performers

ISA   International Songwriters' Association

ISAM, I.S.A.M.   Institute for Studies in American Music

ISB   International Society of Bassists; International Society of Bassists. *Newsletter* (jl.)

ISCM   International Society for Contemporary Music

ISFHC   International Society of Folk Harpers and Craftsmen

ISGC   International Steel Guitar Convention

ISM   Incorporated Society of Musicians; Internationale Stiftung Mozarteum. *Mitteilungen* (jl.)

ISMC   International Society for Music Education

ISMM   International Society for Music in Medicine

ISO   International Society of Organ Builders

ISOB Incorporated Society of Organ Builders

ISOHP International Society for Organ History and Preservation

ISPAA International Society of Performing Arts Administrators

Ist. e Mon. Istituzioni e monumenti dell'arte musicale italiana

ISUM International Society for Uruguayan Music

ISVBM International Society of Violin and Bow Makers

IT International Trombone Association. *Newsletter* (jl.); International Trumpet Guild. *Journal* (jl.); transposed inversion of 12-tone row

ITA International Trombone Association

ITA J International Trombone Association. *Journal* (jl.)

ITA N International Trombone Association. *Newsletter* (jl.)

ITG International Trumpet Guild; International Trumpet Guild. *Journal* (jl.)

ITG J International Trumpet Guild. *Journal* (jl.)

ITG N International Trumpet Guild. *Newsletter* (jl.)

ITO *In Theory Only* (jl.)

Iv Ivrea. Biblioteca capitolare. Codex 115

IVG Internationale Viola Gesellschaft

IVMB Internationale Vereinigung der Musikbibliotheken, Musikarchive und Musikdokumentationszentren

IVRS International Viola Research Society

IVS International Viola Society

IWMA International Western Music Association

IZ *Instrumentenbau-Zeitschrift* (jl.)

IzvestijaInstMBAN Bulgarska Akademiia na Naukite, Sofia. Institute za Musikozname. Izvestiia

J *Jenaer Handschrift* (medieval ms.)

J A Schoenb Arnold Schoenberg Institute. *Journal* (jl.)

J ALS American Liszt Society. *Journal* (jl.)

J Am Mus In American Musical Instrument Society. *Journal* (jl.)

J Am Music American Musicological Society. *Journal* (jl.)

J Amer Musicol Soc American Musicological Society. *Journal* (jl.)

J Arnold Schoenberg Inst   Arnold Schoenberg Institute. *Journal* (jl.)

J B Co.   *Jazz, Blues & Co.* (jl.)

J Band Res   *Journal of Band Research* (jl.)

J Church Mus   *Journal of Church Music* (jl.)

J Echo   *Jazz Echo* (jl.)

J Ed J   *NAJE Educator* (jl.)

J Freak   *Jazz Freak* (jl.)

J Hot   *Jazz Hot, Le* (jl.)

J Indian Musicol Soc   Indian Musicological Society. *Journal* (jl.)

J ITA   International Trombone Association. *Journal* (jl.)

J ITG   International Trumpet Guild. *Journal* (jl.)

J Jazz Stud   *Journal of Jazz Studies* (jl.)

J Jazz Studies   *Journal of Jazz Studies* (jl.)

J Mag   *Jazz Magazine* (Paris) (jl.)

J Mus Theory   *Journal of Music Theory* (jl.)

J Mus Therapy   *Journal of Music Therapy* (jl.)

J Music Res   *Journal of Musicological Research* (jl.)

J Music Ther   *Journal of Music Therapy* (jl.)

J Music Thr   *Journal of Music Theory* (jl.)

J Nu   *Jazz Nu* (jl.)

J Rep   *Jazz Report* (jl.)

J Res   *Jazz Research* (jl.)

J Res Mus Ed   *Journal of Research in Music Education* (jl.)

J Res Music   *Journal of Research in Music Education* (jl.)

J Spot   *Jazz Spotlite News* (jl.)

J Times   *Jazz Times* (jl.)

J Violin S   Violin Society of America. *Journal* (jl.)

J Violin Soc Amer   Violin Society of America. *Journal* (jl.)

J-H   *Jazz* (Hellerup, Denmark) (jl.)

J-S   *Jazz* (Sydney) (jl.)

JA   American Musicological Society. *Journal* (jl.)

Jahrb Volks   *Jahrbuch für Volksliedforschung* (jl.)

JAMS   American Musicological Society. *Journal* (jl.)

JAMTD   Canadian Association for Music Therapy. *Journal* (jl.)

JanM   Jan, Karl von. *Musici scriptores graeci*

JAS   Jazz Arts Society

JASA   Acoustical Society of America. *Journal* (jl.)

JATP   Jazz at the Philharmonic

Jazz J Int   *Jazz Journal International* (jl.)

Jazz Mag (US)   *Jazz Magazine* (Northport, NY) (jl.)

Jazz Mag   *Jazz Magazine* (Paris) (jl.)

Jazz Rept   *Jazz Report* (jl.)

JazzF   *Jazzforschung* (jl.)

JB   *Journal of Band Research* (jl.)

JBandResearch   *Journal of Band Research* (jl.)

JbDeutschenSängerbundes   Deutsches Sängerbund. *Jahrbuch* (jl.)

JbfVf, JbfVldf   *Jahrbuch für Volksliedforschung* (jl.)

JbKomischenOper   *Jahrbuch der Komischen Oper* (jl.)

JbMP   *Jahrbuch der Musikbibliothek Peters* (jl.)

Jb Orff Inst   Orff Institut. *Jahrbuch* (jl.)

JbP   *Jahrbuch der Musikbibliothek Peters* (jl.)

JbVolksliedf   *Jahrbuch für Volksliedforschung* (jl.)

JC   *Journal of Church Music* (jl.)

JChurchM   *Journal of Church Music* (jl.)

JCMA   Japan Contemporary Music Association

JCOA   Jazz Composers Orchestra Association

JEFDSS   English Folk Dance and Song Society. *Journal* (jl.)

JEMF   John Edwards Memorial Foundation

JEMF Q, JEMF Quart   John Edwards Memorial Foundation. *Quarterly* (jl.)

Jeunesse   *Jeunesse et orgue* (jl.)

JF-D   *Jazz Forum* (German ed.)

JF-I   *Jazz Forum* (Int'l. ed.)

Jfreund   *Jazzfreund, Der* (jl.)

JFSS Folk-Song Society. *Journal* (jl.)

JI *Jazz Index*; Jazz Interactions; *Jazz International* (jl.)

JIFMC International Folk Music Council. *Yearbook* (jl.)

JJ *Journal of Jazz Studies* (jl.)

JJI *Jazz Journal International* (jl.)

JluteSocAmer Lute Society of America. *Journal* (jl.)

JM *Journal of Music Theory* (jl.)

JM Theory *Journal of Music Theory* (jl.)

JMA Jewish Music Alliance

JMC Jewish Music Council

JME Juventudes Musicales de España

JMF Jewish Music Forum

JMH Jeunesses Musicales of Hungary

JMI Jeunesses Musicales of Israel

JMP *Jahrbuch der Musikbibliothek Peters* (jl.); Portuguese Musical Youth Association / Juventude Musical Portuguesa

JMS Jeunesses Musicales de Suisse

JMT *Journal of Music Theory* (jl.)

JMTh *Journal of Music Theory* (jl.)

JMTherapy *Journal of Music Therapy* (jl.)

JMW *Jahrbücher für musikalische Wissenschaft* (jl.)

JN *Juilliard News Bulletin* (jl.)

Jnytt *Jazznytt* (jl.)

Jo St *Journal of Jazz Studies* (jl.)

JP *Jazz Podium* (jl.)

JRBM *Journal of Renaissance and Baroque Music* (jl.)

JResearchMEducation *Journal of Research in Music Education* (jl.)

JRM *Journal of Research in Music Education* (jl.)

JRME *Journal of Research in Music Education* (jl.)

JRMEA *Journal of Research in Music Education* (jl.)

JRMEd *Journal of Reserach in Music Education* (jl.)

JRS *Journal of Research in Singing* (jl.)

JS Arnold Schoenberg Institute. *Journal* (jl.)

JT *Journal of Music Therapy* (jl.)

JU *Juilliard Review Annual* (jl.)

Jub. *Jubilate*

JV Violin Society of America. *Journal* (jl.)

JVNM *Bouwsteenen: Jaarboek der Vereniging voor Nederlandshe muziekgeschiedenis* (jl.)

JWS *Jazz World Society*

JZ *Jazz Magazine* (jl.)

K. Kirkpatrick (before a number, identification assigned by Ralph Kirkpatrick to D. Scarlatti's sonatas); *Köchel-Verzeichnis* (i.e., L. von Köchel's chronol. list of Mozart's works)

K. Chor *Kinderchor* (G=children's chorus)

K.V. *Köchel-Verzeichnis* (i.e., L. von Köchel's chronol. list of Mozart's works)

K&S Kistner & Siegel (publ.)

KaM. *Kammermusik* (G=chamber music)

Kant. *Kantate* (G=cantata)

Kb. *Kontrabass* (G=contrabass, double bass)

KbCh *Knabenchor* (G=boys' chorus)

Kbd. keyboard

KBMf *Kölner Beiträge zur Musikforschung* (jl.)

KC *Keyboard Classics* (jl.)

KE *Keeping Up With Orff-Schulwerk in the Classroom* (jl.)

Kf. *Kontrafaktur* (G=contrafactum)

Kfag. *Kontrafagott* (G=contrabassoon)

KgrIMG Internationale Musikgesellschaft. *Kongress* (jl.)

Kir Mus *Der Kirchenmusiker* (jl.)

Kirchor *Der Kirchenchor* (jl.)

KJ *Cäcilien Kalender* (jl.)

KJ, KJb *Kirchenmusikalisches Jahrbuch* (jl.)

Kl *Klarinette* (G=clarinet)

Kl. *Klavier* (G=piano)

Kl. A. *Klavierauszug* (G=piano reduction; vocal score)

Kl. Fl. *kleine Flöte* (G=piccolo)

Kl. Tr. *kleine Trommel* (G=side drum)

Kl-A., Kla. *Klavierauszug* (G=piano reduction; vocal score)

Klank *Klank en Weerklank* (jl.)

Klar. *Klarinette* (G=clarinet)

Klass. *klassisch* (G=classical)

KM *Kirchenmusik* (G=church music); *Kwartalnik muzyczyny* (jl.)

Km. *Der Kirchenmusiker* (jl.)

KMJ *Kirchenmusikalisches Jahrbuch* (jl.)

KMJB, Km Jb *Kirchenmusikalisches Jahrbuch* (jl.)

KmNachrichten *Kirchenmusikalische Nachrichten* (jl.)

Kmp. *Kapellmeister*

Kn. Chor *Knabenchor* (G=boys' chorus)

KochL Koch, Heinrich Christoph. *Musikalisches Lexikon*

Kod. *Kodex* (G=codex)

Komp. *komponiert* (G=composed); *Komponist* (G=composer)

Kompos. *Komposition*

Kons. *Konservatorium* (G=conservatory)

Konz. *Konzert* (G=concert); *konzertierend*

KonzM. *Konzertmeister* (G=concert master)

Kp. *Kontrapunkt* (G=counterpoint); *kontrapunktisch* (G=contrapuntal)

KTAI Keyboard Teachers Association International

Kwart. Muz. *Kwartalnik muzyczyny* (jl.)

KWFM Kurt Weill Foundation for Music

Ky. *Kyrie*

L, L. *Liber Usualis, with introduction and rubrics in English*; long; *longa, longae* (nota.); Longo (I=numbering system of D. Scarlatti's sonatas devised by Alessandro Longo)

L. litany; low

L.c. left channel (tape)

L.h., L.H. left hand / *linke Hand* (G)

L.t. leading tone

L.v. let vibrate

L-dx *longa duplex* (nota.)

La Musica E Basso, A. *Musica: Enciclopedia storica*

LA left arm

LA Leschetizky Association; Lucques. Bibliothèque Capitulaire. Codex 601 (Antiphonaire monastique) (facsim.) (*Paleographie musicale, 9*)

Labor D *Diccionario de la música Labor*

LAMDA London Academy of Music and Dramatic Art

LaMusicaD *La Musica: Dizionario* (sotto la direzione di Guido Maria Gatti)

Las H Angles, Higinio. *El Códex musical de Las Huelgas*

Lat Am Mus, Lat Am Mus R *Latin American Music Review* (jl.) / *Revista de música latinoamericana*

LavE Lavignac, Albert, ed. *Encyclopédie de la musique et dictionnaire du Conservatoire*

LavignacE Lavignac, Albert, ed. *Encyclopédie de la musique et dictionnaire du Conservatoire*

LB *col legno battuto*; *Lose Blätter der Musikantengilde*

LBCM Lang, Paul Henry, ed. *Contemporary Music in Europe*; Licentiate of the Bandsman's College of Music

LC British Museum. Library. Ms. Cotton Titus A. XXVI (ms.)

LCAUS Latvian Choir Association of the U.S.

LCSM Licentiate of the Birmingham School of Music

LD *Erbe deutscher Musik. 2. Reihe. Landschaftsdenkmale*; *Landschaftsdenkmale (Das Erbe deutscher Musik. 2. Reihe)*

Ldb. *Liederbuch* (G=song book)

LDMT Laudes (Chant, Matins)

LDOF Laudes (Chant, Office)

Ldr. leader

LDS Laudes (Chant, Mass)

Legg⁰ leggiero (I=lightly)

Legni *strumenti a fiato di legno* (I=woodwind instruments)

Let Apost *Letania Apostolica*

Let Can *Letania Canonica*

LF Liederkranz Foundation

LFC League of Filipino Composers

LGBA Lesbian and Gay Bands of America

LGSM Licentiate of the Guildhall School of Music and Drama

Li libretto; ligature, ligated; line; *links* (G=left)

Lib. libretto; *ligatura binaria* (nota.)

Libr. libretto

Libr. pr. *libretto proprio* (I=own libretto)

LiedChor *Lied und Chor* (jl.)

List *The Listener* (BBC) (jl.)

Lit. litany

LM *Larousse de la musique*

LM *Lucrări de muzicologie* (jl.)

LMC London Musical Club

LMHF Lauritz Melchior Heldentenor Foundation

Lo British Museum. Library. Ms. Addl. 29987 (ms.)

LoD British Museum. Library. Addl. 27630 (ms.)

LoHa British Museum. Library. Harley 987 (ms.)

Lp long-playing record

LPO London Philharmonic Orchestra

LR *Liber responsorialis pro festis*

LRAM Licentiate of the Royal Academy of Music

LRM *La Rassegna musicale* (jl.)

LRSM Licentiate of the Royal Schools of Music

LS *English School of Lutenist Song Writers* (Edmund H. Fellowes, ed.); Lute Society; Lute Society of America. *Journal* (jl.)

LSA Lute Society of America

LSJ Lute Society. *Journal* (jl.)

LSM Jacquot, Jean, ed. *La luth et sa musique*

LSO London Symphony Orchestra

LSS Leopold Stokowski Society; Lerner, Edward R. *Study Scores of*

Musical Styles

LSSA Leopold Stokowski Society of America

LT *col legno tratto*

Lt., Lt. lute / *Laute* (G) / *luth* (F) / *liuto* (I) / *laúd* (Sp)

LTCL Licentiate of the Trinity College of Music

LU *Liber Usualis missae et officii pro dominicis et festis duplicibus cum cantu gregoriano*; *Liber Usualis, with introduction and rubrics in English*

Luc Lucca. Archivio di stato. Biblioteca. Ms. 184

LuM Guillaume de Machaut. *Musikalische Werke* (Friedrich Ludwig, ed.) *(Publikationen älterer Musik)*

Lusing. *lusingando* (I=tenderly)

LuteSocJ Lute Society. *Journal* (jl.)

Luzrări Muzicol *Lucrări de muzicologie* (jl.)

LVM *Liber vesperalis juxta ritum Sanctae Ecclesiae Mediolanensis*

LW Haberl, F. X., ed. *Lasso, Orlando di. Sämtliche Werke*

LWV Schneider, Herbert. *Chronologisch-thematisches Verzeichnis sämtlicher Werke von Jean-Baptiste Lully*

M *Die Musik* (jl.); Maelzel metronome; measure, measures; medium difficulty; middle; *minima, minimae* (nota.); moderate tempo

M. *main, mains* (F=hand(s)); manual(s); *Mittel* (G=middle)

M Schallplatte *Musica Schallplatte* (jl.)

M. Chor *Männerchor* (G=men's chorus)

M. Harm-ka *Mundharmonika* (G=harmonica)

M.d. *main droite* (F) / *mano destra* (I) / *manu dextra* (L) = right hand

M.D. *mit Dämpfer* (G=with mute, damper pedal)

M.g. *main gauche* (F=left hand), m.g.

M.M. Maelzel metronome; *movimento metronomico*

M.s. *manu sinistra* (I=left hand)

M.v. *mezzo voce* (I=half voice)

M-D medium to difficult

M&L *Music & Letters* (jl.)

Ma   Madrid. Biblioteca Nacional. Ms. 20486 (medieval ms.)

MA   Melodious Accord; *Musical Antiquary* (jl.)

MAB   *Musica antiqua Bohemica*

Madr.   madrigal

Mag.   Magnificat

Magg.   *maggiore* (I=major)

Magn.   *magnetico*; *magnetofono* (I) / *Magnetophon* (G) / *magnétophone* (F) / *magnetofón* (Sp) = tape recorder

Magnif.   Magnificat

MaJ   Marrocco, W. Thomas. *Jacopo da Bologna. Works*

Maj.   major

MAltar   *Musik und Altar* (jl.)

MAM   *Musik alter Meister*

MaMI   Marcuse, Sybil. *Musical Instruments: A Comprehensive Dictionary*

Man.   manual(s)

MANA   Music Advisers' National Association; Musicians Against Nuclear Arms

Manc.   *mancando* (I=growing quieter)

Mand.   mandolin / *Mandoline* (G) / *mandoline* (F) / *mandolino* (I)

MaO   *Magnun opus musicum*

MAP   *Musica antiqua Polonica*; Musical Aptitude Profile

Mar.   maraca(s); marimba

Marc.   *marcato* (I=stressed)

MArte   *Música y arte* (jl.)

MAS   Musical Antiquarian Society. *Publications*

Mat.   *ad matutinum*

MATA   Musical Arena Theatres Association

MB   Bachelor of Music; *Musica Britannica*

MBF   Musicians Benevolent Fund

MBildung   *Musik und Bildung* (jl.)

MBSI   Musical Box Society International

MBühne   *Musikbühne* (jl.)

Mc *musica da camera* (I=chamber music)

MCA Music Corporation of America; Music Critics' Association of North America; Musical Corporation of America; Musicians' Club of America

Mcan *Musicanada* (jl.)

Mcan *Musical Canada* (jl.)

MCB Music Confederation of Belgium

Mch. *Männerchor* (G=men's chorus)

McKee Peter McKee Music Co. (publ.)

MCM Master of Church Music; *Music Clubs Magazine* (jl.)

MCour *Musical Courier* (jl.)

McV British Museum. Library. Ms. Addl. 41667 (*McVeagh Fragment*)

MD *Modern Drummer* (jl.); *Musica disciplina* (jl.), *Musica divina* (jl.); musical director / *Musik Direktor, Musikdirektor* (G); *Musikalische Denkmäler, Musikdirektor* (G=music director)

Md. mandolin / *Mandoline* (G) / *mandoline* (F) / *mandolino* (I)

MDA Music Distributors Association

MdC *musica da camera* (I=chamber music)

ME *Musikerziehung* (jl.); *Muzikal'naya entsiklopediya*

MEA Music Editors' Association

MEC Music Education Council

MEDJA *Music Educators' Journal* (jl.)

MedMM *Mediaeval Musical Manuscripts*

MEF Musicians' Emergency Fund

Mehrst. *mehrstimmig* (G=polyphonic)

MEIEA Music and Entertainment Industry Educators Association

MEJ *Music Educators' Journal* (jl.)

MEL Music Education League

Mel M *Melody Maker* (jl.)

Mel Maker *Melody Maker* (jl.)

Mel. melody

Mel. instr. melody instrument / *mélodie-instrument* (F) / *Melodie-*

Instrument (G)

MelodieRhythmus *Melodie und Rhythmus* (jl.)

Melos/NeueZM *Melos/Neue Zeitschrift für Musik* (jl.)

MEM *Mestres de l'escolania de Montserret*

Memory *Memory Lane: Dance Band, Vocal, & Jazz Review* (jl.)

MENC National Association for Music Education

Mens en Mel *Mens en melodie* (jl.)

MensMelodie *Mens en melodie* (jl.)

Met. Metropolitan Opera

MET Wolf, Johannes, ed. *Music of Earlier Times*

Met. metronome

MEV *Musica elettronica viva*

Mez. *Mezzo-Sopran* (G)

Mezzo sop. *mezzo soprano*

Mf *mezzo forte, mezzoforte*

Mf, MF *Die Musikforschung* (jl.); *Musikforskning* (Norwegian=music research); Musicians Foundation

Mff *mezzo forte, mezzoforte*

MfM, MFM *Monatshefte für Musikgeschichte* (jl.)

MFO Norsk Musikerforbund

Mforskning *Music & forskning* (jl.)

MForum *Music Forum* (jl.)

Mg *Musikforschung* (G=music research); *Musikgeschichte* (G=music history)

MgB *Musikgeschichte in Bildern*

MGC Magisterium in Gregorian Chant, Pontifical School of Sacred Music, Rome (Pontificio Istituto di Musica)

MGes *Musik und Gesellschaft* (jl.)

MGG *Musik in Geschichte und Gegenwart*

MGottesdienst *Musik und Gottesdienst* (jl.)

MH *Musica hispana*; *Musikhandel* (jl.), Musikk-Huset (publ.)

MHMA Benjamin, Rajeczky. *Melodiarium hungariae medii aevi I: Hymnen und Sequenzen*

MI, mi *minim* (nota.); Mönkemeyer, Helmut, ed. *Musica Instrumentalis*; *Monumenta Polyphoniae Italicae*; *Music Index*

MIAC Music Industries Association of Canada / Association canadienne des industries de la musique, ACIM

Mic microphone

MIC Music Industry Conference; Music Industry Council; Music Information Center/Centre

MIDEM Marche international du disque et de l'édition musicale / International Record and Music Publishing Market, IRMPM

MIDI Musical Instrument Digital Interface

Mie. *musicologie* (F=musicology)

Migne. Patr. gr. Migne, Jacques-Paul, ed. *Patrologiae cursus completus, series graeca*

Migne. Patr. lat. Migne, Jacques-Paul, ed. *Patrologiae cursus completus, series latina*

Mil. d. (mil. dr.) military drum

Min. *minima, minimae* (nota.); minor / *minore* (I); minutes

Min. sc. miniature score

MIR Jacquot, Jean, ed. *Musique instrumentale de la Renaissance*; Musical Information Retrieval (comp. program)

Misc Mus *Miscellanea musicologica* (Adelaide) (jl.)

MiscM-A *Miscellanea musicologica* (Adelaide) (jl.)

MiscM-C *Miscellanea musicologica* (Prague) (jl.)

MiscMusicol *Miscellanea musicologica* (Adelaide) (jl.)

MiscMusicol *Miscellanea musicologica* (Prague) (jl.)

Miss R *Missale Romanum ex decreto sacrosancti concilii Tridentini restitutum*

MittDeutschenGesMOrients Deutsche Gesellschaft für Musik des Orients. *Mitteilungen* (jl.)

MittHansPfitznerGes Hans Pfitzner Gesellschaft. *Mitteilungen*

MittIntStiftungMozarteum Internationale Stiftung Mozarteum. *Mitteilungen* (jl.)

Mittl. *Mittler* (G=medium, middle)

MittMaxRegerInst Max-Reger-Institut. *Mitteilungen* (jl.)

MittÖsterreichGesMw Österreichische Gesellschaft für Musikwissenschaft. *Mitteilungen* (jl.)

MittSchweizMfGes Schweizerische Musikforschende Gesellschaft. *Mitteilungsblatt* (jl.)

MittSteirTonkünstlerbundes Steirisches Tonkünstlerbund. *Mitteilungen* (jl.)

MJ *Music Journal* (jl.)

MJA Music Jobbers' Association

MJb *Mozart-Jahrbuch* (jl.)

MJeu *Musique en jeu* (jl.)

MJQ Modern Jazz Quartet

MJudaica *Musica Judaica* (jl.)

MJugend *Musikalische Jugend*

Mk *Die Musik* (jl.)

MK Magyar Kórus, Budapest; *Musik und Kirche* (jl.)

MKirche *Musik und Kirche* (jl.)

ML *Music & Letters* (jl.)

MLA Music Library Association

MLC Maple Leaf Club

MLDMA *Melody Maker* (jl.)

MLetters *Music & Letters* (jl.)

MLex *Musiklexikon* (G=music dictionary)

MLMAI-L *Monumenta lyrica medii aevi italica. I. Latina*

MLMAI-M *Monumenta lyrica medii aevi italica. III. Mensurabilia*

MLMI *Monumenta lyrica medii aevi italica*

MM Parrish, Carl, ed. *Masterpieces of Music Before 1750*; *MM: tidskrift for rytmish musik* (Copenhagen); *Modern Music* (jl.)

MM, M.M. Master of Music

Mm. measure, measures; metronome

MMA *Miscellanea musicologica* (Prague) (jl.); Music Masters' Association (London); Reese, Gustave. *Music in the Middle Ages*

MMB *Monumenta Musicae Belgicae*; *Monumenta Musicae Byzantinae*

MMB-L   *Monumenta Musicae Byzantinae. Lectionaria*

MMB-P   *Monumenta Musicae Byzantinae. Principale*

MMB-S   *Monumenta Musicae Byzantinae. Subsidia*

MMB-T   *Monumenta Musicae Byzantinae. Transcripta*

MMBel, MMBelg.   *Monumenta Musicae Belgicae*

MmBullSIM   *Mercure musical* (jl.)

MMC   Aubry, Pierre, ed. *Mélanges de musicologie critique*; *Miscellanea musicologica* (Prague) (jl.)

MMD   *Musikalische Denkmäler*

MME   *Monumentos de la música española*

MMedii Aevi   *Musica medii aevi*

MMEsp   *Monumentos de la música española*

MMF   Moravian Music Foundation; Mutual Musicians Foundation

MMFTR   Expert, Henri, ed. *Les monuments de la musique française au temps de la Renaissance*

MMg   *Monatshefte für Musikgeschichte* (jl.)

MMI   *Monumenti di Musica Italiana*

MMinima   *musica minima*

MMMA   *Monumenta monodica medii aevi*; Schlager, Karlheinz, ed. *Alleluia-Melodien I (Monumenta monodica medii aevi, 7)*

MMMLF   *Monuments of Music and Music Literature in Facsimile*

MMN   *Monumenta Musicae neerlandicae*

MMO   Music Minus One

MMP   Monumenta Musicae in Polonia

MMR   *Monthly Musical Record* (jl.)

MMS   Hesbert, Dom Rene, ed. *Monumenta musicae sacrae*; *Monumenta Musicae Svecicae*

Mmus., M.Mus.   Master of Music

Mn   Munich. Bayerische Staatsbibliothek, Clm 14274 (olim Mus. Ms. 3232a)

Mn2   Munich. Bayerische Staatsbibliothek. Clm 15611 (ms.)

MNEV   *Musica nostra et vostra*

MNewsl   *Musical Newsletter* (jl.)

Mo *Codex Montpellier* (Montpellier. Bibliothèque de l'École de Médicine, H196)

MO *Musical Opinion* (jl.)

Mo Mus Rec *Monthly Musical Record* (jl.)

MOA Music Operators of America

Mod modulator

Mod. Modena. Biblioteca Estense. [alpha] M. 5.24 (olim lat. 568); *moderato* (I=moderately)

Mod Mus *Modern Music* (jl.)

ModB Modena. Biblioteca Estense olim lat. 471 (medieval ms.)

Modern Drum *Modern Drummer* (jl.)

Modto. *moderato* (I=moderately)

MOG Metropolitan Opera Guild

MOM Hennefield, Norman, ed. *Masterpieces of Organ Music*

MONC Metropolitan Opera National Council

Mono. monophonic

MOpinion *Musical Opinion* (jl.)

Moravian Mus Moravian Music Foundation. *Bulletin* (jl.)

Morg Pierpont Library, Cod. 396

MoserL Moser, Hans Joachim. *Musiklexikon*

MOst, MOstens *Music des Ostens*

Mot. motet, *motetto* (I), *motetus* (L)

MoTO Malipiero, Gian Francesco, ed. *Monteverdi: Tutte le opere*

MOUG Music OCLC Users' Group

Movt. movement

Mozart Versuch Mozart, Leopold. *Versuch einer gründlichen Violinschule*

Mozart-Jb *Mozart-Jahrbuch* (jl.)

Mp *mezzo piano*

MP Music Press (publ.)

MPA Music Publishers' Association of the United States

MPL *Musician, Player and Listener* (jl.)

MPologne *Musique en Pologne* (jl.)

MPPA Music Publishers' Protective Association

MPTF Music Performance Trust Funds

MQ *Musical Quarterly* (jl.)

MR McLaughlin & Reilly (publ.); *Music Review* (jl.); Musikrevy (Stockholm) (jl.); Reese, Gustave. *Music in the Renaissance*

MRCO Member of the Royal College of Organists

MRF Music Research Foundation

MRM Lowinsky, Edward, ed. *Monuments of Renaissance Music*

MRS *Musiche rinascimentali siciliane*

Ms, MS *mezzo soprano*

MS Dittmer, Luther, ed. *Musicological Studies*

MSA Musicological Society of Australia

MSacra *Musica sacra* (jl.)

MSacraeMinisterium *Musicae sacrae ministerium*

MSAS Musicians and Singers Association of Singapore

MScene *Music Scene* (jl.)

MSchule *Musik in der Schule* (jl.)

MSD *Musicological Studies and Documents*

MSO Melbourne Symphony Orchestra; Montréal Symphony Orchestra

Mso. *mezzo soprano*

MSR *miserationes* (chant)

MSV Ennio Society

MT *Music Theory Spectrum* (jl.); *Musical Times* (jl.)

MTA Music Trades Association; Musical Theatre Association

MTC *Meet the Composer*

MTh. *Musiktheorie* (G=music theory)

Mtherapie *Musiktherapie* (G=music therapy)

MThT Dittmer, Luther, ed. *Musical Theorists in Translation*

MTimes *Musical Times* (jl.)

MTNA Music Teachers' National Association

MTousTemps *Musique de tous les temps* (rec. lab.)

MU *Die Musikantengilder* (jl.); Musicians' Union

MUB   *Music for Brass*

MuK   *Musik und Kirche* (jl.)

MUM   *Music Ministry* (jl.)

MUMUA   *Music and Musicians* (jl.)

MUN   *Musical Newsletter* (jl.)

MUniversità   Musica università (Pontina, Italy)

Mus   *Musica* (Kassel) (jl.)

Mus & Dance   *Music and Dance* (jl.)

Mus & Lett   *Music & Letters* (jl.)

Mus & mus, Mus & Mus   *Music and Musicians* (jl.)

Mus AD, Mus A D   Doctor of Musical Arts

Mus Bac   *Musicae Baccalaureus* (L=Bachelor of Music)

Mus Bach   *Musicae Baccalaureus* (L=Bachelor of Music)

Mus Box   Musical Box Society International

Mus D   *Musicae Doctor* (L=Doctor of Music)

Mus d'oggi   *Musica d'oggi* (jl.)

Mus Dealer   *Music Dealer* (jl.)

Mus Denmark   *Musical Denmark* (jl.)

Mus dir   musical director / *Musik Direktor, Musikdirektor* (G)

Mus Disc   *Musica disciplina* (jl.)

Mus Doc   *Musicae Doctor* (L=Doctor of Music)

Mus Ed D   Doctor of Music Education

Mus Ed J   *Music Educators' Journal* (jl.)

Mus Ed M   Master of Music Education

Mus et Lit   *Musique et liturgie* (jl.)

Mus Events   *Musical Events* (jl.)

Mus Forum   *Music Forum* (jl.)

Mus in Ed   *Music in Education* (jl.)

Mus in Schule   *Musik in der Schule* (jl.)

Mus Int   *Musik International-Instrumentenbau-Zeitschrift* (jl.)

Mus J   *Music Journal* (jl.); *Musica Jazz: Rassegna mensile* (jl.)

Mus Jeu   *Musique en jeu* (jl.)

Mus Jl *Music Journal* (jl.)

Mus Judaica *Musica Judaica* (jl.)

Mus Lib Assn Notes Music Library Association. *Notes* (jl.)

Mus M *Musicae magister* (L=Master of Music)

Mus Mag *Music Magazine* (Ontario) (jl.)

Mus Min *Music Ministry* (jl.)

Mus News *Music News* (Chicago) (jl.); *Musical Newsletter* (jl.)

Mus News Prague *Music News from Prague* (jl.)

Mus Oggi *Musica d'oggi* (jl.)

Mus Op *Musical Opinion* (jl.)

Mus Opinion *Musical Opinion* (jl.)

Mus P & L *Musician, Player and Listener* (jl.)

Mus Parade *Music Parade* (jl.)

Mus Q, Mus Qu *Musical Quarterly* (jl.)

Mus Scene *Music Scene* (jl.)

Mus Schall *Musica Schallplatte* (jl.)

Mus Superv J *Music Supervisors' Journal* (jl.)

Mus Survey *Music Survey* (jl.)

Mus T *Musical Times* (jl.)

Mus Tcr *Music Teacher and Piano Student* (jl.)

Mus Teach Nat Assn Proc Music Teachers' National Association. *Proceedings* (jl.)

Mus Theory Spectrum *Music Theory Spectrum* (jl.)

Mus Today NL *Music Today Newsletter* (jl.)

Mus Trade Rev *Music Trade Review* (jl.)

Mus Trades *Music Trades* (jl.)

Mus u Bild *Musik und Bildung* (jl.)

Mus u Ges *Musik und Gesellschaft* (jl.)

Mus u Gottesd *Musik und Gottesdienst* (jl.)

Mus u Kir *Musik und Kirche* (jl.)

Mus West *Music of the West Magazine* (jl.)

MUS *Music Now* (jl.)

Mus. Am. *Musical America* (jl.)

Mus. Brit. *Musica Britannica*

Mus. d'h. *musique d'harmonie*

Mus. de ch. *musique de chambre* (F=chamber music)

Mus. music, musician, musical

Mus. sacr. *musique sacrée* (F=sacred music)

Mus. sacr. cath. *musique sacrée catholique* (F=Catholic sacred music)

Mus.B. *Musicae Baccalaureus* (L=Bachelor of Music)

Muscan *Musicanada* (jl.)

MusClubs Mag *Music Clubs Magazine* (jl.)

Muscrit music critic, music criticis

MUSE Musicians United for Safe Energy

MusG *Musik und Gesellschaft* (jl.)

Music (SMA) *Music* (Schools of Music Association) (jl.)

Music Ed Jnl *Music Educators' Journal* (jl.)

Music Educ *Music Educators' Journal* (jl.)

Music J *Music Journal* (jl.)

Music Lett *Music & Letters* (jl.)

Music Man *Music and Man* (jl.)

Music Quart *Musical Quarterly* (jl.)

Music Rev *Music Review* (jl.)

Music Times *Musical Times* (jl.)

Music. *musicologie* (F=musicology)

Musica E, La *Musica: Enciclopedia storica* (a cura di A. Basso)

MusicaD, La Gatti, Guido Maria. *La Musica: Dizionario*

MusicI *Music Index*

Musician *Musician, Player and Listener* (jl.)

Musicol [AUS] *Musicology Australia* (jl.)

Musicol. musicological, musicologist, musicology

MUSICOMP Music Simulator-Interpreter for Compositional Procedures (comp. lang.)

MusicoSlovaca *Musicologica slovaca* (jl.)

Musikforsch *Die Musikforschung* (jl.)

MusL *Music & Letters* (jl.)

MusLeader *Music Leader* (jl.)

MusMA *Musica medii aevi*

MusR *Music Review* (jl.)

MusRev *Music Review* (jl.)

MusSacra *Musica sacra* (jl.)

MusTimes *Musical Times* (jl.)

Muz Sbornik *Muzikološki zbornik* (jl.)

MuzikolZbornik *Muzikološki zbornik* (jl.)

MuzK *Muzyka Kwartalnik* (jl.)

MVB Muziekverbond van België

MVH *Musica viva historica*

MVM Münchener Veröffentlichungen zur Musikgeschichte

MVSSP *Musiche vocali strumentali sacre e profane*

Mvt. movement

Mw *Das Musikwerk*

Mw. *Musikwissenschaft* (G=musicology), *Musikwissenschaftlich* (G=musicological)

MwArb *Musikwissenschaftliche Arbeiten* (jl.)

MwSb Gennrich, Friedrich, ed. *Musikwissenschaftliche Studienbibliothek*

Mx *maxima* (nota.)

MZ *Muzikološki zbornik* (jl.)

Mżizn *Muzykal'naia żhizn'* (jl.)

Mzv. *mezzo voce* (I=half voice)

N *Nebenstimme* (G=subsidiary voice or part); *noleggio* (I=rental); Novello & Co. (publ.)

N. st. *nouveau style* (F=new style); *novi styli*

Na, NA *Note d'archivio per la storia musicale* (jl.)

NAAC National Association of Accompanists and Coaches

NAACC National Association for American Composers and Conductors

NABBA North American Brass Band Association

NABIM National Association of Band Instrument Manufacturers

NAC National Association of Choirs; National Association of College Wind and Percussion Instructors. *Journal*

NAC Nordic Association of Campanology

NACUSA National Association of Composers/USA

NACWPI National Association of College Wind and Percussion Instructors

NACWPI J National Association of College Wind and Percussion Instructors. *Journal* (jl.)

NAGCR North American Guild of Change Ringers

Nagel *Nagels Musikarchiv*

NAJ *Jazz Educators' Journal* (jl.)

NAJE National Association of Jazz Educators

NAMESCU National Association of Music Executives in State Universities

NAMM International Music Products Association; National Association of Music Merchants

NAMMM National Association of Musical Merchandise Manufacturers

NAMMW National Association of Musical Merchandise Wholesalers

NAMT National Association for Music Therapy

NANM National Association of Negro Musicians

NAO National Accordion Organization

NAPBIRT National Association of Professional Band Instrument Repair Technicians

NAPM National Academy of Popular Music; National Association of Pastoral Musicians

NARM National Association of Record Manufacturers; National Association of Recording Merchandisers

Narr. narrator

NAS National Academy of Songwriters

NASA North American Saxophone Alliance; North American Singers

Association

NASM National Association of Schools of Music; National Association of Schools of Music. *Proceedings* (jl.)

NASMD National Association of School Music Dealers

NASOL Norske Symfoni-Orkestres Landsforbund

NAT National Association of Teachers of Singing. *NATS Bulletin* (jl.)

Nat. natural

NATCA National Association of Teachers of Singing. *NATS Bulletin* (jl.)

NATS National Association of Teachers of Singing; National Association of Teachers of Singing. *NATS Bulletin*

NATSBul National Association of Teachers of Singing. *NATS Bulletin* (jl.)

NAWM National Association of Women in Music; *Norton Anthology of Western Music*

NAYO National Association of Youth Orchestras

NB *Notenbeispiel, -e* (G=musical example, -s)

NBA Bach, Johann Sebastian. *Neue Ausgabe sämtlicher Werke*; National Band Association; *Neue Bach Ausgabe*

NBJb *Neues Beethoven-Jahrbuch* (jl.)

NBMC National Black Music Caucus

Nc note cancrizans (retrograde of a note series)

NC *Nineteenth-Century Music* (jl.); *nuova consonanza*

NCBA National Catholic Band Association; National Catholic Bandmasters' Association

NCM National College of Music (London)

NCMC Nordic Council for Music Conservatoires

NCMI National Council of Music Importers

NCMIE National Council of Music Importers and Exporters

NCS *Novello Chorister Series*

NCSSM National Council of State Supervisors of Music

NDR Norddeutscher Rundfunk; Nordwestdeutscher Rundfunk

Neue MZ *Neue Musikzeitung* (jl.)

NeueZM *Neue Zeitschrift für Musik* (jl.)

News ITA International Trombone Association. *Newsletter* (jl.)

News ITG International Trumpet Guild. *Newsletter* (jl.)

NFA National Flute Association

NFIMA National Federation Interscholastic Music Association

NFMC National Federation of Music Clubs

NFMS National Federation of Music Societies

NFSM National Fraternity of Student Musicians

NG *New Grove Dictionary of Music and Musicians*

NGPT National Guild of Piano Teachers

Ni, NI note (pitch) series, inversion of a; Naouka i Izkoustvo, Sofia (publ.)

Nine Cen Mus, Nine Ct Mus *Nineteenth-Century Music* (jl.)

NJSO National Jazz Service Organization

NKF Norwegian Society of Composers / Norsk Komponistforening

NKK Nordiska Kor Kommitten

NKR Nordisk Konservatorierad

Nm *nastro magnetico* (I=magnetic tape)

NM *Nagels Musikarchiv*; Norsk Musikerforbund / Norwegian Musicians Union

NMA Mozart, Wolfgang Amadeus. *Neue Ausgabe sämtlicher Werke*; *Nagels Musikarchiv*; National Musicamp Association; *Neue Mozart-Ausgabe*

NMC National Music Camp (Interlochen, Mich.); National Music Council; National Music Council. *Bulletin* (jl.)

NMCGB National Music Council of Great Britain

NMDS New Music Distribution Service

NMI Norsk Musikinformasjon

NMIC Norwegian Music Information Center

NML National Music League

NMPA National Music Publishers' Association

NMPATA National Music Printers and Allied Trades Association

NMZ *Neue Musikzeitung* (jl.)

NNRF *Nouvelle nouvelle revue française* (jl.)

NO Music Library Association. *Notes* (jl.)

NO-TFA National Old-Time Fiddlers' Association

NOA National Opera Association, National Orchestral Association

Noct *ad nocturnos*

NODA National Operatic and Dramatic Association

NOH, NOHM *New Oxford History of Music*

NOI, National Opera Institute

NOMUS Nordic Music Committee / Nordisk Musikkomite

Non div. *non divisi*

NOPA Forening for norske komponister og tekstforfattere / Norske Populerautorer

Norm. *normale* (nota.)

Norsk Mus *Norsk musikerblad* (jl.)

NorskMt *Norsk musiktidsskrift* (jl.)

NOS National Oratorio Society

NOSB Northeastern Sängerbund of America

Not. notation

Notaz. *notazione* (I=notation)

Notes Music Library Association. *Notes* (jl.)

Nouv. éd. pr. *Nouvelle édition pratique* (F=new performing edition)

Nov. Novello & Co. (publ.)

NPF National Piano Foundation

NPM Apel, Willi. *Notation of Polyphonic Music, 900-1600*; National Association of Pastoral Musicians

NPMA National Piano Manufacturers' Association of America

NPTA National Piano Travelers Association

NPV Dutch Pianola Society / Nederlandse Pianola Vereniging

NRF *Nouvelle revue française* (jl.)

NRMI, nRMI *Nuova rivista musicale italiana* (jl.)

Ns note series (pitch series in orig. version)

NS Kamien, Roger, ed. *The Norton Scores*

NSAA Norwegian Singers Association of America

NSBBA National School Brass Band Association

NSMS National Sheet Music Society

NSO National School Orchestra Association. *Bulletin* (jl.)

NSOA National School Orchestra Association; National School Orchestra Association. *Bulletin* (jl.)

NSSK National Society of Student Keyboardists

NTL Gerber, Ernst Ludwig. *Neues historisch-biographisches Lexikon der Tonkünstler*

Numus *Numus West* (jl.)

Nunc *Nunc dimittis*

Nuov Riv M, Nuova Riv M *Nuova rivista musicale italiana* (jl.)

Nuova RM Italiana, NuovaRMItaliana *Nuova rivista musicale italiana* (jl.)

NutidaMus *Nutida musik* (jl.)

Nv *non vibrato*

NVGD Dutch Association of Gramophone Records / Nederlandse Vereniging van Grammofoonplaten

NWDR Nordwestdeutscher Rundfunk

NWMF National Women's Music Festival

NYO National Youth Orchestra of Great Britain

NYPO New York Philharmonic Orchestra

NZ *Neue Zeitschrift für Musik* (jl.)

NZ Muzik *Neue Zeitschrift für Musik* (jl.)

NZfM *Neue Zeitschrift für Musik* (jl.)

NZH Nakladni zavod hrvatske, Zagreb (publ.)

NZM *Neue Zeitschrift für Musik* (jl.)

NZSME New Zealand Society for Music Education

NZSMT New Zealand Society for Music Therapy

O original (form of 12-tone row)

O. Nr. *ohne Nummer* (G=unnumbered)

O.D. *ohne Dämpfer* (G=without mute, damper pedal)

O.s. Old style

OAKE   Organization of American Kodaly Educators

Ob. d'am.   *oboe d'amore*

Ob. da cac.   *oboe da caccia*

Ob.   oboe

Obbl.   *obbligato* (I) / *obligat* (F) / *Obligat* (G) / *obligado* (Sp)

Oberst.   *Oberstimme* (G=upper part)

Oberw.   *Oberwerk* (G=upper manual, part)

Obl.   *obbligato* (I) / *obligat* (F) / *Obligat* (G) / *obligado* (Sp); *Oblong* (rec. label)

Obr.   Wolf, Johannes, ed. *Obrecht, Jacob. Werken*

Obw.   *Oberwerk* (G=upper manual, part)

OCHLLC   Organ Clearing House LLC

Oct   *ad octavam*

ODMS   Onderwys Diploma in Musiek, Stellenbosch, South Africa

OEA   Orchestral Employers' Association

OeMZ   *Österreichische Musikzeitschrift* (jl.)

Oeuv. ch.   *oeuvres choisies* (F=selected works)

Oeuv. compl.   *oeuvres complètes* (F=complete works)

Of., off.   offertory, *offertorium*

Offert.   offertory, *offertorium*

Ofv   offertory verse

OGM   Österreichische Gesellschaft für Musik

OGMW   Österreichische Gesellschaft für Musikwissenschaft

OH, OHM   *Oxford History of Music*

OHS   *Officium hebdomadae sanctae et octavae Paschae*; Organ Historical Society

OHTA   Organ Historical Trust of Australia

OJ   *Opera Journal* (jl.)

OJCE   Orchestre des jeunes de la Communaute européenne

OL   Dufourcq, Norbert, *et al. Orgue et liturgie*

OLF   Organ Literature Foundation

OLI   Litaize, Gaston, ed. *L'Organiste liturgique*

OM   *Opus musicum* (Brno, Czech Rep.) (jl.)

OMM Marrocco, W. Thomas. *Oxford Anthology of Medieval Music*

Ömz *Österreichische Musikzeitschrift* (jl.)

ON *Orchestra News* (jl.)

Ongaku-gei *Ongaku-geijutsu* (jl.)

Op *Opera News* (jl.); *opus* (L=work)

Op. buf. *opera buffa*

Op. posth. *opus posthumous*

Op. ser. *opera seria*

Op.-com. *opéra comique*

Oper u Konzert *Oper und Konzert* (jl.)

Opera Can *Opera Canada* (jl.)

Opera J *Opera Journal* (jl.)

Opera N *Opera News* (jl.)

Opp. *opera* (pl. of opus; L=works)

Opt. optional

Opus mus *Opus musicum* (Brno, Czech Rep.) (jl.)

OpusM *Opus musicum* (Brno, Czech Rep.) (jl.)

Or. oratorio, *oratorium*

Orat. oratorium, *oratorium*

Orbis mus *Orbis musicae* (jl.)

Orch. orchestra / *orchestra* (I) / *Orchester* (G) / *orchestre* (F); orchestral

Orch. b. orchestra bells (G=Glockenspiel)

Orch. Bes. *Orchesterbesetzung* (G=orchestral scoring)

Orchd. orchestrated (by)

Org. organ / *Orgel* (G) / *orgue* (F) / *organo* (I) / *órgano* (Sp)

Organ. organology

Organ Yb, OrganYB *Organ Yearbook* (jl.)

Organists R *Organists' Review* (jl.)

Orgm. *organum*; Seiffert, Max, *et al. Organum*

Orgt organist

Ork J *Orkester Journalen: tidskrift för jazzmusik* (jl.)

Orn. ornament, ornamentation / *ornement* (F) / *ornamento* (I)

ÖSB Österreichischer Sängerbund

OSM Orchestre symphonique de Montréal

Öster. Musik. *Österreichische Musikzeitschrift* (jl.)

ÖsterreichBlasm *Österreichische Blasmusik*

Ot, OT transposed original form of 12-tone row

OTM *Old Time Music* (jl.)

Ott Ott, Carolus, ed. *Offertoriale sive versus offertoriorum cantus Gregoriani*

Ott. *ottava* (I=octave); *ottavino* (I=piccolo flute)

Ottoni *strumenti a fiato di ottoni* (I=brass instruments)

Ouv. *ouverture* (F) / *Ouvertüre* (G)

OV *Ovation* (jl.)

Ov. overture

OxfB Oxford. Bodleian Library. Lat. liturg. d. 5 (ms.)

P Palestrina, Giovanni Pierluigi da. *Werke*; *pausa*, pedal; *piano* (I=soft); Pincherle, Marc. *Antonio Vivaldi et la musique instrumentale. v. 2. Inventaire thématique*; *positif* (F=choir organ); prime (12-tone row in its original form at its original pitch)

P. *pars* (L=part); *Partitur* (G=score); *poussé* (F=upstroke of a bow)

P. sinf. *poema sinfonico*

P.-V. Pincherle, Marc. *Antonio Vivaldi et la musique instrumentale. v. 2. Inventaire thématique*

P.a. *punctus additionis* (nota.)

P.d. *punctus divisionis* (nota.)

P.r. *positif-récit*

P Roy Music Royal Musical Association. *Proceedings*

Pa piano, pianoforte (the instrument)

PA *Pastoral Music* (jl.)

PAC *ad pacem*

PadA Oxford. Bodleian Library. Can. Pat. lat. 229 (ms.)

Pal m *Paléographie musicale*

PalMus   *Paléographie musicale*

PäM, PÄM, PAM   *Publikationen älterer Musik*

PAME   Portuguese Association of Music Education

PAMS   American Musicological Society. *Papers* (jl.)

PÄMw   Gesellschaft für Musikforschung. *Publikationen älterer praktischer und theoretischer Musikwerke* (Robert Eitner, ed.)

PAN   *Pastoral Music Notebook* (jl.)

PanoramaMInstruments   *Panorama de la musique et des instruments*

Part.   *partition* (F=score), *Partitur* (G=score)

PAS   Percussive Arts Society

Pas mus   *Pastoral Music* (jl.)

Patr. gr.   Migne, Jacques-Paul, ed. *Patrologiae cursus completus, series graeca*

Patr. lat.   Migne, Jacques-Paul, ed. *Patrologiae cursus completus, series latina*

PAVAS   Performing and Visual Arts Society

PaW   Palestrina, Giovanni Pierluigi da. *Werke*

PBC   Biblioteca de Catalunya. Departamento de música. *Publicationes*

Pc   percussion (E, F) / *percussione* (I) / *percusión* (Sp); pitch class

PC, P-C   Pillet, Alfred & H. Carstens. *Bibliographie der Troubadours* (identification number)

PCM   Polskie Centrum Muzyczne

PDQ Bach   pen name of Peter Schickele

PE   *Percussionist* (jl.)

Ped.   pedal

Péd   *pédale* (F)

Perc.   percussion (E, F) *percussione* (I) / *percusión* (Sp)

Perc notes   *Percussive Notes* (jl.)

Perd.   *perdendosi* (I=dying away)

Perf.   performance, performed (by)

Pers New Mus   *Perspectives of New Music* (jl.)

Persp N Mus   *Perspectives of New Music* (jl.)

Perspectives   *Perspectives of New Music* (jl.)

PET *Peters Notes*

Pf *poco forte, più forte*

Pf. piano, pianoforte (the instrument)

Pf4 piano, 4-hands / pianoforte 4 mani (I)

Pfitzner Hans Pfitzner Gesellschaft. *Mitteilungen*

Pfte pianoforte

PG Migne, Jacques-Paul, ed. *Patrologiae cursus completus, series graeca*

PGfM Gesellschaft für Musikforschung. *Publikationen älterer praktischer und theoretischer Musikwerke* (Robert Eitner, ed.)

PGM Gesellschaft für Musikforschung. *Publikationen älterer praktischer und theoretischer Musikwerke* (Robert Eitner, ed.)

Phil Philharmonic

PI point of inversion

Piano Quart *Piano Quarterly* (jl.)

PianoQ *Piano Quarterly* (jl.)

Pic. fl. *Piccoloflöte* (G) / *piccolo flûte* (F) / *piccolo flauto* (I)

Pic., picc. piccolo

PIEG Pianoforte Industries Export Group

PIISM Istituto italiano per la storia della musica. *Pubblicazione*

PIMG Internationale Musikgesellschaft. *Publikationen* (jl.)

Pizz. *pizzicato* (I=pinched, plucked)

PJB *Jahrbuch der Musikbibliothek Peters* (jl.)

Pk., Pkn. *Pauken* (G=kettledrums; timpani)

PKL Pi Kappa Lambda

PL Migne, Jacques-Paul, ed. *Patrologiae cursus completus, series latina*

Pli. *plica, plicata* (I=ornamental passing tone)

Pli-dx. *plica duplex*

PM *Paléographie musicale; Portuguliae musicae; Processionale monasticum ad usum congregationis Gallicae*

PMA Musical Association. *Proceedings* (jl.); Pianoforte Manufacturers' Association; Royal Musical Association. *Proceedings*

PMAI Pianoforte Manufacturers' Association International

PMAP *Publications de la musique ancienne polonaise*

PMC Conseil polonais de la musique / Polish Music Centre; Philatelic Music Circle; Polish Music Council

PMFC *Polyphonic Music of the Fourteenth Century*

PMLA Production Music Library Association

PMM *Polyphonic Music of the Fourteenth Century*

PMMM *Publications of Medieval Music Manuscripts*

PMMS Plainsong and Medieval Music Society

PMS *Polyphonic Music of the Fourteenth Century*

PN *Percussive Notes* (jl.)

PNM *Perspectives of New Music* (jl.)

Pno *pianissimo* (I=very soft)

Pno. piano, pianoforte (the instrument)

PO Philharmonic Orchestra

Point *Le Point du Jazz* (jl.)

Pol. Rocznik Muzykol. Polski rocznik muzykologiczny

Polish mus *Polish Music* (jl.) / *Polnische musik*

Pont. *ponticello* (I=on the bridge); *sul ponticello* (I=on the bridge)

Pop Mus & Soc *Popular Music and Society* (jl.)

Pop Music S *Popular Music and Society* (jl.)

PoradnikM *Poradnik muzyczny* (jl.)

Pos. *Posaune* (G=trombone); *positif* (F=choir organ); position

Post. *postumo*

Pp *pianissimo* (I=very soft)

PP *Pan Pipes of Sigma Alpha Iota* (jl.)

PPA Pianoforte Publicity Association

PPG Player Piano Group

Ppp *pianississimo* (I=extremely soft)

PQ *Piano Quarterly* (jl.)

PR American Society of University Composers. *Proceedings* (jl.)

Präp. Kl. *präpariertes Klavier* (G=prepared piano)

PRCS *preces* (chant)

Prel. *preludio* (I=prelude)

Prescr. *prescrizioni* (I=directions for playing)

Prim *ad primam*

Princ *principale*

PRLG *Praelegenda* (chant)

PRM Polski rocznik muzykologiczny; Polskie Rada Muzyczna

PRMA Royal Musical Association. *Proceedings*

PRO Canada Performing Rights Organziation of Canada

Proc Mus Assn Musical Association. *Proceedings* (jl.)

Proc. Mus. Ass. Musical Association. *Proceedings* (jl.)

Proc. Mus. Assoc. Musical Association. *Proceedings* (jl.)

Proc. R. Mus Royal Musical Association. *Proceedings*

Proc. R. Mus. Assoc. Royal Music Association. *Proceedings*

ProcAmerSocUComposers American Society of University Composers. *Proceedings* (jl.)

ProcOrganInstNSW Organ Institute of New South Wales. *Proceedings* (jl.)

ProcRoyalMAssoc Royal Musical Association. *Proceedings*

Progr. program, programme

PRS Performing Rights Society

PrW Praetorius, Michael. *Werke*

Ps. *Posaune* (G=trombone); psalter / *psautier* (F)

PSAA Polish Singers Alliance of America

PSFM French Society of Musicology. *Publications* (jl.)

PSGA Pedal Steel Guitar Association

PSLD *psallendi* (chant)

PSLM *psalmi* (chant)

PSM *Princeton Studies in Music*

PSMfG Schweizerische Musikforschende Gesellschaft. *Publikationen*

PsychologyM *Psychology of Music* (jl.)

Pt *partitura* (I=score)

Pt. petit; *sul ponticello* (I=on the bridge)

Pt., pts. part, parts

PTA Pianoforte Tuners' Association

Ptbk. partbook

PTG Piano Technician Guild

Pti *piatti* (I=cymbals)

PTJ *Piano Technicians' Journal* (jl.)

Pto *piatto* (I=cymbal)

PTSA Piano Trade Suppliers' Association

Ptt *partitura tascabile* (I=miniature score, pocket score)

PubAPTM Gesellschaft für Musikforschung. *Publikationen älterer praktischer und theoretischer Musikwerke*

PWM Polish Music Publishers / Polskie Wydawnictwo Muzyczne

PWN Polskie Wydawnictwo Naukowe

PWS Peter Warlock Society

PWSA Professional Women Singers Association

Q.H. Queen's Hall (London)

Qnt. quintet

Qntte *quintette* (G=quintets)

Qt. quartet

Qtte *quartette* (G=quartets)

Quad *Quadrivium: rivista di filogia e musicologia medievale* (jl.)

Quaderni della RaM *Quaderni della Rassegna musicale* (jl.)

Quantz-Versuch Quantz, Johann Joachim. *Versuch einer Anweisung die Flöte traversière zu spielen*

Quart *ad quartam*

Quart. *quartetto* (I=quartet)

Quat. *ligatura quaternaria* (nota.); *quatuor* (F=quartet)

Quin. *ligatura quintenaria* (nota.)

Quint *ad quintam*

Quint. *quintetto* (I=quintet)

R Raynaud, Gaston. *Bibliographie des altfranzösischen Liedes*; *récit, recitative*; response, responsory / *responsorium*; retrograde; Ricordi (publ.); rim (of perc. instrument); Rinaldi, Mario. *Catalogo numerico tematico delle composizione di Antonio Vivaldi*; *ripieno*

R Belge Mus *Revue belge de musicologie / Belgisch Tijdschrift voor muziek-wetenschap / Belgian Review of Musicology* (jl.)

R Mus Chile *Revista musical chilena* (jl.)

R de Mus *Revue de musicologie* (jl.)

R Ital Mus *Rivista italiana di musicologia* (jl.)

R Mus *La Revue musicale* (jl.)

R Mus de Suisse Romande *Revue musicale de Suisse romande* (jl.)

R Mus Ital *Nuova rivista musicale italiana* (jl.)

R.c. right channel (tape)

R.C.M. Royal College of Music

R.h. right hand

R.s. rimshot

RA right arm

Rad. *radiophonique* (F)

Radiof. *radiofonico* (I)

Rall. *rallentando* (I=becoming slower)

RaM, RAM *La Rassegna musicale* (jl.)

RAM Royal Academy of Music

RAMH Krummel, Don W., *Resources of American Music History*

Rass mus Curci *Rassegna musicale Curci* (jl.)

Rass. Greg. *Rassegna gregoriana* (jl.)

RassegnaMCurci *Rassegna musicale Curci* (jl.)

Ratch. ratchet

RB *Revue belge de musicologie / Belgisch Tijdschrift voor muziek-wetenschap / Belgian Review of Musicology* (jl.)

RbelgeMusicol *Revue belge de musicologie / Belgisch Tijdschrift voor muziek-wetenschap / Belgian Review of Musicology* (jl.)

RBM, RMBie *Revue belge de musicologie / Belgisch Tijdschrift voor muziek-wetenschap / Belgian Review of Musicology* (jl.)

RCA Royal Choral Association

RCC Record Collectors' Club

RCCO Royal Canadian College of Organists

Rcdg. recording

RCG *Revue du chant grégorien* (jl.)

RCGrég *Revue du chant grégorien* (jl.)

RCM *Royal College of Music Magazine* (jl.)

RCMI Research Center for Musical Iconography

RCO Royal College of Organists

RCS Royal Choral Society

RD *Reichsdenkmale (Das Erbe deutscher Musik, 1. Reihe)*

RdM French Society of Musicology. *Rapports et communications* (jl.)

RdM *Revue de musicologie* (jl.)

Re great responsory

Re. *rechts* (G=right)

Rec R *Record Review* (jl.)

Rec Res *Record Research* (jl.)

Réc. *récitant*

Recherches *Recherches sur la musique française classique*

Recit. *recitative*

Reconcil penit *ad reconciliandum penitentem*

Recorder & Mus *Recorder and Music Magazine* (jl.)

RecorderMMagazine *Recorder and Music Magazine* (jl.)

Red. reduction, reduced

Réd. *réduction*

Réduit *réduction*

ReM *La Revue musicale* (jl.)

ReMMA Reese, Gustave. *Music in the Middle Ages*

ReMR Reese, Gustave. *Music in the Renaissance*

Rep *repertorio*

Repr. reprise

Resp. responsory / *responsorium*

Rev verse of great responsory

Rev music *Revue de musicologie* (jl.)

Rev musicale *La Revue musicale* (jl.)

Rev. Bras. de Música *Revista Brasileira de Música* (jl.)

Rev. de musicol *Revue de musicologie* (jl.)

Rev. Internat. Mus. *Revue internationale de musique* (jl.)

Rev. Mus. Chilena *Revista musical chilena* (jl.)

Rez. *Rezitativ* (G=recitative)

Rf., rfz. *rinforzando* (I=suddenly louder)

RFJ *Radio Free Jazz* (jl.)

RG *Revue grégorienne* (jl.)

RGMP *Revue et gazette musicale de Paris* (jl.)

Rh transcription committed to one of a number of rhythmic interpretations (nota.)

RHCM *Revue d'histoire et de critique musicales* (jl.)

Ri retrograde inversion

RIAA Recording Industry Association of America

RIAM Royal Irish Academy of Music

Ric. Ricordi (publ.)

Ricordi E *Enciclopedia della musica* (Ricordi)

Rid. *riduzione* (I=reduction), *ridotto* (I=reduced)

RidIM Répertoire Internationale d'Iconographie Musicale / International Repertory of Musical Iconography

Riemann Beisp Riemann, Hugo. *Musikgeschichte in Beispielen*

Riemann HdM Riemann, Hugo. *Handbuch der Musikgeschichte*

RiemannB Riemann, Hugo. *Musikgeschichte in Beispielen*

RiemannH, Riemann HdM Riemann, Hugo. *Handbuch der Musikgeschichte*

RiemannL *Riemann Musik Lexikon*

RiHM Riemann, Hugo. *Handbuch der Musikgeschichte*

RIM *Revue internationale de musique* (jl.); *Rivista italiana di musicologia* (jl.)

RiMB Riemann, Hugo. *Musikgeschichte in Beispielen*

Rin Rinaldi, Mario. *Catalogo numerico tematico delle composizione di Antonio Vivaldi*

Rip. *ripieno*

Rit, RIT transposed retrograde inversion of 12-tone row

Rit. *ritardando* (I=becoming slower); *ritenuto* (I=suddenly and extremely slower)

RItalianaMusicol *Rivista italiana di musicologia* (jl.)

Riv Mus Italiana *Rivista musicale italiana* (jl.)

RLPO Royal Liverpool Philharmonic Orchestra (and Society)

RM *La Revue musicale* (jl.)

RMA Royal Musical Association; Royal Musical Association. *Proceedings*

RMARC Royal Musical Association. *RMA Research Chronicle*

RMA Research Royal Musical Association. *RMA Research Chronicle*

RMAResearchChron Royal Musical Association. *RMA Research Chronicle*

RMAW Sachs, Curt. *Rise of Music in the Ancient World*

RMC *La Revue musicale* (jl.); *Revue d'histoire et de critique musicales* (jl.)

RMChilena *Revista musical chilena* (jl.)

RMCM Royal Manchester College of Music

RMFC *Recherches sur la musique française classique*

RMG *Russkaya muzikal'naya gazeta* (jl.)

RMI *Revue de musicologie* (jl.); *Rivista musicale italiana* (jl.)

RMie *Revue de musicologie* (jl.)

RMS *Renaissance manuscript studies*; *Revue musicale suisse* (jl.)

RMSA Rural Music Schools Association

RMSC Royal Military School of Music

RMSuisse *Revue musicale suisse* (jl.)

RMSuisseRomande *Revue musicale de Suisse romande* (jl.)

RMusicol *Revue de musicologie* (jl.)

RNCM Royal Northern College of Music

RO Radio Orchestra

ROPE Reunion of Professional Entertainers

ROS Reed Organ Society

Rpm revolutions per minute

RPMDA Retail Print Music Dealers Association

RPO Rochester Philharmonic Orchestra; Royal Philharmonic Orchestra

RPS Royal Philharmonic Society

RR *Record Research* (jl.)

RRMB *Recent Researches in the Music of the Baroque Era*

RRMBE *Recent Researches in the Music of the Baroque Era*

RRMM *Recent Researches in the Music of the Middle Ages and Early Renaissance*

RRMR *Recent Researches in the Music of the Renaissance*

RS Ragtime Society; *responds* (chant)

RSAMD Royal Scottish Academy of Music and Drama

RSCM Royal School of Church Music

RSIM *Revue musicale S.I.M.* (jl.); Société internationale de musique revue

RSM Royal Society of Musicians of Great Britain

RSMGB Royal Society of Musicians of Great Britain

RSO Radio Symphony Orchestra

Rt transposed retrograde inversion of 12-tone row

RTP Waite, William. *The Rhythm of Twelfth-Century Polyphony*

Ruch muz *Ruch muzyczny* (jl.)

RuchM *Ruch muzyczny* (jl.)

RV Ryom, Peter. *Répertoire des oeuvres d'Antonio Vivaldi / Verzeichnis der Werke Antonio Vivaldis*

S *semibrevis* (nota.); *subito* (I=suddenly), subject; very slow

S. Schmieder, Wolfgang. *Thematisch-systematisches Verzeichnis der musikalischen Werke von J. S. Bach*; *segno* (I=sign); *Singstimme* (G=singing voice); *sinistra* (I=left); solo; soprano; *superius*

S.c. *signum congruentiae* (nota.)

S.d. snare drum

S.p. *sul ponticello* (I=on the bridge)

S.s. *senza sordino* (I=without mute)

S.t. *senza tempo*

S.v. *senza vibrato*

S.W.V. Bittinger, Werner, ed. Schütz, Heinrich. *Heinrich Schütz-Werke-Verzeichnis*

S-Z, SZ Editions Suvini Zerboni (publ.)

S. cym. suspended cymbal

S. int. *senza interruzione*

SA Mus Tcr *South African Music Teacher* (jl.)

SAA Suzuki Association of the Americas

SACEM Société des auteurs, compositeurs et éditeurs de musique

Sachs *Real-Lexikon der Musikinstrumente* (Curt Sachs)

Sachs Hdb. Sachs, Curt. *Handbuch der Musikinstrumentenkunde*

Sachs R Sachs, Curt. *Real-Lexikon der Musikinstrumente*

SachsH Sachs, Curt. *Handbuch der Musikinstrumentenkunde*

SachsL Sachs, Curt. *Real-Lexikon der Musikinstrumente*

SACM South African College of Music

SADA Southern Appalachian Dulcimer Association

SaHMI Sachs, Curt. *History of Musical Instruments*

SAI Sigma Alpha Iota

SAKOJ Yugoslavian Composers' Association / Savez kompozitora Jugoslavije

SAL-MAR "Real time machine" combining analog production and digital control of sounds, devised by SALvatore MARtirano, Josef Sekon, and others

SAM Society for Asian Music

SAMA Scottish Amateur Music Association

SAME *South African Music Encyclopedia*

SamNam Samrådet for Nordisk Amatørmusik

SAMT *South African Music Teacher* (jl.)

San Fran Opera *San Francisco Opera* (jl.)

SAN Sonic Arts Network

Sandp. bl. sandpaper blocks

SängerMusikantenZ *Sänger- und Musikantenzeitung* (jl.)

SaRM *Real-Lexikon der Musikinstrumente* (Curt Sachs)

SartoriB Sartori, Claudio. *Bibliografia della musica strumentale italiana stampata . . .*

SASMT South African Society of Music Teachers

SATB soprano, alto, tenor, bass

Sax saxophone / *sassofono* (I)

Sb *semibreve* (nota.)

SB *Selmer's Bandwagon* (jl.); Stainer and Bell (publ.)

SBIMG Internationale Musikgesellschaft. *Sammelbände* (jl.)

SBM Société belge de musicologie

Sbr. *semibrevis* (nota.)

SbW Schubert, Franz. *Werke*

Sc score

SC Soviet Composer Publishers / Izdatyelstvo "Sovyetskii kompozitor"

SCA Screen Composers of America

SCG Society for the Classic Guitar

Schallplatte u Kir *Schallplatte und Kirche* (jl.)

Schering B, Schering Beisp. Schering, Arnold. *Geschichte der Musik in Beispielen*

SchGMB Schering, Arnold. *Geschichte der Musik in Beispielen*

SchillingE Schilling, Gustav. *Encyclopädie der gesammten musikalischen Wissenschaften*

SchL Schrade, Leo, ed. *Francesco Landini. Works* (*Polyphonic Music of the Fourteenth Century, v. 4*)

Schl. *Schlagzeug* (G=percussion)

Schl. Instr. *Schlaginstrumente* (G=percussion instruments)

SchmidlD Schmidl, Carlo. *Dizionario dei musicisti*

SchmidlDS Schmidl, Carlo. *Dizionario dei musicisti. Supplement*

Schoenberg Inst Arnold Schoenberg Institute. *Journal* (jl.)

School Mus *School Musician, Director, and Teacher* (jl.)

Schw Musikz *Schweizerische Musikzeitung* (jl.)

Schweiz Mus *Schweizerische Musikzeitung* (jl.)

SCI Society of Composers, Inc.

SCJ *Congregatio Sacerdotum a Sacro Corde Jesu*

SCL Southeastern Composers' League

SCM *School Musician, Director, and Teacher* (jl.)

SCMA Smith College Music Archives

SCMF Société canadienne de musique folklorique

SCNM Society for Commissioning New Music

SCR *Sacrificia* (chant)

SCTM Société canadienne pour les traditions musicales

SCV Schweizerische Chorvereinigung

ScW Schütz, Heinrich. *Sämtliche Werke*

SD *Satzdauer* (G=phrase length)

SDE Canada Société de droits d'exécution du Canada

SDR Süddeutscher Rundfunk

SEAMUS Society for Electro-Acoustic Music in the United States

Sec *ad secundam*; *Second Line* (jl.)

SEC *Studies in Eastern Chant* (jl.)

SeegerL Seeger, Horst. *Musiklexikon*

SEM Society for Ethnomusicology; *University of California Series of Early Music*

Sept *ad septimam*

SEQ *String Education Quarterly* (jl.)

Seq. sequence / *Sequenz* (G)

SESAC Society of European Stage Authors and Composers

Sest. *sestetto* (I=sextet)

Sext *ad sextam*

Sf *semifusa* (nota.); *sforzato* (I=forced)

SFC Swiss Federation of Choirs

SFIRE U.S. Scottish Fiddling Revival

SFM Société française de musicologie

Sfp *sforzato piano*

SfVMw Sammelbände für vergleichende Musikwissenschaft

Sfz *sforzato* (I=forced)

Sfz. p. *sforzato piano*

SGM Society for General Music

Sgst. *Singstimme* (G=singing voice)

Sh sharp

SH Slovenská hudba

Shellac *Shellac Stack* (jl.)

SHMRG Sound, Harmony, Melody, Rhythm, Growth (analytical system set forth by Jan La Rue)

Si *simplex, simplices* (nota.)

SI *Sing Out!* (jl.)

SIBMAS Société Internationale des Bibliothèques et des Musées des Arts du Spectacle / International Association of Libraries and Museums of the Performing Arts

SIC Society of Icelandic Composers

SIEM Société internationale pour l'éducation musicale

SIK Société Internationale Kodály

SIM Internationale Musikgesellschaft. *Sammelbände* (jl.); Société internationale de musique; Société internationale de musique revue

SIMC Società internazionale di musica contemporanea; Société internationale pour la musique contemporaine

SIMG Internationale Musikgesellschaft. *Sammelbände* (jl.)

Sin. *sinistra* (I=left)

Sinf. *sinfonia, sinfonico*

Sing Kir *Singende Kirche*

Singst. *Singstimme* (G=singing voice)

Sist. sistrum

Sizz. cym. sizzle cymbal

SJ *Saxophone Journal* (jl.); *Schweizerisches Jahrbuch für Musikwissenschaft* (jl.)

SJbMw *Schweizerisches Jahrbuch für Musikwissenschaft* (jl.)

SK Školska Knijiga (Zagreb) (publ.)

SKAP Föreningen Svenska Kompositörer av Populärmusik

SKJ Yugoslavian Composers' Association / Savez kompozitora Jugoslavije

Sl *soprano leggiero*

Sl. bells sleigh bells

Sl. whistle slidewhistle, slide whistle

SLC Songwriters and Lyricists Club

Slovak Mus *Slovak Music* (jl.)

SlovenskáHud Slovenská hudba

Sm *semiminum* (nota.)

SM *Sacred Music* (jl.); *Sovetskaia muzyka* (jl.); *Studia musicologica academiae scientiarum hungaricae* (jl.); Süddeutscher Musikverlag (publ.)

SMA Schools Music Association; *Studies in Music* (Nedlands, Australia); Swiss Musicians' Association

SmB *Schweizer Musikbuch*

SMB Bachelor of Sacred Music

SMC Swiss Music Council

SMd *Schweizerische Musikdenkmäler*

SMD Doctor of Sacred Music; League of Music Societies (Yugo.) / Savez muzičkih društava

SMDTB *School Musician, Director, and Teacher* (jl.)

SMFF Svensk Musikförläggare Föreningen

SML Schuh, Willi, ed. *Schweizer Musiker-Lexikon*; Suomen Musiikkioppilaitosten Liitto

SMM, SMMA Gennrich, Friedrich, ed. *Summa musicae medii aevi*

SMN *Studia musicologica norvegica* (jl.)

Smorz. *smorzando* (I=fading away)

SMP Slownik muzyków polskich

SMPA Swedish Music Publishers Association

SMPV Swiss Association for Music Education

SMT Society for Music Theory

SMTE Society for Music Teachers Education

SMUC Société de musique des universites canadiennes

SmW Schumann, Robert. *Werke*

SMw *Studien zur Musikwissenschaft* (jl.)

SmwAbh *Sammlung musikwissenschaftlicher Abhandlungen*

SMz *Schweizerische Musikzeitung* (jl.)

SMZ *Schweizer Musikpädagogische Blätter*

Sn. off snares off

SNAPM Society of Norwegian Authors of Popular Music

SNCT *ad sanctus*

SNKLHU State Publishers of Literature, Music & Fine Arts, Prague / Státni Nakladatelstvi Krásné Literatury, Hudby a Umění

SNO Scottish National Orchestra (now, Royal Scottish National Orchestra, RSNO)

SNS Symphony Nova Scotia

So symphony orchestra

SOB *Süddeutsche Orgelmeister des Barock*

Soc. Fr. de Mie Société française de musicologie

SOCAN Society of Composers, Authors and Music Publishers of Canada

Solf. *solfège* (F) / *solfeggio* (I)

SOM Swedish Independent Music Producers Organisation

Son. sonata

Songwriters R *Songwriter's Review* (jl.)

Sop., sopr. soprano

SOR Sveriges Orkesterforeningars Riksforbund

Sord. *sordino, sordini* (I=mute(s))

Sost. *sostenuto* (I=sustained)

SoT *Sloejd och Ton* (jl.)

Sound Brass *Sounding Brass and the Conductor* (jl.)

South Rag *Southern Rag* (jl.); South Rag

Sovet Muz *Sovetskaia muzyka* (jl.)

SovetskajaM *Sovetskaia muzyka* (jl.)

SovM *Sovetskaia muzyka* (jl.)

Sp	*sine perfectione* (nota.)

Sp.	*Sopran* (G=soprano); *Spitze* (G=point)

SPAH	Society for the Preservation and Advancement of the Harmonica

SPAM	Society for the Publication of American Music

SPBA	Scottish Pipe Band Association

SPDM	Society for the Publication of Danish Music

SPEBSQSA	Society for the Preservation and Encouragement of Barber Shop Quartet Singing in America

SpettatoreM	*Lo Spettatore musicale* (jl.)

Spic, spicc.	*spiccato* (I=rebounding off the string)

SPICMACAY	Society for the Promotion of Indian Music and Culture Amongst Youth

SPNM	Society for the Promotion of New Music

Spr	*sine proprietate* (nota.)

Spr.	*Sprecher* (G=speaker)

Sq.	*Codex Squarcialupi* (Florence. Biblioteca Mediceo-Laurenziana. Pal. 87); transcription in square note-symbols that are not diplomatic, without rhythmic value (nota.)

Sr	short responsory

SR	*Songwriter's Review* (jl.); *Source Readings in Music History* (Oliver Strunk)

SRA	*Source Readings in Music History* (Oliver Strunk)

SRB	*Source Readings in Music History* (Oliver Strunk)

SRC	*Source Readings in Music History* (Oliver Strunk)

SS	Society for Strings; Sonneck Society

SSC	Society of Slovene Composers, Society of Swedish Composers

SSCP	Swedish Society of Composers and Publishers

SSM	Société suisse de musicologie; Swedish Society for Musicology

SSMT	Swiss Society of Music Teachers in Secondary Schools

SSPM	Société suisse de pédagogie musicale

SSPMC	Swedish Society of Popular Music Composers

SSR	New Composers' Federation / Shinko Sakkyoku Renmei; *Source*

Readings in Music History (Oliver Strunk)

SSRe *Source Readings in Music History* (Oliver Strunk)

SSRo *Source Readings in Music History* (Oliver Strunk)

St z M *Studien zur Musikwissenschaft* (jl.)

St. stanza

St. *Stimme* (G=separate voice, part); *Stimmen* (G=voices, parts)

St. diap. stopped diapason

St.M2 Paris. Bibliothèque nationale. Lat. 3549 (ms.)

ST Stäblein, Bruno, ed. *Hymnen (I): Die mittelalterlichen Hymnenmelodien des Abendlandes (Monumenta monodica medii aevi, 1)*; *sul tasto* (I=over the fingerboard)

ST. *Stereo* (jl.)

Stacc. *staccato*

Stb. *Stimmbuch* (G=partbook)

StereoR, Stereo R *Stereo Review* (jl.)

Stg. *stimmig*, as in 4stg. (G=voiced, e.g., 4-voiced)

Stgn. *stimmigen*, as in 4stg. (G=voiced, e.g., 4-voiced)

STIM Svenska Tonsättares Internationella Musikbyrå

StM *Studien zur Musikwissenschaft* (jl.)

STM Society for Traditional Music

STMf *Svensk tidskrift för musikforskning*

StMl *Studia musicologica* (jl.); *Studia musicologica* (Budapest) (jl.)

StMw, STMW *Studien zur Musikwissenschaft* (jl.)

Story *Storyville* (jl.)

STR *Stereo Review* (jl.)

Str. qt. string quartet

Str. *Streich, -er* (G=string, strings), string (-s); strophe; *strumento* (I=instrument)

Streichor. *Streichorchester* (G=string orchestra)

String. *stringendo*

StrQu *Streichquartett* (G=string quartet)

Strqua string quartet / *Streichquartett* (G)

Strqui string quintet / *Streichquintett* (G)

Strum. *strumentale* (I=instrumental)

Stsp. *Stabspiel*

Stu Mus *Studia musicologica* (Budapest) (jl.)

STUBA Swiss Tuba and Baritone Association

Stud. Studie

StudCercetăriIstoriaArtei *Studii și cercetări de istoria artei* (jl.)

Studia mus *Studia musicologica* (jl.)

Studia Mus *Studia musicologica* (Budapest) (jl.)

Studia Mus Nor *Studia musicologica norvegica* (jl.)

Studies Mus *Studies in Music* (Nedlands, Australia)

StudiM *Studi musicali* (Florence) (jl.)

StudM [AUS] *Studies in Music* (Nedlands, Australia)

StudM [CND] *Studies in Music* (London, Ont.)

StudMus *Studia musicologica* (jl.)

StudMusicol *Studia musicologica* (Budapest) (jl.)

StudMusicolNorvegica *Studia musicologica norvegica* (jl.)

StudMuzicol *Studii de muzicologie* (Bucharest)

StuMw *Studien zur Musikwissenschaft* (jl.)

Stutt Stuttgart. Landesbibliothek. I Asc. 95 (ms.)

STV Schweizerischer Tonkünstlerverein

SU *Suzuki World* (jl.)

SUDM Samfundet til Udgivelse af Dansk Musik

SULASOL Suomen Laulajain ja Soittajain Liitto

SUMC Sociedad Uruguaya de Música Contemporánea

Sup. *superius*

Sv stressed vibrato

Sven Tids M *Svensk tidskrift för musikforskning*

Svensk Tid *Svensk tidskrift för musikforskning*

SvenskTMf *Svensk tidskrift för musikforskning*

SvensktMHistorisktArkivBul Svenskt musikhistoriskt arkiv.
    Bulletin (jl.)

SVMM Schweizerische Vereinigung der Musiklehrerinnen und
    Musiklehrer an den Mittelschulen

SW Sadler's Wells (London)

Sw. swell organ

Swingt. *Swingtime: maandblad voor jazz en blues* (jl.)

Swk. *Sammelwerk* (G=collected works)

SWM Society of Women Musicians

SwW Sweelinck, Jan P. *Werke*

SYG Paris. Bibliothèque nationale. Codex 903 *(Graduel de Saint-Yrieix)* facsim. (in *Paléographie musicale, 13*)

Sym. symphony, symphonic

Sym mag *Symphony Magazine* (jl.)

Sym news *Symphony News* (jl.)

Synch. synchronize, synchronization

Synth. synthesizer

Syst. system, *Systeme* (G=staff, staves)

SZ Suvini Zerboni (publ.)

Sz. *Schlagzeug* (G=percussion)

T *tempus*

T. *sul tasto* (I=over the fingerboard); *tasto* (I=keyboard); *tempora*; tenor (E, G) / *ténor* (F) / *tenore* (I); *tief* (G=low); tiré

(F=downbow); tonic; *tutti*

T.b. temple block

T.c. *tre corde*

T.d. tenor drum

T.s., t.s., T.S. *tasto solo*

T.t. tom-tom(s) / *tomtom* (Sp)

T.ts. tamtam(s)

T.U.B.A. Tubists Universal Brotherhood Association

T.W.V. *Telemann-Werke-Verzeichnis*

Ta tuba

TaAM Tagliapietra, G., ed. *Antologia di musica . . . per pianoforte*

Tab. tablature (E, F) / *Tablatur* (G)

Tam. t. tamtam(s)

Tamb. *tambour* (F) / *tamburo* (I) / *tambor* (Sp) = drum, kettledrum; tambourine

Tast. Instr. *Tasteninstrumente* (G=keyboard instruments)

Tasto *strumenti a tastiera* (I=keyboard instruments)

Tb troubadour

Tb. tuba

Tba. tuba

TBS Sir Thomas Beecham Society

TCM *Tudor Church Music* (jl.)

TE *Tempo* (jl.)

TeD *Te Deum*

TEM Parrish, Carl. *Treasury of Early Music*

Tem. I° *tempo primo*

Temp. bl. temple block

Ten. dr. tenor drum

Ten. tenor (E, G) / *ténor* (F) / *tenore* (I), *tenuto* (I=sustained)

Ter. *ligatura ternaria* (nota.)

Tert *ad tertiam*

TesoroSacroM *Tesoro sacro musical*

TG Tribune de Saint-Gervais

Th. *Theil* (G=part [Teil]); theme

Th. mus. *théorie musicale, théorie de la musique*

Thd, THD total harmonic distortion (acoustics)

TÎ Tonskaldafelag Islands

TiFC Frederic Chopin Society / Towarzystwo imienia Fryderyka Chopina

Timb. timbales

Timp. *timpani* (I=kettledrums)

TJMS Traditional Japanese Music Society

Tl., Tle. *Teil, -e* (G=part, -s)

Tm *tambour* (F) / *tamburo* (I) / *tambor* (Sp) = drum, kettledrum

TM *Thesauri musici*

TMP   Transcontinental Music Publishing Co. (publ.)

TMw   Vereniging voor nederlandse muziekgeschiedenis. *Tijdschrift* (jl.)

Tnr.   tenor (E, G) / *ténor* (F) / *tenore* (I)

Tomt.   tom-tom(s) / *tomtom* (Sp)

Tonphys.   *Tonphysiologie* (G=physiology of music)

Tonpsych.   *Tonpsychologie* (G=psychology of music)

Torchi   Torchi, Luigi, ed. *L'arte musicale in Italia*

Tôyô ongaku   *Tôyô ongaku kenkyû* (jl.)

Tp   *tonus perigrinus* (church mode)

Tp.   *timpani* (I=kettledrums)

Tpi.   *timpani* (I=kettledrums)

Tr   tract / *tractus*

Tr.   transpose; treble; trill; *tromba, -e* (I=trumpet, trumpets); *Trommel* (G=drum); *tropus*, trope

TR   *Triad* (jl.)

Tract.   tract / *tractus*

Trad mus   *Traditional Music* (jl.)

Transc, transcc   transcription(s)

Transp.   transposed / *transponiert* (G)

Transpon.   *transponiere* (G=transpose; adj.), *transponieren* (G=to transpose)

Transpos.   transposition

Trascr.   (I=transcription) *trascrizione*

Trb., trbe.   *tromba, -e* (I=trumpet, trumpets), trombone (E, F, I) / *trombón* (Sp)

Trbn.   trombone (E, F, I) / *trombón* (Sp)

Trem.   *tremolo*

Trg.   triangle

Tri.   triangle

TRI-M   Tri-M Music Honor Society

Triangle   *Triangle of Mu Phi Epsilon* (jl.)

Trib mus   *Tribune musical* (Buenos Aires) (jl.)

TribSTG *Tribune de Saint-Gervais*

Tribune orgue *Tribune de l'orgue* (jl.)

Tripl. *triplum*

Trmb. trombone (E, F, I) / *trombón* (Sp)

TRN *Threni* (chant)

Tromb. *tromba, -e* (I=trumpet, trumpets), trombone (E, F, I) / trombón (Sp)

Trp., trp. *Trompete* (G) / *trompette* (F) = trumpet

Tv trouvère

TV Vereniging voor nederlandse muziekgeschiedenis. *Tijdschrift* (jl.), Vereniging voor Noord-nederlands

TVer Vereniging voor nederlandse muziekgeschiedenis. *Tijdschrift* (jl.)

TVerNederlandseMg Vereniging voor nederlandse muziekgeschiedenis. *Tijdschrift* (jl.)

TVMN Vereniging voor nederlandse muziekgeschiedenis. *Tijdschrift* (jl.)

U Universal Edition (publ.)

U.c., U.C. *una corda*

UA *Uraufführung* (G=first performance)

UALM University Accompanists' Licentiate in Music

UBC Union of Bulgarian Composers

UCB Unie van Belgische Componisten / Union des compositeurs belges

UCPM *University of California Publications in Music*

UE Universal Edition (publ.)

Ue. *Übertragung* (G=transcription)

UGHA United in Group Harmony Association

UKBiH Udruženje kompizotora Bosne i Hercegovine

UKH Udruženje kompizotora Hrvatske

UKM Udruženje kompizotora Makedonije

UME Union Musical Española

Unac, unacc. unaccompanied

Unis. *unisono* (I=unison)

Unterst. *Unterstimme* (G=lower part)

UPC *University of Pennsylvania Choral Series*; Union of Polish Composers

UPLM University Performers' Licentiate in Music

Us *Liber Usualis missae et officii pro dominicis et festis duplicibus cum cantu gregoriano*

USC Union suisse des chorales

UTLM University Teachers' Licentiate in Music

UVM Vereniging voor nederlandse muziekgeschiedenis. *Uitgaven* (jl.)

UVNM Vereniging voor nederlandse muziekgeschiedenis. *Uitgaven* (jl.)

V verse, *versicle*

V & R Vandenhoeck & Rupprecht (publ.)

V. *verte* (F=turn over [the page]); violin / *violon* (F) / *violino* (I) / *Violine* (G) / *violín* (Sp) *voci* (I=voices); *voix* (F=voice); *vox* (L=voice)

V.l. *vibrato lento* (I=slow vibrato)

V.s. *voce sola*; *volti subito* (I=turn the page quickly)

V¹ *violini primi*

V² *violini secondi*

Va da gba *viola da gamba*

Va. viola

Vab *viola da braccio*

Vag *viola da gamba*

VAR *Varia* (chant)

Var. variant, *variazione* (I=variation)

Vb vibraphone / *vibrafono* (I)

Vbs vibrations per second

Vc. violoncello / *violoncelle* (F) / *violonchelo* (Sp)

VCA voltage-controlled amplifier

Vcelle *violoncelle* (F=violoncello)

VCF voltage-controlled filter

Vcl. violoncello / *violoncelle* (F) / *violonchelo* (Sp)

Vcle *versicle*

VCO voltage-controlled oscillator

VdASA Viola d'Amore Society of America

Vdgsa, VdGSA Viola da Gamba Society of America

VDKC Verband Deutscher Konzertchöre / German Society of Concert Choirs

VDS Viola d'Amore Society; Verband Deutscher Schulmusiker

VDSA Viola d'Amore Society of America

Verdi Newsl *Verdi Newsletter* (jl.)

Vesp. vespers / *vesperae*

VfMw, VFWM *Vierteljahrsschrift für Musikwissenschaft* (jl.)

Vgl. Mf. *Vergleichende Musikforschung* (G=comparative musicology)

VI *Viol* (jl.)

Vib. vibraphone / *vibrafono* (I), *vibrato*

Vibes vibraphone / *vibrafono* (I)

Vibr. vibraphone / *vibrafono* (I)

Vie viella

VieM *Vie musicale* (Canada) (jl.)

Vierst. *vierstimmig* (G=4 pts., 4 voices)

Vio violin(s)

Viola *viola d'amore*

ViolaDaGambaSocJ Chelys, the Viola da Gamba Society Journal (jl.)

VIR *Virtuoso* (jl.)

Viv. *vivace*

ViW Victoria, Thomas L. *Opera omnia*

Vla d'a *viola d'amore*

VlaamsMT *Vlaams Muziektijdschrift* (jl.)

Vlc. violoncello / *violoncelle* (F) / *violonchelo* (Sp)

Vle. *violone*; viole

VLMS Villa-Lobos Music Society

Vlon *violon* (F=violin)

Vm *voce media* (I=middle voice)

VMN Association of Music Dealers and Publishers in the Netherlands / Vereniging van Muziekhandelaren en -uitgavens Nederland

VMPH Hirsch, Paul. *Publications of the Paul Hirsch Music Library / Veröffentlichungen der Musik-Bibliothek Paul Hirsch*

VMw, VWM *Vierteljahrsschrift für Musikwissenschaft* (jl.)

Vn *vibrato normale* (I=normal vibrato)

Vni *violini* (I=violins)

VNM Verlag Neue Musik (publ.)

Vo *violino*; *versione organistica + solo* (I=orchestral parts reduced for organ; organ reduction)

VO *Voice: The Magazine of Vocal Music* (jl.)

Voc. vocal / *vocale* (I)

VogelB Vogel, Emil. *Bibliothek der gedruckten weltlichen Vokalmusik Italiens . . .*

Voice *Voice: The Magazine of Vocal Music* (jl.)

Vok. *vokal*

Volksm *Volksmusik*

Vp *versione pianistica + solo* (I=orchestral parts reduced for piano; piano reduction)

VP *Variae preces ex liturgia tum hodierna tum antiqua collectae aut usu receptae* (chant)

VPR *vespertini* (chant)

Vr *vibrato rapido* (I=rapid vibrato); *voce recitante* (I=reciting voice)

VR verses (chant)

VRS *versus* (chant)

VS Violoncello Society

VSA Violin Society of America, Violin Society of America. *Journal* (jl.)

Vv. violins

W M. Witmark & Sons (publ.)

W. chimes wind chimes

W. snare with snare

W.b. wood block(s)

W.s. with snare

W¹ Wolfenbüttel. Herzog-August-Bibliothek. Mss (677 (Helms. 628)) (medieval ms.)

W² Wolfenbüttel. Herzog-August-Bibliothek. Mss (1099 (Helms. 1206)) (medieval ms.)

WA Worcester. Cathedral Library. Codex F. 160. facsimile (*Paleographie musicale*, 12)

WaltherL Walther, Johann Gottfried. *Musicalisches Lexikon oder Musicalische Bibliothek*

WaltherML Walther, Johann Gottfried. *Musicalisches Lexikon oder Musicalische Bibliothek*

WASO Women's Association for Symphony Orchestras

WBDI Women Band Directors International

WBP *Woodwind World — Brass and Percussion* (jl.)

WDMP Wydawnictwo dawnej muzyki polskiej

WDR Nordwestdeutscher Rundfunk; Westdeutscher Rundfunk

WE *Wellesley Edition*

WECIS *Wellesley Edition Cantata Index Series*

WelshM *Welsh Music* (jl.)

WFIMC World Federation of International Music Competitions

WFMA World Folk Music Association

WIM Western International Music Co. (publ.)

WLSM *World Library of Sacred Music*

WM Wolf, Johannes, ed. *Music of Earlier Times*

WMA Western Music Association; Workers' Music Association

WMS Willem Mengelberg Society

WNOC Welsh National Opera Company

WO *World of Opera*

WoB Innsbruck. Universitätsbibliothek. *Wolkenstein-Codex*

WoG, WoGM Wolf, Johannes. *Geschichte der Mensural-Notation von 1250-1460*

WoH, WoHN Wolf, Johannes. *Handbuch der Notationskunde*

WolfM Wolf, Johannes. *Geschichte der Mensural-Notation von 1250-1460*

WolfN Wolf, Johannes. *Handbuch der Notationskunde*

WoO, W.o.O. *Werke ohne Opuszahl* (G=works without opus number)

Wood World Brass *Woodwind World — Brass and Percussion* (jl.)

Woodwind W *Woodwind World — Brass and Percussion* (jl.)

Worc. Worcester. Cathedral Library. Additional 68 (ms.)

WorcO Oxford. Bodleian Library. Lat. liturg. d.20 (ms.)

World Mus *World of Music*

World Music *World of Music*

WorldM *World of Music*

Wotq. Wotquenne, Alfred. *Catalogue thématique de l'oeuvre de Carl Philipp Emanuel Bach*

Wq Wotquenne, Alfred. *Thematisches Verzeichnis der Werke von Carl Philipp Emanuel Bach*

WQ *Wind Quarterly* (jl.)

WTC, WtK Bach, Johann Sebastian. *Wohltemperierte Clavier*

WürttembergBlätterKm *Württembergische Blätter für Kirchenmusik*

Ww woodwind

Ww quin woodwind quintet

WWBDA *Woodwind World — Brass and Percussion* (jl.)

WychowanieMSzkole Wychowanie muzyczne w szkole

Xil. *xilofono* (I=xylophone)

Xyl. xylophone

YbInterAmerMResearch *Yearbook for Inter-American Musical Research* (jl.)

YCA Young Concert Artists

YMF   Young Musicians' Foundation

Z.   Zimmerman, Franklin B. *Henry Purcell: An Analytical Catalogue of his Music*

Z.f.MTH   *Zeitschrift für Musiktheorie* (jl.)

Zeit f. Hausmusik   *Zeitschrift für Hausmusik* (jl.)

Zeit f. Musik   *Zeitschrift für Musik* (jl.)

Zf Mus Theorie   *Zeitschrift für Musiktheorie* (jl.)

ZfI, ZfIb   *Zeitschrift für Instrumentenbau* (jl.)

ZfM, ZFM   *Zeitschrift für Musik* (jl.)

ZfMth   *Zeitschrift für Musiktheorie* (jl.)

ZfMw, ZFMW   *Zeitschrift für Musikwissenschaft* (jl.)

ZHMP   Zrodła do historii muzyki polskiej

ZI   *Zeitschrift für Instrumentenbau* (jl.)

ZKP   Zwiazek Kompozytorow Polskich

ZL   *Zenei Lexikon*

ZM   *Zeitschrift für Musik* (jl.)

ZMtheorie   *Zeitschrift für Musiktheorie* (jl.)

ZMw, ZMW   *Zeitschrift für Musikwissenschaft* (jl.)

Zupfinstr.   *Zupfinstrumente* (G=plectral instruments)

Zweist.   *zweistimmig* (G=two-part)

Zykl.   *zyklisch* (G=cyclic)

THE REVERSE DICTIONARY

45-rpm recordings   45s
78-rpm recordings   78s

A cappella   a cap., a capp.

A parte ante (nota.)   a.p.a.

A parte post (nota.)   a.p.p.

A tempo (I=return to original tempo)   a.t., a tem.

À Cœur Joie International   ACJI

About Time (rec. lab.)   About

Abr. Lundquist AB (publ.)   AL

Abtheilung (G=part, section, division)   Abt., Abth., Abtlg.

Academy of Wind and Percussion Arts   AWAPA

Ace of Diamonds (rec. lab.)   A of D

Accelerando (I=faster)   accel., accel°

Accent (rec. lab.)   Ac, ACC

Accent on Worship, Music, and the Arts (jl.)   AC

Accompaniment   acc., accomp., accpt.

Accompany   acc.

Accord (F=chord)   acc.

Accordion(s) acc.

Accordion Federation of North America AFNA

Accordion Society of Australia ASA

Accordionists and Teachers Guild, International ATG

Accordo (I=chord) acc.

Accresciuto (I=increased) accres.

Acompañamiento (Sp=accompaniment) acomp.

Acoustical Society of America A.S.A.

Acoustical Society of America. *Journal* (jl.) JASA

Acoustic(s) / acoustique (F) / Akustik (G) / acustica (I) / acústica (Sp)
    ac., acoust., Ak., Akust.

Acta Mozartiana (jl.) Act Mozart

Acta musicologica (jl.) AcM, Act Music, Acta, Acta mus,
    ActaMusicol, AM, AML

Acustica, acústica *see* acoustic(s)

A. Dvořák: Thematic Catalogue of Works (Jarmil Burghauser) B.

Ad accendentes ACC

Ad confractiones panis CFP

Ad decimam dec.

Ad libitum (L=at liberty) ad l., ad lib.

Ad matutinum mat.

Ad nocturnos noct

Ad octavam oct

Ad pacem PAC

Ad primam prim

Ad quartam quart

Ad quintam quint

Ad reconciliandum penitentem reconcil penit

Ad sanctus SNCT

Ad secundam sec

Ad septimam sept

Ad sextam sext

Ad tertiam tert

Adagio   adag., adgo, adgᵒ, adᵒ, ado

Additional manuscripts (British Museum)   Add.

Adelaide Symphony Orchestra   ASO

Adelphi (rec. lab.)   Adel

Adler, Guido. *Handbuch der Musikgeschichte*   AdHM, AdlerH, AdlerHdb, Adler HMG

Adlung, Jacob. *Musica mechanica organoedi*   Adlung Mus. mech. org.

Adsit scribendi Virgo Beata mihi   ASVBM

Advance (rec. lab.)   Adv

Affettuoso   affettᵒ

Affrettando   affrettᵒ

Aflevering   aflg.

African Music (jl.)   AfricanM

African-American Music Society   AAMS

Afro-American Music Opportunities Association   AAMOA

Aggregate (vertical combination of pitches)   A

Agitato   Agᵒ

Agnus Dei   Ag

Aircheck (rec. lab.)   Air.

Akkord (G=chord)   Ak.

Akkordeon (G=accordion)   Akk.

Akustik see acoustic(s)

Akustisch   ak., akust.

Al segno   al seg.

Algemeen Nederlands Zangverbond *see* General Dutch Singing Society

Algemeine Musikgesellschaft   AMG

Algemene muziekencyclopedie   AMe

Algemene muziekencyclopedie: Supplement   AMes

Algord Music (publ.)   Algord

Alkan Society   AS

All Ears (rec. lab.)   All E.

All' ottava   all' ot, all' ott., All' 8va

Allegretto   allgtto., allgtt°

Allegro   all°

Alleluia   aeuia, al., all.

Alleluia-Melodien I (Monumenta monodica medii aevi, 7) (Karlheinz Schlager, ed.)   MMMA

Alleluia verse   alv

Alleluiatici **(chant)**   ALL

Allgemeine Musikzeitung (jl.)   AM, Amz, AMZ

Allgemeiner Deutscher Musikverein   ADMV

Alliance for Canadian New-Music Projects   ACNMP

Alligator (rec. lab.)   Alli.

Almglocke(n) (G=herd bells)   Almgl.

Alpha-Numeric System for the Classification of Records   ANSCR

Alto   a, alt.

Alto viola   a. vla.

Altus   A.

Amateur Chamber Music Players   ACMP

Amateur Organists and Keyboard Association International   AOAI

Ambient Sound (rec. lab.)   Ambient S.

American Academy of Teachers of Singing   AATS

American Accordion Musicological Society   AAMS

American Accordionists' Association   AAA

American Association for Music Therapy (earlier, Urban Federation of Music Therapy, UFMT)   AAMT

American Bach Foundation   ABF

American Bandmasters Association   ABA

American Banjo Fraternity   ABF

American Beethoven Society   ABS

American Berlin Opera Foundation   ABOF

American Boychoir Federation   ABF

American Choral Directors' Association   ACDA

American Choral Review (jl.)   ACR, Am Choral R, AmerChoralR

American College of Musicians   ACM

American Composers' Alliance   ACA

American Composers' Alliance. Composers' Facsimile Edition
   ACA-CFE

American Disc Jockey Association   ADJA

American Ensemble (Chamber Music America) (jl.)   AE, Am Ens

American Federation of Jazz Societies   AFJS

American Federation of Musicians of the United States and Canada
   (earlier, American Federation of Musicians)   AFM, AF of M

American Federation of Pueri Cantores   AFPC

American Federation of Violin and Bow Makers   AFVBM

American Festival of Microtonal Music   AFMM

American Guild of Authors and Composers   AGAC

American Guild of English Handbell Ringers   AGEHR

American Guild of Music   AGM

American Guild of Musical Artists   AGMA

American Guild of Organists   A.G.O., AGO

American Guitar Society   AGS

American Harp Journal (jl.)   Am Harp J

American Harp Society   AHS

American Industrial Music Association   AIMA

American Institute for Verdi Studies   AIVS

American Institute of Musical Studies   AIMS

American Institute of Musicology   AIM

American Institute of Organbuilder   AIO

American Israel Opera Foundation   AIOF

American Liszt Society   ALS

American Liszt Society. *Journal* (jl.)   J ALS

American Lithuanian Musicians Alliance   ALMA

American Matthay Association   AMA

American Music Center   AMC

American Music Center. *Newsletter* (jl.)   AMC

American Music Conference   AMC

American Music Editions   AME

American Music Festival Association   AMFA

American Music Scholarship Association   AMSA

American Music Teacher (jl.)   Am Mus Tcr, AMT, AMUTA

American Music Therapy Association   AMTA

American Musical Instrument Society   AMIS

American Musical Instrument Society. *Journal* (jl.)   AMIS J, J Am
   Mus In

American Musical Instrument Society. *Newsletter* (jl.)   AMIS N

American Musicians' Union   AMU

American Musicological Society   AMS

American Musicological Society. *Bulletin* (jl.)   BAMS

American Musicological Society. *Journal* (jl.)   JA, JAMS, J Am
   Music, J Amer Musicol Soc

American Musicological Society. *Papers* (jl.)   PAMS

American Orff-Schulwerk Association   AOSA

American Organist (jl.; earlier, *Music: The A.G.O. and R.C.C.O.*
   Magazine)   Am Org

American Pianists Association   APA

American Record Guide (jl.)   Am Rec G, ARG

American Recorder (jl.)   Am Recorder, AmerRecorder, AR

American Recorder Society   ARS

American Recorder Society Editions   ARS

American Recorder Teachers Association   ARTA

American School Band Directors' Association   ASBDA

American Society for Jewish Music   ASJM

American Society of Ancient Instruments   ASAI

American Society of Composers, Authors, and Publishers   ASCAP

American Society of Music Arrangers and Composers   ASMAC

American Society of Music Copyists   ASMC

American Society of University Composers   ASUC

American Society of University Composers. *Proceedings* (jl.)   PR,

ProcAmerSocUComposers

American String Teacher (jl.) AS, AST

American String Teachers' Association ASTA

American Suzuki Journal (jl.) ASJ

American Symphony Orchestra League ASOL

American Theatre Organ Enthusiasts ATOE

American Theatre Organ Society ATOS

American Viola Society AVS

American Women Composers AWC

Amphion (rec. lab.) Amp.

Amplified amp., ampli.

Analecta hymnica medii aevi (jl.) AH, Anal. hymn.

Analecta musicologica (jl.) AnalectaMusicol, AnMc

Analog computer anacom

Analog to digital a/d

Analog-digital converter adc

Analog-to-digital recorder adr

Analysis anal.

Ancia doppia (I=double reed) ancia d.

Andante and., andte

Andantino andno., and[no]

Andrew's Music (rec. lab.) Andr.

Angles, Higinio. *El Códex musical de Las Huelgas* Ahu, AHu, Las H

Anglo-Canadian Music Publishers' Association (later, Anglo-Canadian Music Co.) Ang-Can

Anhaltisch (G=continuous) anhalt.

Animato anim.

Annales Chopin *see Rocznik Chopinowski*

Annales Hindemith / *Hindemith Jahrbuch* (jl.) HindemithJb

Annales musicologiques (jl.) Amu, AnnM, AnnMl, Ann. mus.

Année musicale (jl.) AM

Annuit Coeptis (rec. lab.) Annu.

Anstalt zur Wahrung der Aufführungsrechte auf dem Gebiet der

Musik   AWA

Anthologia vocalis (jl.)   AV

Anthology of Canadian Music   ACM / *Anthologie de la musique canadienne*, AMC (rec. lab.)

Anthology of Medieval Music (Richard H. Hoppin, ed.)   AMM

Antilles (rec. lab.)   Ant.

Antiphon   an., ant.

Antiphon verse   anv

Antiphonale missarum juxta ritum Sanctae Ecclesiae Mediolanensis AMM, Ant. Vat.

Antiphonale monasticum pro diurnis horis   AM, Ant M

Antiphonale sacrosanctae romanae ecclesiae pro diurnis horis   A, Ant R, AR

Antiphonarium ad usum sacri et canonici ordinis Praemonstratensis AntP

Antiphoniale Sarisburiense (jl.)   AS

Antiphons   ANT

Antiquae musicae italicae (jl.)   Ant MI

Antiquae musicae italicae scriptores (jl.)   AMIS

Antique cymbals   ant. cym.

Antique Phonograph Collectors Club   APCC

Antiquitates musicae in Polonia (jl.)   AMP

Antologia di musica . . . per pianoforte (G. Tagliapietra, ed.)   TaAM

Antonio Vivaldi. Catalogo numerico-tematico delle opere strumentale (Antonio Fanna)   F.

Antonio Vivaldi et la musique instrumentale. v. 2. Inventaire thématique (Marc Pincherle)   P, P.-V.

Anuario musical (jl.)   AnM, Anu Mus, Anuario Mus., Anuario M

Apel, Willi. *French Secular Music of the Late Fourteenth CenturyP* ApF

Apel, Willi. *Gregorian Chant*   ApelG, ApGC

Apel, Willi. *Harvard Dictionary of Music*   HDM

Apel, Willi. *Masters of the Keyboard*   ApelMK

Apel, Willi. *Musik aus früher Zeit für Klavier*   ApMZ

Apel, Willi. *Notation der polyphonen Musik, 900-1600* ApelN

Apel, Willi. *Notation of Polyphonic Music, 900-1600* ApelN, ApN, ApNPM, NPM

Apocrypha Apoc.

Apogee Press (publ.) Apogee

Appena aperta (I=[mouth] slightly open) a.a.

Arabesque (rec. lab.) Ara.

Arbeit, -en (G=work, works) Arb.

Arbeitsgemeinschaft Deutscher Chorverband ADC

Arbeits Gemeinschaft Europäischer Chorverbände *see* Federation of European Choral Associations

Arbeitsgemeinschaft für rheinische Musikgeschichte. *Mitteilungen* (jl.) MittRheinischeMg

Arcato, coll' arco (I=with the bow, bowed) arc.

Arch form ABCBA

Archambault Musique (publ.) Archambault

Archbishop of Canterbury's Diploma in Church Music ADCM

Archets arch.

Archiv für Musikforschung (jl.) AfMf, Amf, Archiv fMF

Archiv für Musikwissenschaft (jl.) AfMW, Amw, Arch Mus, Arch Musik, Archiv fMW

Archiv für Musikwissenschaft. Beihefte (jl.) BzAfMW

Archive of Folk & Jazz Music (rec. lab.) Arc. Folk

Archive of Piano Music (rec. lab.) Arc. Piano

Archive of Recorder Consorts ARC

Archives and Research Centre for Ethnomusicology ARCE

Archives des maîtres de l'orgue des XVIe, XVIIe, et XVIIIe siècles (A. Guilmant et A. Pirro, ed.) Guilmant-Pirro

Archivio musicale lateranense Arch. mus. lat.

Archivium Musices Metropolitanum Mediolanense AMMM

Arco (I=bow) a, ar

Ardito ard^o

Arhoolie (rec. lab.) Arhoo

Arista (rec. lab.)   Ari.

Arista/Freedom (rec. lab.)   Ari./Free.

Arista/GRP (rec. lab.)   Ari/GRP

Arista/Novus (rec. lab.)   Ari/No

Armonia (I=harmony)   arm.

Armonica a bocca (I=harmonica)   ab

Armonio (I, Sp=harmonium)   arm.

Arnold Schoenberg Institute. *Journal* (jl.)   J A Schoenb, J Arnold
   Schoenberg Inst, JS, Schoenberg Inst

Arpa (I=harp)   ar

Arpeggio   arp., arpio.

Arranged, arrangement, *arrangiert* (G)   arr.

Arte musicale in Italia (Luigi Torchi, ed.)   AMI, Torchi

Arthur Jordan Choral Series   AJ

Arti musices (jl.)   Arti mus

Artist-Direct (rec. lab.)   Art/Dir

Artists House (rec. lab.)   Artists

As loud as possible   alap

As soft as possible   asap

As soon as possible   asap

Ascendens, ascendentes   asc

Ashbourne (rec. lab.)   Ashb

Asian Music (jl.)   AsianM, Asian Mus, ASM

Asian Musician (jl.)   ASIJB

Aspects of Medieval and Renaissance Music (Jan LaRue, ed.)
   AMRM

Associação Portuguesa de Educação Musical *see* Portugese
   Association of Music Education

Associate, American Guild of Organists   AAGO

Associate in Music   A Mus

Associate in Music of the London College of Music (now, London
   College of Music and Media, within Thames Valley University),
   AMusLCM

Associate of the Canadian College of Organists (later, ARCCO, Associate of the Royal Canadian College of Organists) ACCO

Associate of the Guildhall School of Music and Drama AGSM

Associate of the London Academy of Music and Drama ALAM

Associate of the London College of Music (now, London College of Music and Media, within Thames Valley University) ALCM

Associate of the Royal Academy of Music ARAM

Associate of the Royal Canadian College of Organists (formerly ACCO, Associate of the Canadian College of Organists) ARCCO

Associate of the Royal College of Music ARCM

Associate of the Royal College of Organists ARCO

Associate of the Royal Manchester College of Music ARMCM (RMCM merged with the Northern School of Music, now Royal Northern College of Music)

Associate of the Royal School of Church Music ARSCM

Associate of the Tonic Sol-fa College of Music ATSC

Associated Audio Archives AAA

Associated Music Publishers (publ.) AM, AMP

Associated Pipe Organ Builders of America APOBA

Association canadienne des bibliothèques, archives et centres de documentation musicaux *see* Canadian Association of Music Libraries

Association canadienne des écoles universitaires de musique *see* Canadian Association of University Schools of Music

Association canadienne des éditeurs de musique *see* Canadian Music Publishers' Association

Association canadienne des éducateurs de musique *see* Canadian Music Educators Association

Association canadienne des industries de la musique *see* Music Industries Association of Canada

Association de l'industrie canadienne de l'enregistrement *see* Canadian Recording Industry Association

Association de Musicothérapie du Canada *see* Canadian Association for Music Therapy

Association des musiciens suisses *see* Swiss Musicians' Association

Association des musiciens suisses *see* Swiss Musicians' Association

Association des orchestres canadiens *see* Association of Canadian Orchestras

Association européenne des conservatoires *see* European Association of Conservatoires

Association européenne des directeurs de bureaux de concerts et spectacles AEDBCS

Association européenne des festivals *see* European Festivals Association

Association for British Music ABM

Association for Dutch Music History ADMH / Vereniging voor nederlandse muziekgeschiedenis VNM

Association for Latin-American Music & Art ALMA

Association for Recorded Sound Collections ARS, ARSC

Association for Recorded Sound Collections. *Journal* (jl.) Assoc Recor

Association for Technology in Music Instruction ATMI

Association for the Advancement of Creative Music AACM

Association for the Furtherment of Bel Canto AFBC

Association internationale des directeurs d'opéra *see* International Association of Opera Directors

Association internationale pour l'étude de la musique popular *see* International Association for the Study of Popular Music

Association Internationale des Bibliothéque, Archives et Centres de Documentation Musicaux *see* International Association of Music Libraries, Archives, and Documentation Centres

Association of Anglican Musicians AAM

Association of Blind Piano Tuners ABPT

Association of Canadian Orchestras ACO / Association des orchestres canadiens AOC

Association of Canadian Women Composers ACWC

Association of Choral Conductors ACC

Association of College and University and Community Arts Administrators ACUCAA

Association of Concert Bands   ACB

Association of Conductors and Instructors   ACI / Bond van Orkestdirigenten en Instructeurs   BvO

Association of Croatian Composers   ACC / Udruženje kompizotora Hrvatske   UKH

Association of Finnish Music Schools   AFMS / Suomen Musiikkioppilaitosten Liitto   SML

Association of Finnish Symphony Orchestras   AFSO

Association of German Music Dealers   GDM

Association of German Music Publishers   DMV

Association of Independent Composers and Performers   AICP

Association of Irish Musical Societies   AIMS

Association of Macedonian Composers   AMC / Udruženje kompizotora Makedonije   UKM

Association of Music Dealers and Publishers in the Netherlands / Vereniging van Muziekhandelaren en -uitgevens Nederland   VMN

Association of Musical Instrument Industries   AMII

Association of Piano Class Teachers   APCT

Association of Professional Music Therapists   APMT

Association of Professional Vocal Ensembles   APVE

Association of String Class Teachers   ASCT

Association of Swedish Symphony Orchestras   ASSO / Sveriges Orkesterforeningars Riksforbund   SOR

Association of Wind Teachers   AWT

Association pour la diffusion des accordéonistes francophones   ADAF

Asylum (rec. lab.)   Asy

Atlantic (rec. lab.)   At

Aubry, Pierre, ed. *Mélanges de musicologie critique*   MMC

Audio Directions (rec. lab.)   AudioD

Audio Fidelity (rec. lab.)   Audio Fi

Audio Manufacturers' Group   AMG

Audiophile (rec. lab.)   Audiop

Aufführung (G=performance)   Auff.

Aufgeführt (G=performed)   aufgef.

Augener (publ.)   Au

Augment   aug.

Augmented   augm.

Augsburg (rec. lab.)   Augsb

Augsburg Publishing House (publ.)   Augsburg

Aural Explorer (rec. lab.)   Aural

Ausgewählte (G=selected)   ausgew., ausgw.

Ausgewählte Werke (G=collected works)   AW

Australasian Performing Rights Association   APRA

Australian Journal of Music Education (jl.)   Australian J Mus Ed

Australian Music Retailers Association   AMRA

Australian Music Therapy Association   AMTA

Australian Musical Association   AMA

Australian Society for Music Education   ASME

Austrasian Performing Rights Association. *APRA Journal* (jl.)
   APRA J

Austrian Association for Musicology   AAM / Österreichische
   Gesellschaft für Musikwissenschaft   OGMW

Austrian Choral Society   ACS / Österreichischer Sängerbund   ÖSB

Auswahl (G=selected)   Ausw.

Authors' Agency of the Polish Music Publishers   AA

Automatic Music Instrument Collectors' Association   AMICA

Avant-Garde (rec. lab.)   Av

Ave Maria   A.M.

Azerbaijan Composers' Union   ACU

Bach (Riemenschneider Bach Institute) (jl.)   BA

Bach, Beethoven & Brahms   BBB

Bach, Carl Philipp Emanuel. *Versuch über die wahre Art das Clavier
   zu spielen*   Bach Versuch

Bach Guild (rec. lab.)   Bach

Bach, Johann Sebastian. *Neue Ausgabe sämtlicher Werke*   NBA

Bach, Johann Sebastian. *Werke* (ed. by the Bach Gesellschaft)   BG

Bach, Johann Sebastian. *Wohltemperierte Clavier*   WTC, WtK

Bach-Gesellschaft   B.G.

Bach-Jahrbuch (jl.)   BachJb, BJ, BjB

Bach Werke-Verzeichnis   BWV

Bachelor of Arts in Music   BAM

Bachelor of Music   BM, B Mus, MB

Bachelor of Music in Education   BME, B Mus Ed, BMusEd

Bachelor of Music in Public School Music   BMus (PSM)

Bachelor of Sacred Music   BSM, BSMu, BS Mu, BSMus, BS Mus, SMB

Bachelor of School Music   BSM, BSMus, BS Mus

Back   B.

Backstreet (rec. lab.)   Back.

Bainbridge (rec. lab.)   Bain.

Bajo (Sp=low; bass)   b., B

Bajo cifrado (Sp=figured bass)   b. cif.

Bajo continuo   see basso continuo

Balalaika and Domra Association of America   BDAA

Bălgarska muzyka (jl.)   BălgarskaM

Ballo (I=dance)   bl

Bamberg Codex, Ed. IV6   Ba

Bands of America   BA

Banjo   bjo.

Banjo Newsletter (jl.)   BNL

Bantock Society   BS

Barcelona. Biblioteca central, M. 853 (ms.)   BarcA

Barcinonense   barc.

Bärenreiter Verlag (publ.)   Bä, Br, BV, B.V.K.

Barger & Barclay (publ.)   Bar & Bar

Baritone / *Bariton* (G) / *barriton* (F) / *baritono* (I)   Bar., Bari., bari., Br

Baroque (rec. lab.)   Bar

Bartók Archives Z-Symbol Rhythm Extraction   BARZREX

Bass / *basse* (F), *Bass* (G) / *basso* (I)   b, B, bs

Bass clarinet   bc, bs. cl.

Bass drum   B.D.

Bass guitar   b. guit.

Bass trombone   Btb.

Basse chiffrée (F=figured bass)   b. ch.

Basse continue *see* basso continuo

Basset horn   BHr

Bassklarinette (G=bass clarinet)   Basskl., Bkl

Basso   B.

Basso, A. *Musica: Enciclopedia storica*   La Musica E

Basso continuo (I) / *basse continue* (F) / *bajo continuo* (Sp)   bc, Bc, B.c.

Bassoon(s) / *Fagott* (G) / *fagotto* (I) / *fagot* (Sp)   bn., bons., bsn., fag., Fag., fg., Fg.

Bayerische Volksmusik (jl.)   BayerischeVolksm

Bearsville (rec. lab.)   Bears.

Bee Hive (rec. lab.)   Bee

Beethoven, Ludwig van. Werke (Guido Adler, ed.)   BeW

Beethoven-Jahrbuch (jl.)   BeethovenJb, BeJB, Be JB

Begleitung (G=accompaniment)   Begl.

Beispiel (G=example)   Beisp., Bsp.

Beispielsammlung zur älteren Musikgeschichte (Alfred Einstein)   Einstein Beisp.

Beispielsammlung zur Musikgeschichte (Alfred Einstein)   EiMB, Einstein Beisp.

Beiträge zur Musikwissenschaft (jl.)   Beitr. Musik, Beitr. Mw, Bmw, BzMw

Beiträge zur Rheinischen Musikgeschichte (jl.)   BRMg

Belfagor; Rassegna di varia umanità (jl.)   Bel

Belgian Review of Musicology *see* *Revue belge de musicologie*

Belgian Society of Musicology   BSM / Société belge de musicologie

SBM

Belgisch Tijdschrift voor muziek-wetenschap see *Revue belge de musicologie*

Bell plate(s) bell p., bell pl.

Bemerkung (G=comment, note) Bem.

Bémol, Bemol (F, G=flat) Bem.

Bemolle (I=flat) bem.

Benedicite Bte.

Benedictiones (chant, Mass) BNMT, BNS

Benedictus Be, Bs

Bénévent. Bibliothèque Capitulaire. Codex VI.34 *(Graduel de Bénévent avec prosaire et tropaire)* GB

Benjamin, Rajeczky. *Melodiarium hungariae medii aevi I: Hymnen und Sequenzen* MHMA

Bennington College Series of New Music BCS

Bennington Review (jl.) BR

Berandol Music (publ.) Ber

Beserk (rec. lab.) Beserk

Besetzung (G=scoring, instrumentation) Bes.

Besseler, Heinrich. *Die Musik des Mittelalters und der Renaissance* BeMMR

Bibliografia della musica strumentale italiana stampata . . . (Claudio Sartori) SartoriB

Bibliographie der Musiksammelwerke des XVI. und XVII. Jahrhunderts (Robert Eitner) EitnerBg, Eitner S

Bibliographie der Troubadours (Alfred Pillet & H. Carstens) PC, P-C

Bibliographie des altfranzösischen Liedes (Gaston Raynaud) R

Biblioteca de Catalunya. Departamento de música. *Publicationes* PBC

Biblioteca musica Bononiensis BMB

Bibliothek der gedruckten weltlichen Vokalmusik Italiens . . . (Emil Vogel) VogelB

Big Band Academy of America BBAA

Big Tree (rec. lab.) Big

Billboard (jl.) BB, BILLA

Billboard Information Network BIN

Biograph (rec. lab.) Bio.

Biographie universelle des musiciens (François J. Fétis) FétisB, FétisBS

Biographisch-bibliographisches Quellenlexikon (Robert Eitner) EitnerQ

Bipartite form, binary form AB

Birmingham School of Music BSM

Biscuit City (rec. lab.) Bisc.

Bittinger, Werner, ed. *Schütz, Heinrich. Heinrich Schütz-Werke-Verzeichnis* S.W.V.

Black Music Association BMA

Black Music Research Journal (jl.) BMR

Black Perspective in Music (jl.) Bl, Black per in music, Black Per M, BlackPerspectiveM

Blackbird (rec. lab.) Black.

Blarney Castle (rec. lab.) Blar.

Bläserquartett (G=woodwind quartet) Bläqua

Bläserquintett (G=woodwind quintet) Bläqui

Blasinstrumente (G=wind instruments) Bl., Blasinstru.

Blätter der Sackpfeife BS

Blechblasinstrumente Blechbl.

Blind Pig (rec. lab.) Blind

Blockflöte (G=recorder) Blofl.

Blue Goose (rec. lab.) Blue G

Blue Note (rec. lab.) Blue

Blue Thumb (rec. lab.) Blue Th.

Bluebird (rec. lab.) Blueb.

Bluegrass Unlimited Bluegrass

BMI Canada BMIC

BMI: The Many Worlds of Music (jl.) BMI

Board clapper bd. clp.

Bocca chuisa (I=mouth closed) b.c., b.ch.

Böhmische Choralnotation *see* Bohemian plainsong notation, BChN

Bohemian plainsong notation BPN / böhmische Choralnotation BChN

Bohemian Ragtime Society BRS

Boletin interamericano de música (jl.) BolInteramerM

Boletin latino-americano de música (Bogotà) (jl.) Bol. Lat.-Am. Mús.

Bolletino bibliografico musicale (jl.) Boll. Bibl. Mus.

Bond van Orkestdirigenten en Instructeurs *see* Association of Conductors and Instructors

Boosey & Hawkes (publ.) B&H, Bo & Ha, Bo&H, BoHa

Boston International (rec. lab.) Boston I.

Boston Music Co. (publ.) BM, BMC

Boston Symphony Orchestra BSO

Bote & Bock (publ.) B&B, BB, B & B, Bo&Bo

Bouche fermée (closed mouth) b.f.

Boulevard (rec. lab.) Boul.

Bournemouth Symphony Orchestra BSO

Bouwsteenen: Jaarboek der Vereniging voor Nederlandshe muziekgeschiedenis (jl.) Bouwsteenen: JVNM

Brahms-Studien (jl.) Brahms-Stud

Brainard, Paul. *Le Sonate per violino di Giuseppe Tartini* B.

Brake drum(s) brake dr.

Brass instruments br.

Brass and Percussion (jl.) B and P

Brass and Wind News (jl.) BW

Brass and Woodwind Quarterly (jl.) BrassWoodwindQ, BWQ

Brass Bulletin (jl.) Brass B

Brass Quarterly (jl.) BQ

Bratsche (G=viola) Br.

Breitkopf & Härtel (publ.) Br. & H.

Breve, breves, brevis (nota.) br

Breviarum monasticum   Brev M

Breviarum romanum   Brev R

Brevis (nota.)   b, B, br

Brevis altera (nota.)   br-a

British & Continental Music Agencies   BCMA

British Association of Barbershop Singers   BABS

British Association of Concert Agents   BACA

British Association of Record Dealers   BARD

British Association of Symphonic Bands and Wind Ensembles
   BASBWE

British Broadcasting Corporation. Scottish Symphony Orchestra
   BBCSSO

British Broadcasting Corporation. Symphony Orchestra   BBC S.O.

British Catalogue of Music   BCM

British Federation of Music Festivals   BFMF

British Institute of Jazz Studies   BIJS

British Institute of Recorded Sound   BIRS

British Institute of Recorded Sound. *Bulletin* (jl.)   BIRS

British Journal of Music Therapy (jl.)   BJMTD

British Museum. Library. Addl. 12194 (*Graduale Sarisburiense*)
   (ms.)   GS

British Museum. Library. Addl. 27630 (ms.)   LoD

British Museum. Library. Harley 987 (ms.)   LoHa

British Museum. Library. Ms. Addl. 29987 (ms.)   Lo

British Museum. Library. Ms. Addl. 41667 (*McVeagh Fragment*)
   McV

British Museum. Library. Ms. Cotton Titus A. XXVI (ms.)   LC

British Music Society   BMS

British Musicians' Pensions Society   BMPS

British National Opera Company   BNOC

British Suzuki Institute   BSI

*British Union-Catalogue of Early Music Printed Before the Year
   1801* (Edith Schnapper, ed.)   BUC, BUCEM

Broadcast Music, Inc. BMI

Broekmans & Van Poppel (publ.) B&VP

Broude Brothers (publ.) BB

Brown, Howard Mayer. *Instrumental Music Printed Before 1600: A Bibliography* BrownI

Bruckner Society of America BSA

Brussels. Museum of Musical Instruments. *Bulletin* (jl.) Brus Museum, BrusselsMuseumMInstrumentsBul

Bryant, Giles. *Healey Willan Catalogue* B.

Bücken, Ernst, ed. *Handbuch der Musikwissenschaft* BüHM, BückenH, Bücken Hdb, HÜHM, HdMw, HMw

Buenos Aires musical (jl.) Buenos Aires Mus, BuenosAiresM

Bukofzer, Manfred. *Music in the Baroque Era* BuMBE

Bulgarska Akademiia na Naukite, Sofia. Institute za Musikozname. *Izvestiia* IIM, IzvestijaInstMBAN

Bulgarska Muzika (jl.) Bulgar Muz

Bulletin de la vie musicale belge / *Bulletin van het Belgisch Muziekleven* (jl.) BulVieMBelge

Bundesverband der Deutschen Musikinstrumenten-Hersteller *see* National Association of German Musical Instrument Manufacturers

Burghauser, Jarmil. *A. Dvořák: Thematic Catalogue of Works* B.

Burney, Charles. *A General History of Music From the Earliest Ages to the Present* BurneyH

C.F. Peters (publ.) CFP

Cabaza (perc. instr.) cab.

Cäcilien Kalender (jl.) KJ

Cadence cad.

Cahiers canadiens de musique *see* Canada Music Book

Cahiers Debussy (jl.) CahDebussy

Calando (I=gradually diminishing) cal.

Cambrai. Bibliothéque Municipale. Ms. 1328 (1176) Ca.

Cambridge University Musical Society CUMS

Camden (rec. lab.) Cam

Campana (I, Sp=bell)   camp.

Campane (I=bells)   cmp

Canada Folk Bulletin (jl.)   Can Folk B

Canada Music Book   Can Mus Bk   CMB / *Cahiers canadiens de musique*   CahCanadiensM

Canadian Amateur Musicians / Musiciens amateurs du Canada MAC

Canadian Association for Music Therapy / Association de Musicothérapie du Canada   AMC

Canadian Association for Music Therapy. *Journal* (jl.)   JAMTD

Canadian Association of Music Libraries, Archives, and Documentation Centres   CAML / Association canadienne des bibliothèques, archives et centres de documentation musicaux ACBM (earlier, Canadian Music Library Association, CMLA / Association canadienne des bibliothèques musicaux, ACBM)

Canadian Association of University Schools of Music   CAUSM / Association canadienne des écoles universitaires de musique ACEUM

Canadian Band Association   CBA

Canadian Band Directors' Association (formerly CBA)   CBDA

Canadian Bandmaster (jl.)   CanB

Canadian Bandmasters' Association   CBA

Canadian Bandsman (jl.)   CanB

Canadian Broadcasting Corporation Symphony Orchestra CBCSO

Canadian Bureau for the Advancement of Music   CBAM

Canadian College of Organists / Collège Canadien des Organistes (later, RCCO)   CCO

Canadian Composer (jl.) / *Le Compositeur Canadien*, Can Composer CanComp

Canadian Federation of Music Teachers' Association   CFMTA / Fédération canadienne des professeurs de musique   FCAPM

Canadian Folk Music Journal (jl.)   Can Folk Mus, CFMJ

Canadian Folk Music Society   CFMS / Société canadienne de musique folklorique   SCMF

Canadian Journal of Music (jl.)   CanJM

Canadian League of Composers / Ligue canadienne de compositeurs
CLComp

Canadian Music Centre / Centre musical canadien (later, Centre de
musique canadienne)   CMC, CMCentre

Canadian Music Council / Conseil canadien de la musique   CMC,
CMCouncil

Canadian Music Educator (jl.) / *L'Educateur de musique au Canada*
CME

Canadian Music Educators Association   CMEA / Association
canadienne des éducateurs de musique   ACEM

Canadian Music Journal (jl.)   CMJ

Canadian Music Library Association   *see*   Canadian Association of
Music Libraries, Archives, and Documentation Centres

Canadian Music Publishers' Association   CMPA

Canadian Music Sales Corp. (publ.)   CMS

Canadian Music Trades Journal (jl.)   CMTJ

Canadian Musical Reproduction Rights Agency   CMRRA

Canadian Musician (jl.)   Can Mus

Canadian On-line Musicians' Association   COMA

Canadian Opera Company   COC

Canadian Record Manufacturers' Association (later, CRIA)   CRM
Assn

Canadian Recording Industry Association   CRIA / Association de
l'industrie canadienne de l'enregistrement   AICE

Canadian Review of Music and Art (jl.)   CRMA

Canadian Society for Musical Traditions   CSMT / Société
canadienne pour les traditions musicales   SCTM

Canadian Society of Folk Music   CSFM / Société canadienne de
musique folklorique   SCMF

Canadian String Teachers' Association   CSTA

Canadian Talent Library (rec. lab.)   CTL

Canadian University Music Society   CUMS / Société de musique des universites canadiennes   SMUC

Cancionero   canc.

Canna ad anima di legno (I=flute pipe, wood) (organ)   canna d. l.

Canna ad anima di metallo (I=flute pipe, metal) (organ)   canna d. m.

Canna d'organo (I=organ pipe)   canna

Cantabile (I=singing)   cantab.

Cantata   cant.

Cantate   Cant.

Cantate Domino   CanD

Canticle (jl.)   Can

Cantique   cant.

Canto (I=high voice)   cant.

Canto Gregoriano   Canto Greg

Canto organo (I=for voice and organ)   co

Canto primo   C° I^{mo}, cp

Cantus   c

Cantus firmus   c.f.

Capitol (rec. lab.)   Cap.

Capolavori polifonici del secolo XVI   CP

Cappella   capp.

Carl Fischer (publ.)   CF

Carmina medii aevi posterioris latina I/I (Hans Walther, ed.)   CMA

Carnet musical (jl.)   Carnet mus

Carstens, H. *Bibliographie der Troubadours* (Alfred Pillet & H. Carstens)   PC, P-C

Catalogo numerico tematico delle composizione di Antonio Vivaldi (Mario Rinaldi)   Rin

Catalogue-thématique de l'oeuvre de Carl Philipp Emanuel Bach (Alfred Wotquenne)   Wotq.

Catalogus musicus   Ca M, CaM

Catch Society of America   CSA

Catgut Acoustical Society   CAS

Celeste / celesta (I)   cel.

Cembalo (G=harpsichord) Cem., Cemb.

Center (of perc. instr.) c

Center for Contemporary Opera CCO

Center for Preservation and Propagation of Iranian Music CPPIM

Central Opera Service COS

Central Opera Service Bulletin (jl.) CE, Central Opera

Centre Belge de Documentation Musicale CBDM, Cebedem, CeBeDeM

Centre international de recherche musicale CIRM

Centre musical canadien *see* Canadian Music Centre

Centre national de la recherche scientifique CNRS

Cercetări de muzicologie CercetăriMuzicol, CMz

Certificat d'aptitude pédagogique à l'enseignement de la musique CAPEM

Certification Board for Music Therapists CBMT

Československé Hudebni Informační Středisko *see* Czech Music Information Centre

Československý Hudebni Slovnik čSHS

Československý Hudebni Slovník Osob a Instituci čHS

Český Hudebni Fond ČHF

Chalumeau chal.

Chamber cham.

Chamber music ch.

Chamber Music America CMA

Chanson (F=song) chans.

Chansonnier chans.

Chant ch., cht.

Chant populaire ch. pop.

Chanteur (F=singer) ch.

Chantilly. Musée Condé. Bibliothèque. Ms. 564 (olim 1047) Ch

Chappell & Co. (publ.) Chap.

Chelys, the Viola da Gamba Society Journal (jl.)
  ViolaDaGambaSocJ

Chevalier, Ulysse. *Repertorium hymnologicum*   Chev

China Nationalities Orchestra   CNOS

Chinese cymbal   chin. cym.

Chinese Music Society of North America   CMSNA

Chitarra (I=guitar)   chit., ct.

Chitarrone (Sp=Mexican bass guitar)   chit.

Choeur d'enfants (F=children's chorus)   choeur d'enf.

Choeur d'hommes (F=men's chorus)   choeur d'h., h

Choeur de femmes (F=women's chorus)   choeur de f., f

Choeur des muses   CM

Choeur mixte (F=mixed chorus)   choeur m.

Choir director   ChDir

Choirmaster's diploma of the American Guild of Organists   Ch.M.

Choirmaster's diploma of the Royal Canadian College of Organists
    Ch.M.

Choirmaster's diploma of the Royal College of Organists   CHM

Choral Journal (jl.)   Choral J., CJ

Chorbuch, -bücher (G=choirbook(s))   Chb.

Chord / *accord* (F) / *accordo* (I)   acc

Chordirektor   ChDir

Chordirigent (G=choir conductor)   Chdgt.

Choristers' Guild Letters (jl.)   CGL

Chorus   ch., chor.

Chorwerk, Das   Chw., Cw, CW

Chromatic   chrom.

Chromatik (G=chromatic; noun)   Chrom.

Chromatisch (G=chromatic; adj.), chrom.

Chronologisch-thematisches Verzeichnis sämtlicher Werke von Jean-Baptiste Lully (Herbert Schneider)   LWV

Chrysander, Friedrich, ed. *Händel, Georg Friedrich. Werke*   HäW

Church Music (jl.)   CHU, Church Mus

Church Music Association   CMA

Church Music Association of America   CMAA

Church Music Publishers' Association CMPA

Church Music Trust CMT

Church Musician (jl.) CM

Cimbalom cimb.

City of Birmingham Symphony Orchestra CBSO

Clamores (chant, Mass) CLM

Clamores (chant, Office) CLMO

Clarasch Society CS

Clarinet / clarinette (F) / clarinete (Sp) / clarinetto (I) cl.

Clarinetto basso (I=bass clarinet) clb

Clarinetto contrabasso (I=contrabass clarinet) cl. cb.

Clarino claro., clno.

Clarion Music Society CMS

Classical Music Lovers' Exchange CMLE

Classici della musica italiana CDMI

Classici musicali italiani CMI

Classiques français du moyen age CFMA

Clavecin (F) / *clavicembalo* (I), *clavecín* (Sp) (=harpsichord) clv.

Clavicembalo (I=harpsichord) clav, clv., cv

Clavichord clvd.

Clavier clav.

Clavier (jl.) CL, CLAVA

Co-Operating Danish Amateur-Orchestras CDAO

Cobbett's Cyclopedic Survey of Chamber Music CCSCM

Coda: The Jazz Magazine (jl.) Coda

Codex cod.

Codex Aosta (15th cent. ms.) Ao

Codex Huelgas (Codex Burgos) Hu

Codex Montpellier (Montpellier. Bibliothèque de l'École de Médicine, H196) Mo

Códex musical de Las Huelgas (Higinio Angles) Ahu, AHu, Las H

Codex Squarcialupi (Florence. Biblioteca Mediceo-Laurenziana. Pal. 87) Sq.

Codice cod.

Col basso (I=with the bass) c.b., c.B.

Col canto col c.

Col legno c.l.

Col legno battuto c.l.b., clb, LB

Col legno tratto clt., c.l.t., LT

Coll'arco, arcato (I=with the bow, bowed) arc.

Coll'ottava (doubled at the octave) col. ott^a, c. 8va

Colla destra c.d.

Colla sinistra (I=with the left hand) c.s.

Colla voce col. vo.

Collana coll.

Colleague of the American Guild of Organists CAGO

Collectanea historiae musicae (jl.) CHM

Collected edition(s) ce

Collection d'études musicologiques CEM / *Sammlung musikwissenschaftlicher Abhandlungen* SMwAbh

Collectors Record Club CRC

College Band Directors National Association CBDNA

College Music Society C.M.S., CMS

College Music Symposium (jl.) CMS, coll. mus., Coll Music, College MSymposium, College Mus

Collège Canadien des Organistes *see* Canadian College of Organists

Collegium musicum CM, coll. mus.

Colmarer Handschrift (Cgm 4997) (medieval ms.) C

Coloration (nota.) col

Colored (nota.) col

Columbia (rec. lab.) Col.

Come primo co. I^{mo}

Come sopra co. so.

Comhaltas Ceoltóiri Eireann *see* Traditional Irish Singing and Dancing Society

Comique com.

Comité internacional de museos y colecciones de instrumentos musicales *see* International Committee of Musical Instrument Museums and Collections

Comité international des musées et collections d'instruments de musique *see* International Committee of Musical Instrument Museums and Collections

Comité national de la musique *see* French National Music Committee

Communion verse cov

Comodo com.

Compact disc CD

Company of Fifers and Drummers CFD

Complete edition comp. ed.

Completorium (compline; last of the canonical hours) Compl.

Composed (by, in) comp.

Composer compr.

Composer, The (jl.) COM

Composer/USA (National Association of Composers) (jl.) CUS

Composer-Performer Edition CPE

Composers' and Lyricists' Guild of America CLGA

Composers, Authors, and Artists of America CAAA

Composers, Authors, and Publishers Association of Canada CAPAC / Association des compositeurs, auteurs et éditeurs de Canada ACAEC

Composers' Autograph Publications CAP

Composers' Autograph Publications Records Association CAPRA

Composers' Cooperative Society CCS

Composers' Facsimile Edition CFE

Composers' Guild of Great Britain CGGB

Composers' Recordings, Inc. (rec. lab.) CRI

Composers' Symphony Orchestra C.S.O.

Composers Theatre CT

Compositeur Canadien *see* Canadian Composer

Composition   comp., compn.

Compositore (I=composer)   comp.

Composizione (I=composition)   comps.

Computer Music (jl.)   Comput Mus, Computer mus

Computer Music Journal (jl.)   Computer Mus J

Computer Music Society   CMS

Con espressione (I=with expression)   con esp.

Con sordino (I=with the mute)   c.s.

Concentus musicus   CM

Concert Artist Guild   CAG

Concert Artists' Association   CAA

Concert Music Broadcasters' Association   CMBA

Concertante   conc.

Concertato   conc.

Concerto   conc., ct°

Concerts symphoniques de Montréal (later, MSO, Montréal Symphony Orchestra)   CSM

Concordia Publishing House (publ.)   Con

Conductor   condr.

Confédération internationale de musique electroacoustique *see* International Confederation for Electroacoustic Music

Confédération internationale des accordeonistes *see* International Confederation of Accordionists

Confédération internationale des sociétes musicales *see* International Confederation of Societies of Music

Confédération internationale des sociétiés d'auteurs et compositeurs *see* International Confederation of Societies of Authors and Composers

Confédération internationale des sociétiés populaires de musique *see* International Confederation of Popular Music Societies

Congregatio Sacerdotum a Sacro Corde Jesu   SCJ

Connaissance de l'orgue   ConnaissanceOrgue

Connchord (jl.)   CH

Conseil canadien de la musique *see* Canadian Music Council

Conseil international de la musique *see* International Music Council

Conseil international des compositeurs *see* International Council of Composers

Conseil polonais de la musique *see* Polish Music Council

Conseil suisse de la musique *see* Swiss Music Council

Consejo interamericano de música *see* Inter-American Music Council

Consejo Nacional de Cultura, Havana CNC

Conservatory / *conservatoire* (F) / *conservatorio* (I) cons.

Consolidated Music Publishers CMP

Consortium to Distribute Computer Music CDCM

Contemporary A Cappella Society of America CASA

Contemporary Keyboard (jl.; later, *Keyboard*) CK, Cont. Key, Cont. Keybd.

Contemporary Music in Europe (Paul Henry Lang, ed.) LBCM

Contemporary Music Project CMP

Contextual Harmonic Analysis CONHAN

Continuo cont.

Contrabass *see* double bass

Contrabassoon c.bn.

Contrafagotto (I=contrabassoon) c. fag., cfg

Contralto cto.

Contrappunto *see* counterpoint

Contratenor *see* countertenor

Contrebasse *see* double bass

Contrepoint *see* counterpoint

Contributions to Music Education CMUED, Con Mus Ed

Cor anglais (F=English horn) c.a., cor angl.

Cordes (F=strings) c.

Cornetti (I=horns) crti

Cornetto (I=horn) cnto

Corno (I, Sp=horn) co., cor., cr

Corno inglese (I=English horn) ci., cor. i.

Coronet (rec. lab.)   Cor

Corpus des luthistes français   CLF

Corpus mensurabilis musical   CMM

Corpus of Early Keyboard Music   CEK, CEKM

Corpus of Early Music in Facsimile   CEMF

Corpus scriptorum de musica   CSM

Corpus troporum   CT

Corruption   corr.

Costruzione (I=[instrument] making)   costr

Council for Research in Music Education   CRME

Council for Research in Music Education. *Bulletin* (jl.)   BRM, CMUEB, CouncilResearchMEducationBul, CRME

Council for the Encouragement of Music and the Arts   CEMA

Counterpoint / *contrappunto* (I) / *contrapunto* (Sp) / *contrepoint* (F)   cp, cpt., ctpt.

Countersubject   cs

Countertenor / *contratenor* (I)   ct.

Courrier musical de France (jl.)   Cour Mus France, CourrierMFrance

Coussemaker, Charles Edmond Henri. *Scriptorum de musica medii aevi. Nova series*   CousseS, Coussemaker Scr, CS

Covent Garden (Royal Opera House), London   CG

Cowbell(s)   c.b., cowb.

Crash cymbal(s)   c. cym.

Creative Audio and Music Electronics Organization   CAMEO

Creative Guitar International   CGI

Creative Music Foundation   CMF

Creative Music Index   CMI

Creative Musicians Coalition   CMC

Credo   Cr.

Creed Taylor, Inc. (rec. lab.)   CTI

Crescendo   cres., cresc.

Crescendo International (jl.)   Cresc.

Croatian Music Institute / Hrvatski Glazbeni zavod   HGZ

Croatian Singing Society / Hrvatsko pjevačko društvo   HPD

Crotale(s)   crot.

Cuerda   c.

Cum opposita proprietate (nota.)   cop.

Cum perfectione (nota.)   cp

Cum proprietate (nota.)   cpr

Cum Notis Variorum (jl.)   CNV

Cumann Cheol Tire Eireann   *see* Folk Music Society of Ireland

Curci, Edizioni (publ.)   EC

Current Musicology (jl.)   CM, CMc, CU, Curr. Music, Current Musicol

Curwen, J., and Sons (publ.)   Cu

Cycles per second   cps

Cyclic / *cyclique* (F)   cycl.

Cymbal tongs   cym. tngs.

Cymbals   cym.

Cymbals / *cymbales* (F)   cymb.

Cymbals, antique   ant. cym.

Cymbals, finger   fing. cyms.

Czech Music Information Centre / Československé Hudební Informační Středisko   ČHIS

Da capo (I=from the beginning)   DC, D.C.

Daffodil (rec. lab.)   Daf.

Dal segno (I=go back to the sign and repeat)   dal s., d.s.

Dämpfer (G=mute)   Dpf.

Danish Musicological Society / Dansk Selskab for Musikforskning   DSM

Danish Society for Jazz, Rock, and Folk Composers   DSJRFC

Danish Songwriters Guild   DSG

Dansk aarbog for musikforskning (jl.)   DAM, DanskAarbogMf

Dansk musiktidsskrift (jl.)   Dansk Mus, DMT

Dansk Selskab for Musikforskning / Danish Musicological Society

DSM

Danske Jazz, Beat og Folkemusik Autorer DJBFA

Darmstädter Beiträge zur neuen Musik (jl.)
DarmstädterBeitrNeuenM

Davison, Archibald T. *Historical Anthology of Music* Apel Anth,
ApelAnth, DA, HAM

De cantu et musica sacra (Martin Gerbert) Gerbert, De cantu

Dead Composers Society DCS

Decibel dB, db

Decrescendo (I=becoming softer) decr.

Dějiny české hudby v přikladech DCHP

Delicatamente delic.

Delius Society DS

Delius Society. *Journal* (jl.) Delius

Denkmäler der Tonkunst in Bayern DTB

Denkmäler der Tonkunst in Österreich DTOe, DTÖ

Denkmäler deutscher Tonkunst DdT, DDT

Derry Music Co. (publ.) Der

Descendens, descendentes desc

Destra (I=right) d., dest.

Deus misuratur DeM

Deutsch, Erich Otto. *Franz Schubert: Thematisches Verzeichnis
seiner Werke* D., Deutsch

Deutsche Choral-Mensurale Mischnotation (G=German mixed
plainsong and mensural notation) DMN

Deutsche Gesellschaft für Musik des Orients. *Mitteilungen* (jl.)
MittDeutschenGesMOrients

Deutsche Grammophon Gesellschaft (rec. lab.) DG, DGG

Deutsche Militärmusikerzeitung (jl.) DMMZ

Deutsche Mozart Gesellschaft *see* German Mozart Society

Deutsche Musikkultur (jl.) DMK

Deutscher Musikverlegerverband DMV

Deutscher Tonkünstlerverband *see* German Musicians' Association

Deutscher Verlag für Musik (publ.) DVFM, DVM

Deutsches Jahrbuch der Musikwissenschaft (jl.) DeutschesJbMu, DJbM, DJbMw

Deutsches Jahrbuch für Volkskunde (jl.) Deutsches Jb. Volkskunde, DeutschesJbVolkskunde

Deutsches Mozartfest der deutschen Mozart-Gesellschaft DMG

Deutsches Sängerbund. *Jahrbuch* (jl.) JbDeutschenSängerbundes

Dialogue in Instrumental Music Education DIME

Diapason, The (jl.) DI, Diap

Diapasons (organ pipes, stops) diap.

Diccionario de la música Labor Labor D

Dicionário biográfico de musicos portuguezes DBP

Dictionary of Contemporary Music (John Vinton, ed.) DCM

Dictionnaire de la musique (Bordas) BordasD

Dictionnaire des musiciens suisses (Willi Schuch, ed.) DMS

Difficult D

Digital Alternate Representation of Music Symbols (computer-based notational system) DARMS

Diletto musicale DM

Diminuendo (I) dim., dimin.

Diminuieren (G) dim.

Diminution Dim.

Diplomatic transcription (facsimiles traced or copied freehand) dipl.

Diplomatische Umschrift (G=diplomatic transcription; nota.) dipl. U.

Dirección (Sp) / direzione (I) / direction (F) = conducting dir.

Direction (F) / direzione (I) / dirección (Sp) = conducting dir.

Directors dirs.

Direzione (I=conducting) dir.

Dirigent (G=conductor) Dgt.

Dirigierend (G=conducting) dir.

Discantus D

Discographical Forum (jl.) Disc

Discoteca alta fedeltà (jl.) Discoteca

Diskant (G=discantus) D

Diskantus / Diskantz (G=discantus) D.

Dittmer, Luther, ed. *Musical Theorists in Translation* MThT

Dittmer, Luther, ed. *Musicological Studies* MS

Divertimento div., divert.

Divisi div.

Dizionario dei musicisti (Carlo Schmidl) SchmidlD

Dizionario dei musicisti. Supplement (Carlo Schmidl) SchmidlDS

Django Reinhardt Society DRS

Doblinger (publ.) Dob

Doctor Jazz (jl.) Doctor

Doctor of Music *Musicae Doctor*

Doctor of Music Education Mus Ed D

Doctor of Musical Arts D.M.A., Mus A D, Mus AD

Doctor of Sacred Music SMD

Documenta musicologica (jl.) DM, DMl

Dodecafonia (I, Sp=12-tone music) dod.

Dodekaphonie (G=12-tone music) Dodekaph.

Dodekaphonisch (G=12-tone) dodekaph.

Dolce (I=sweet, -ly) dol.

Dolmetsch Foundation. *Bulletin* (jl.) Dolmetsch B

Dominant, V (i.e., five) D

Dominion (rec. lab.) Dom.

Donizetti Society DonSoc

Doppio pedale dopp. ped.

Dorian (mode) dor.

Dotted dot

Double bass (contrabass) / *contrebasse* (F) / *contrabasso* (I) / *contrabajo* (Sp) cb, c.b., dbl. bass

Double bassoon (contrabassoon) dbn.

Down Beat (jl.) DB, Down Bt.

Dreistimmig (G=three-part) dreist.

Drinker Library of Choral Music DLCM

Drum dr.

Drum Corps International DCI

Društvo Slovenskih Skladateljev *see* Society of Slovene Composers

Dufourcq, Norbert, *et al. Orgue et liturgie* OL

Duplex longa (nota.) D

Duplum (nota.) du

Duration series (nota.) ds

Duration series, inversion of a (nota.) di

Dutch Association of Gramophone Records / Nederlandse Vereniging van Grammofoonplaten NVGD

Dutch Composers' Society / Genootschap van Nederlandse Componisten GeNeCo

Dutch Pianola Society / Nederlandse Pianola Vereniging NPV

E. C. Schirmer (publ.) ECS, ES

Ear Magazine (jl.) EA

Early Bodleian Music EBM

Early English Church Music (jl.) EECM

Early English Harmony From the 10th to the 15th Century (Harry Ellis Wooldridge, ed.) EEH

Early Keyboard Music (jl.) EKM

Early Keyboard Society EKS

Early Music (jl.) Early M, Earl Mus, EM

Early Music Gazette (jl.) Early Mus G

Early Musical Masterworks EMW

Eastman School of Music ESM

Eastman School of Music. *Studies* (jl.) ESME

Easy E

Easy to medium (difficulty) E-M

Edición culturales argentinas ECA

Ediciones cubanas de música ECM

Ediciones musicales Demetrio, S.A. (publ.) E.M.D.E.S.A.

Edition Cotta'sche (publ.) ECo

Éditions complètes (F=complete editions) éd. compl.

Éditions de L'Oiseau Lyre EOL

Éditions des Archives du Palais de Monaco Éd. Arch. Palais Monaco

Éditions françaises de musique (publ.) Éd. fr. de mus., EFMEditions J. Buyst, EB

Editions Suvini Zerboni (publ.) S-Z, SZ

Éditions Transatlantiques (publ.) Éd. Transatl.

Editore G. Zanibon (publ.) EGZ

Editorial Argentina de Música (publ.) EAM

Editorial Argentina de Música Internacional (publ.) EAMI

Editorial Cooperativa Interamericana de Compositores ECIC

Editorial musical del centro (publ.) EDIMCE

Editura Societatii Compozitorilor Romini ESCR

Edizione moderne (I=modern edition) e.m.

Edizioni Curci (publ.) EC

Educateur de musique au Canada *see* Canadian Music Educator

Éducation musicale, L' (jl.) ÉducationM

Educational Group of the Music Industries Association EGMIA

Educazione musicale, L' (jl.) Educazione M

Edward B. Marks (publ.) EBM

Eggebricht, Hans Heinrich. *Handwörterbuch der musikalische Terminologie* HmT, HMT

Einleitung (G=introduction) Einl.

Einstein, Alfred. *Beispielsammlung zur älteren Musikgeschichte* Einstein Beisp.

Einstein, Alfred. *Beispielsammlung zur Musikgeschichte* EiMB, Einstein Beisp.

Einstimmig (G=monodic) einst.

Eitner, Robert. *Bibliographie der Musiksammelwerke des XVI. und XVII. Jahrhunderts* EitnerBg, Eitner S

Eitner, Robert. *Biographisch-bibliographisches Quellenlexikon* EitnerQ

Eitner, Robert. Gesellschaft für Musikforschung. *Publikationen älterer praktischer und theoretischer Musikwerke* EP, PubAPTM

Elaborazione elab.

Electric piano elec. pno.

Electrical and Musical Industries EMI

Electronic Music Consortium EMC

Ellinwood, L., ed. *Landini, Francesco. Works* Ell

Emil Gilels Society EGS

Empire State Publishers (publ.) Emp.

Empresa de grabaciones y ediciones musicales EGREM

Enciclopedia della musica (Ricordi) Ricordi E

Encyclopädie der gesammten musikalischen Wissenschaften (Gustav Schilling) SchillingE

Encyclopedia of Music in Canada / *Encyclopédie de la musique au Canada* EMC

Encyclopédie de la musique (Fasquelle) EF, FasquelleE

Encyclopédie de la musique au Canada see *Encyclopedia of Music in Canada*

Encyclopédie de la musique et dictionnaire du Conservatoire (Albert Lavignac, ed.) EC, EMDC, LavE, LavignacE

Encyclopédie de la Pleiade: Histoire de la musique EP

Enforcer silencieusement (F=depress the keys silently) e.s.

English Chamber Orchestra ECO

English Church Music (jl.) EnglishChurchM

English Dance and Song (jl.) Eng Dance, EnglishDanceSong

English Folk Dance and Song Society EFDSS

English Folk Dance and Song Society. *Journal* (jl.) JEFDSS

English Folk Dance Society EFDS

English horn / *Englisch Horn* (G) eh, E.Hr., eng. hn., Englh.

English Keyboard Music (jl.) EKM

English Lute-Songs EL

English Madrigal School (Edmund H. Fellowes, ed.) EMS

English Madrigalists EM

English Music Journal (jl.) EnglishMJ

English National Opera ENO

English School of Lutenist Song Writers (Edmund H. Fellowes, ed.)
   EFL, EL, ESLS, LS

English String Teachers' Association ESTA

Ennio Society MSV

Ensemble ens.

Equal (voices, parts) eq

Erbe deutsche Musik, Das (jl.) EdM, EDM

Erbe deutscher Musik. 2. Reihe. Landschaftsdenkmale LD

Erst Aufführung, Erstaufführung (G=first performance) EA

Esecutore (I=performer) esec.

Esecuzione (I=performance) esec.

Espressivo (I=expressively) espr.

Estonian Music Center, U.S.A. EMCUSA

Estremamente sul ponticello (I=far up on the bridge) ep

Estremamente sul tasto (I=far up on the fingerboard) et

Estremamente vibrato ev

Ethnomusicology (jl.) EM, ET, Ethmus., Ethnomus., Ethnomusic.

Études de philologie musicale EPM

Études grégoriennes EG

Eulenberg (publ.) Ebg.

Eulenberg-Verlag (publ.) Eul.

Europäische Föderation Junger Chöre *see* European Federation of
   Young Choirs

Europäische Musikschul-Union EMU

European Association of Conservatoires EAC / Association
   européenne des conservatoires AEC

European Association of Music Festivals EAMF

European Community Youth Orchestra ECYO / Orchestre des
   jeunes de la Communaute européenne OJCE

European Federation of Young Choirs / Europäische Föderation
   Junger Chöre EFYC

European Festivals Association EFA / Association européenne des
   festivals AEF

European Music Festival for the Youth EMFY / Europees MuzPiek voor de Jeugd EMFJ

European Piano Teachers Association EPTA

European Society for the Cognitive Sciences of Music ESCOM

European Suzuki Association ESA

European Union of Music Schools EUMS

Europees Muziek voor de Jeugd *see* European Music Festival for the Youth

Exempla musica neerlandica EMN

Expert, Henri, ed. *Les maîtres musiciens de la renaissance française* ExpertMMRF

Expert, Henri, ed. *Les monuments de la musique française au temps de la Renaissance* ExpertMMFR, ExpertMonuments, MMFTR

Expert, Henri, ed. *Répertoire populaire de la musique de la Renaissance* ExRP

Exposition exp., expn, expos.

Facsimile Editions FE

Faenza. Biblitoeca Comunale. Cod. 117 Fa.

Fagott, Fagotto *see* Bassoon(s)

Fair Organ Preservation Society FOPS

Falck Verzeichnis (Martin Falck's cat. of W.F. Bach's works) F.

Fanfare fanf.

Fanna, Antonio. *Antonio Vivaldi. Catalogo numerico-tematico delle opere strumentali* F.

Federación nacional de músicos *see* National Federation of Music

Federal Music Society FMS

Federatio internationalis Pueri Cantores *see* International Federation of "Little Singers"

Federation of Canadian Music Festivals FCMF

Federation of European Choral Associations / Arbeits Gemeinschaft Europäischer Chorverbände ECA

Federation of Master Organ Builders FMOB

Federation of Recorded Music Societies FRMS

Fédération canadienne des professeurs de musique *see* Canadian Federation of Music Teachers' Association

Fédération internationale de l'harmonica *see* International Harmonica Foundation

Fédération internationale des choeurs d'enfants *see* International Federation of Children's Choirs

Fédération internationale des jeunesses musicales *see* International Federation of Jeunesses Musicales

Fédération internationale des musiciens *see* International Federation of Musicians

Fédération mondiale des concours internationaux de musique *see* World Federation of International Music Competitions

Fédération nationale d'associations culturelles d'expansion musicale *see* National Federation of Cultural Associations for the Promotion of Music

Fellerer, Karl, ed. *Anthology of Music* AnthM

Fellow of the American Guild of Organists FAGO

Fellow of the Birmingham Conservatoire FBC

Fellow of the Birmingham School of Music FBSM

Fellow of the Canadian College of Organists FCCO

Fellow of the Guildhall School of Music FGSM

Fellow of the London College of Music FLCM

Fellow of the Royal Academy of Music FRAM

Fellow of the Royal Canadian College of Organists FRCCO

Fellow of the Royal College of Music FRCM

Fellow of the Royal College of Organists FRCO

Fellow of the Royal Manchester College of Music FRMCM

Fellow of the Royal School of Church Music FRSCM

Fellow of the Tonic Sol-fa College of Music FTSC

Fellow of the Trinity College of Music FTCM (earlier, Fellow of Trinity College, London, FTCL)

Fellowes, Edmund Horace, ed. *English Madrigal School* EMS

Fellowes, Edmund Horace, ed. *English School of Lutenist Song Writers* EFL, EL, ESLS, LS

Fellowship of Christian Musicians FCM

Fellowship of Makers and Researchers of Historical Instruments FoMRHI

Festival International de Jazz de Montréal FIJM

Fétis, François J. *Biographie universelle des musiciens* FétisB, FétisBS

Feuilles musicales FM

Feuillets suisses de pédagogie musicale FSPM

Finale fin.

Finger cymbals fing. cyms.

Fingerboard fb

Finnish Amateur Musicians' Association FAMA / Suomen Laulajain ja Soittajain Liitto SULASOL

First Chair of America, Inc. FCA

First performance, first performed (in, by) f.p.

Fisarmonica (I=accordion) fis

Fischbacher (publ.) Fischb.

Fitzwilliam Virginal Book FVB

Five voices or parts 5-v

Flat, fl. / *bémol* (F) / *Bemol* (G) / *bemolle* (I)

Flauto diritto (I=recorder) fl.d.

Flauto dolce (I=recorder) fld

Flexatone flex.

Florence. Biblioteca Mediceo-Laurenziana Bibl. Laur.

Florence. Biblioteca Mediceo-Laurenziana, ms. (plut.29.1) (medieval ms.) F, Flo.

Florence. Biblioteca Mediceo-Laurenziana. Pal. 87. (Quarcialupi Codex) Sq.

Florence. Biblioteca nazionale centrale. Panciatichi 26 (ms) FP

Florilège du concert vocal de la renaissance FCVR

Flügelhorn(s) Flhn.

Flute(s) / *flauto* (I) / *flûte* (F) / *flauta* (Sp) / *Flöte* (G) fl., Fl., fls.

Flûte droite (F=recorder) fl.d.

Flute Journal (jl.)   FJ

Flûte traversière (F=flute)   fl. trav.

Fluttertongue   fl.

Folk Harp Journal (jl.)   Folk Harp J

Folk Music (jl.)   Folk Music

Folk Music Journal (jl.)   Folk Mus J

Folk Music Society of Ireland   FMSI / Cumann Cheol Tire Eireann CCTE

Folk-Song Society. *Journal* (jl.)   JFSS

Folkways (rec. lab.)   Folk

Fontes artis musicae (jl.)   FAM, Fon art mus, Fontes, Fontes artis m

For 4 (voices)   a 4

Forening for norske komponister og tekstforfattere / Norske Populerautorer   NOPA

Foreningen Samiske Komponister   *see*   Union of Lapp Composers

Föreningen Svenska Kompositörer av Populärmusik   *see*   Swedish Society of Popular Music Composers

Föreningen Svenska Tonsättare   *see*   Society of Swedish Composers

Forschungsbeiträge zur Musikwissenschaft   FMw

Forte (I=loud)   f.

Fortepiano (I)   fp

Fortissimo (I)   ff, fmo.

Fortississimo (I)   fff

Fortsetzer (G)   Forts.

Fortsetzung (G=continuation)   Forts.

Forum musicum (jl.)   ForumM

Forzatissimo (I)   ffz

Forzato (I)   fz

Four voices or parts   4-v.

Frames per second   fps

Frammento (I=fragment)   framm.

Franz Schubert: Thematisches Verzeichnis seiner Werke (Erich Otto Deutsch)   D., Deutsch

Frauenchor (G), women's chorus   F. Chor, FrCh.

Frederic Chopin Society / Towarzystwo imienia Fryderyka Chopina   TiFC

Frederick Harris Music Co. (publ.)   FH

French National Music Committee   FNMC / Comité national de la musique   CNM

French Secular Music of the Late Fourteenth Century (Willi Apel)   ApF

French Society of Musicology   FSM / Société française de musicologie   SFM, Soc. Fr. de Mie

French Society of Musicology. *Publications* (jl.)   PSFM

French Society of Musicology. *Rapports et communications* (jl.)   RdM

Frere, Walter Howard, ed. *Graduale Sarisburiense: A Reproduction in Facsimile*   GS

Fretted Instrument Guild of America   FIGA

Fribourg, Switz. Gregorianische Akademie. *Veröffentlichungen*   GAkF

Front (of a perc. instr.)   F

FRoots *see* **Southern Rag**

Full organ, *organo pleno*   f.o., f. org.

Fusa (nota.)   f, fu

G. Schirmer (publ.)   GS

Galpin Society   GS

Galpin Society Journal (jl.)   GalpinSJ, Galpin Soc, GalpinSocJ, GSJ

Gatti, Guido Maria. *La Musica: Dizionario*   LaMusicaD

Gauche (F=left)   g.

Gaudeamus Foundation   GF

Gavotte (rec. lab.)   Gav

Gay and Lesbian Association of Choruses   GALA

Gegensatz (G=contrasting theme)   Ggs., GS

Gemischt (G=mixed)   gem.

Gemischter Chor (G=mixed chorus)   gemCh, gem. Chor

Gemshorn (jl.) GEM

General Dutch Singing Society GDSS / Algemeen Nederlands Zangverbond ANZ

General History of Music from the Earliest Ages to the Present (Charles Burney) BurneyH

General History of the Science and Practice of Music (John Hawkins) HawkinsH

Generalbass Gb.

Generalmusikdirektor, General-Musik-Direktor GMD

Generalpause (G=rest for entire ensemble) G.P.

Gennrich, Friedrich, ed. *Musikwissenschaftliche Studienbibliothek* MwSb

Gennrich, Friedrich, ed. *Summa musicae medii aevi* SMM, SMMA

Genootschap van Nederlandse Componisten *see* Dutch Composers' Society

Georg Kallmeyer Verlag (publ.) GKV

Gérard, Yves. *Thematic, Bibliographical, and Critical Catalogue of the Works of Luigi Boccherini* G.

Gerber, Ernst Ludwig. *Historisch-biographisches Lexikon der Tonkünstler* GerberL

Gerber, Ernst Ludwig. *Neues historisch-biographisches Lexikon der Tonkünstler* GerberNL, GerberNTL, NTL

Gerbert, Martin. *De cantu et musica sacra* Gerbert, De cantu

Gerbert, Martin. *Monumenta liturgiae* GerbertMon

Gerbert, Martin. *Scriptores ecclesiastici de musica sacra potissimum* GerbertS, GS

German Mozart Society GMS / Deutsche Mozart Gesellschaft DMG

German Musicians' Association / Deutscher Tonkünstlerverband DTKV

German Society of Concert Choirs / Verband Deutscher Konzert-Chöre GSCC

German Society of School Music Educators GSSME / Verband Deutscher Schulmusiker VDS

Gérold, T. *Histoire de la musique des origins à la fin du XIVᵉ siècle* Géhm, GéHM

Gesammelte Werke (G=collected works)   GW

Gesamtausgabe (G=collected ed.)   GA

Gesamtdauer (G=total length)   GD

Gesamtverband Deutscher Musikfachgeschäfte   GDM

Gesang (G=song)   Ges.

Gesangbuch (G=song book)   GsgB.

Gesänge (G=songs)   Gsge.

Gesangspädagogik (G=teaching of singing)   Ges-Päd.

Geschichte der Mensural-Notation von 1250-1460 (Johannes Wolf) WoG, WoGM, WolfM

Geschichte der Musik in Bayern (Arnold Schering)   GMB

Geschichte der Musik in Beispielen (Arnold Schering)   ScheringB, Schering Beisp, SchGMB

Gesellschaft für bayerischer Musikgeschichte. *Mitteilungsblatt* (jl.) MittGesBayerischeMg

Gesellschaft für musikalische Aufführungs- und mechanische Vervielfältigungsrechte   GEMA

Gesellschaft für Musikforschung Kongressbericht   GfMKB

Gesellschaft für Musikforschung. Publikationen älterer praktischer und theoretischer Musikwerke (Robert Eitner, ed.)   EP, PgfM, PÄMw, PGM, PubAPTM

Gesellschaft für Selbstspielende Musikinstrumente *see* Society for Self-Playing Musical Instruments

Gestopft (G=muted)   gest.

Gestrichen (G=bowed strings)   gestr.

Geteilt (G=divided)   get.

Gewöhnliche Notenschrift (G=normal notation)   gew. Notenschr.

Giegling, Franz. *Giegling Verzeichnis* (Franz Giegling's cat. of Giuseppe Torelli's works)   G.

Gilbert & Sullivan Journal (jl.)   G & S J

Ginzburg, S. L. *Istoriya russkoy muziki v notnikh obraztsakh*   IRMO

Gitarre (G=guitar)   Git.

Glareanus dodecachordon glar.

Glazounov Society GS

Glissando (I) gliss.

Glockenspiel Gl., Glk., Glock., Glsp., Gsp.

Gloria Gl.

Gopher Music Notes (jl.) GM

Gordon V. Thompson (publ.) GVT

Gospel Music Association GMA

Gospel Music Workshop of America GMWA

Gothic plainsong notation / *gothische Choralnotation* GChN

Gothische Choralnotation / Gothic plainsong notation GChN

Gottesdienst und Kirchenmusik (jl.) Gottesd u Kir, GottesdienstKm

Grackle, The: Improvised Music in Transition (jl.) Gra

Gradual gr., grad.

Gradual verse grv

Graduale Grad.

Graduale sacrosanctae romanae ecclesiae de tempore et de sanctis
   G, GR, Grad. Vat.

Graduale Sarisburiense: A Reproduction in Facsimile (Walter
   Howard Frere, ed.) GS

Graduate of the Birmingham School of Music GBSM

Graduate of the Guildhall School of Music G.G.S.M.

Graduate of the Royal Northern College of Music GRNCM

Graduate of the Royal Schools of Music GRSM

Grainger Journal (jl.) Grainger J

Grammofono, gramófono, gramophone (I, Sp=phonograph) gram.

Gran cassa, grancassa (I=bass drum) grc

Grand gd.

Grand orgue g.o.

Grand positif g.p.

Grand récitatif g.r.

Gray, H. W., Co. (publ.) Gray

Great organ g.o., g. org., gr., gt.

Great responsory re
Gregorian Chant (Willi Apel)   ApelG, ApGC
Grosse Trommel   gr.Tr.
Groupe d'acoustique musicale   GAM
Groupe d'acoustique musicale. *Bulletin* (jl.)   GAM
Groupe de recherches musicales   GRM
Groups gps
Grout, Donald Jay. *History of Western Music*   GrHWM
Grove's Dictionary of Music and Musicians   GD, Grove
Gruppo gr.
Guild for the Promotion of Welsh Music   GPWM
Guild of American Luthiers   GAL
Guild of Carillonneurs in North America   GCNA
Guildhall School of Music and Drama   GSM
Guillaume de Machaut. *Musikalische Werke* (Friedrich Ludwig, ed.)
    (*Publikationen älterer Musik*)   LuM
Guilmant, Alexandre, ed. *Archives des maîtres de l'orgue des XVIe,*
    XVIIe, et XVIIIe siécles (Alexandre Guilmant et André Pirro, ed.)
    Guilmant-Pirro
Guitar / *guitare* (F)   gui, guit.
Guitar and Accessories Marketing Association   GAMA
Guitar and Accessory Manufacturers' Association of America
    GAMA
Guitar & Lute (jl.)   GL
Guitar Foundation of America   GFA
Guitar Player (jl.)   GP, Guitar
Guitar Review (jl.)   GU, GuitarR

H. W. Gray Co. (publ.)   Gray
Haberl, F. X., ed. *Lasso, Orlando di. Sämtliche Werke*   LW
Halfway (on perc. instr.)   H
Hallische Händel-Ausgabe   HHA
Handbell(s) handb.

Handbuch der Musikgeschichte (Guido Adler)   AdHM, AdlerH, AdlerHdb, Adler HMG

Handbuch der Musikgeschichte (Hugo Riemann)   RiemannH, Riemann HdM, RiHM

Handbuch der Musikinstrumentenkunde (Curt Sachs)   SachsH, Sachs Hdb.

Handbuch der Musikwissenschaft (Ernst Bücken, ed.)   BüHM, BückenH, BückenHdb, BÜHM, HbMw, HMw

Handbuch der Notationskunde (Johannes Wolf)   WoH, WoHN

Händel, Georg Friedrich. *Werke* (Friedrich Chrysander, ed.)   HäW

Händel-Jahrbuch (jl.)   HändelJb, HJb

Händelgesellschaft (G=Breitkopf & Härtel's ed. of Händel's works)   H.G.

Händen (G=hands)   Hdn.

Händig (G=handed)   Hd.

Handwörterbuch der musikalischen Terminologie (Hans Heinrich Eggebricht)   HmT, HMT

Hans Pfitzner Gesellschaft. *Mitteilungen*   MittHansPfitznerGes, Pfitzner

Hardanger Fiddle Association of America   HFAA

Harfe (G=harp)   Hf., Hfe.

Hargail Music Press (publ.)   Har

Harmonic mean   hm

Harmonie (G=harmony)   Harmon.

Harmonika-Jahrbuch (jl.)   HarmonikaJb

Harmonisch (G=harmonic)   harm.

Harmonium   harm.

Harp Renaissance Society   HRS

Harpsichord   hpcd., hpd., hpsd.

Harpsichord (jl.)   HD

Harvard Dictionary of Music (Willi Apel)   HDM

Harvard Publications in Music   HPM

Hauptrhythmus (G=principal rhythm)   HR

Hauptsatz (G=principal theme) HS

Hauptstimme H

Hauptwerk (G=great organ) Hauptw., Hk., Hptw.

Hausmusik Hausm.

Haut (F=high) h.

Hautbois (F=oboe) haut., hb., htb.

Haute-contre (F=alto) h.c.

Hawkes & Harris Music Co. (publ.) H & H

Hawkins, John. *A General History of the Science and Practice of Music* HawkinsH

Haydn Studien (jl.) Haydn Stud

Haydn Yearbook (jl.) / *Haydn Jahrbuch* Haydn Yb

Healey Willan Catalogue (Giles Bryant) B.

Hellenic Association for Contemporary Music HACM

Helm, Eugene. *New Thematic Catalog of the Works of Carl Philipp Emanuel Bach* H.

Hennefield, Norman, ed. *Masterpieces of Organ Music* MOM

Henry Purcell: An Analytical Catalogue of his Music (Franklin B. Zimmerman) Z

Henry Watson Music Library, Manchester Public Libraries HWML

Herd bell(s) herd b.

Hertz (cycles per second) Hz

Hesbert, Dom Rene, ed. *Monumenta musicae sacrae* MMS

High h.

High fidelity hi fi

High Fidelity/Musical America (jl.) HF, HF/MA, Hi Fi/Mus Am, HIFMA

Hindemith Jahrbuch (jl.) / *Annales Hindemith* HindemithJb

Hinrichsen's Musical Year Book (jl.) HMY, HMYB

Hirsch, Paul. *Publications of the Paul Hirsch Music Library* / *Veröffentlichungen der Musik-Bibliothek Paul Hirsch* VMPH

Hirsch, Paul. *Veröffentlichungen der Musik-Bibliothek Paul Hirsch*

see Publications of the Paul Hirsch Music Library

His Master's Voice (rec. lab.) H.M.V.

Historic Brass Society HBS

Historical Anthology of Music (Archibald T. Davison) Apel Anth, ApelAnth, DA, HAM

Historisch-biographisches Lexikon der Tonkünstler (Ernst Ludwig Gerber) GerberN

History of Musical Instruments (Curt Sachs) SaHMI

History of Western Music (Donald Jay Grout) GrHWM

Hoboken, Anthony van. *Joseph Haydn: Thematisches Werkverzeichnis* H., Hob.

Hoch (G=high) h.

Holzblasinstrumente (G=woodwind instr.) Holzbl.

Hoppin, Richard H., ed. *Anthology of Medieval Music* AMM

Horn Hr.

Horn Call (jl.) HC

Hörner (G=horns) Hr.

Hortus musicus HM

Hrvatski Glazbeni zavod *see* Croatian Music Institute

Hrvatsko pjevačko društvo *see* Croatian Singing Society

Hudební Matice Uniělecké Besedy (publ.) HMUB

Hudební nástroje HudNástroje

Hudební revue (jl.) HR

Hudební rozhledy (jl.) HR, Hud Roz, HudR

Hudební věda Hud veda, Hudveda, HV

Hudební život Hud Zivot

Hymn, *hymnus* H, hy

Hymn Society of America HSA

Hymn Society of Great Britain and Ireland. *Bulletin* (jl.) Hymn S

Hymn, The (jl.) HY

Hymnen (I): Die mittelalterlichen Hymnenmelodien des Abendlandes (Bruno Stäblein, ed.) (*Monumenta monodica medii aevi, I*) ST

Hymns hymn

Hymns Ancient and Modern Hymns A & M

Iceland Music Information Centre IMIC

Imperial Russian Music Society IRMS

In praktischer Neuausgabe i. pr. NA

In Theory Only (jl.) ITO

Inches per second ips

Incipit inc, incip

Incipit-Verzeichnis (G) / *index des incipit* (F) / *incipit index* IncV

Incorporated Association of Organists IAO

Incorporated Phonographic Society IPS

Incorporated Society of Musicians ISM

Incorporated Society of Organ Builders ISOB

Independent Music Association IMA

Index des incipit see *Incipit-Verzeichnis*

Indian Music Journal (jl.) IndianMJ

Indian Musicological Society. *Journal* (jl.) Indian MS, J Indian
   Musicol Soc

Innsbruck. Universitätsbibliothek. *Wolkenstein-Codex* WoB

Input/output (data proc.) I/O

Institut de psycho-acoustique et de musique electronicque *see*
   Institute for Psycho-Acoustics & Electronic Music

Institut de recherche de coordination acoustique de musique
   IRCAM

Instituta et monumenta IM, IMa

Institute for Psycho-Acoustics & Electronic Music / Instituut voor
   Psychoakoestiek en Elekronische Muziek / Institut de psycho-
   acoustique et de musique electronique IPEM

Institute for Studies in American Music I.S.A.M., ISAM

Institute of Jazz Studies IJS

Institute of Medieval Music IMM

Institute of Musical Instrument Technology IMIT

Institute of the American Musical IAM

Instituto de extensión musical IEM

Instituto Interamericano de Musicología IIM

Instituut voor Psychoakoestiek en Elektronische Muziek *see* Institute for Psycho-Acoustics & Electronic Music

Instrument (E, F) / *Instrument* (G) instr., instr.

Instrument (undesignated) I

Instrumental (E, G) instl., instr.

Instrumental Music Printed Before 1600: A Bibliography (Howard Mayer Brown) BrownI

Instrumentalist (jl.) INS, Instrument

Instrumentation instr.

Instrumentenbau-Zeitschrift (jl.) InstrumententbauZ, IZ

Instrumentenkunde Instrk.

Intabulation, keyboard intab

Inter-American Music Bulletin (jl.) InterAmerMBul

Inter-American Music Center CIDEM

Inter-American Music Council IAMC / Consejo interamericano de música CIDEM

Inter-American Music Review (jl.) Intam Mus R

Intercollegiate Men's Chorus, an International Association of Male Choruses IMC

Intercollegiate Musical Council IMC

Intermediary Musical Language (computer prog. lang) IML

International Alban Berg Society IABS

International Alliance of Women in Music IAWM

International Association for Music Instrument Collections I.A.M.I.C.

International Association for the Study of Popular Music / Association internationale pour l'étude de la musique popular IASPM

International Association of Concert and Festival Managers (later, ISPAA) IACFM

International Association of Concert Managers (later, ISPAA) IACM

International Association of Electronic Keyboard Manufacturers
   IAEKM

International Association of Jazz Appreciation   IAOJA

International Association of Jazz Educators   IAJE

International Association of Jazz Record Collectors   IAJRC

International Association of Jazz Record Collectors. *The IAJRC Journal* (jl.)   IAJRC

International Association of Libraries and Museums of the Performing Arts / Société Internationale des Bibliothèques et des Musées des Arts du Spectacle   SIBMAS

International Association of Music Libraries, Archives, and Documentation Centres   IAML / Association Internationale des Bibliothéque, Archives et Centres de Documentation Musicaux AIBM / Internationale Vereinigung der Musikbibliotheken, Musikarchive und Musikdokumentationszentren   IVMB

International Association of Opera Directors   IAOD / Association internationale des directeurs d'opéra   AIDO

International Association of Organ Teachers USA   IAOT(U)

International Association of Piano Builders and Technicians   IAPBT

International Association of Sound Archives   IASA

International Bach Society   IBS

International Banjo (jl.)   Int Banjo

International Bruckner Gesellschaft   IBG

International Bureau of Mechanical Reproduction   IBMR

International Cello Centre   ICC

International Clarinet Association   ICA

International Clarinet Society   ICS

International Classic Guitar Association   ICGA

International Committee of Musical Instrument Museums and Collections / Comité international des musées et collections d'instruments de musique / Comité internacional de museos y colecciones de instrumentos musicales   CIMCIM

International Computer Music Association   ICMA

International Confederation for Electroacoustic Music /
Confédération internationale de musique electroacoustique ICEM

International Confederation of Accordionists ICA / Confédération
internationale des accordeonistes CIA

International Confederation of Music Publishers ICMP

International Confederation of Popular Music Societies ICPMS /
Confédération internationale des sociétiés populaires de musique
CISPM

International Confederation of Societies of Authors and Composers
ICSAC / Confédération internationale des sociétiés d'auteurs et
compositeurs CISAC

International Confederation of Societies of Music ICSM /
Confédération internationale des sociétes musicales CISM

International Conference of Symphony and Opera Musicians
ICSOM

International Contemporary Music Exchange ICME

International Council for Traditional Music ICTM

International Council of Composers ICC / Conseil international des
compositeurs CIC

International Double Reed Society IDRS

International Fasch Society / Internationale Fasch-Gesellschaft IFG

International Federation for Choral Music IFCM

International Federation of "Little Singers" / Federatio
internationalis Pueri Cantores IFLS

International Federation of Children's Choirs IFCC / Fédération
internationale des choeurs d'enfants FICE

International Federation of Jeunesses Musicales / Fédération
internationale des jeunesses musicales FIJM

International Federation of Musicians IFM / Fédération
internationale des musiciens FIM

International Federation of Ragtime IFR

International Federation of the Phonographic Industry IFPI

International Folk Music Centre IFMC

International Folk Music Council IFMC

International Folk Music Council. *Yearbook* (jl.) IFMC, JIFMC, YbInFolkMCouncil, YIFMC

International Gustav Mahler Society / Internationale Gustav Mahler Gesellschaft IGMG

International Harmonica Foundation IHF / Fédération internationale de l'harmonica FIH

International Heinrich Schütz Society / Internationale Heinrich Schütz Gesellschaft IHSG

International Horn Society IHS

International Hugo Wolf Society / Internationale Hugo Wolf Gesellschaft IHWG

International Institute for Traditional Music IITM

International Kodály Society IKS / Société Internationale Kodály SIK

International League of Women Composers ILWC

International Manuel Poncé Society IMPS

International MIDI Association IMA

International Music Association IMA

International Music Centre IMC / Internationales Musikzentrum IMZ

International Music Council IMC / Conseil international de la musique CIM

International Music Educator (jl.) Int Mus Ed

International Music Products Association (*also* National Association of Music Merchants) NAMM

International Musical Society. *Congress Report* (jl.) IMusSCR

International Musician (jl.) IM, Int Mus

International Musicological Society IMS *see also* Internationale Gesellschaft für Musikwissenschaft IGW *see also* Société internationale de musique SIM

International Organ Festival Society IOFS

International Piano Guild IPG

International Piano Teachers Association IPTA

International Piano Teachers Foundation IPTF

International Planned Music Association   IPMA

International Polka Association   IPA

International Record and Music Publishing Market   IRMPM /
Marche international du disque et de l'édition musicale   MIDEM

International Repertory of Musical Iconography   *see* Répertoire
International d'Iconographie Musicale

International Review of the Aesthetics and Sociology of Music (jl.)
Int R Aesthetics & Soc, Int Rev Aes, Int. Rev. of Music Aesth. &
Sociol., IntRAestheticsSociologyM, IRASM

International Richard Strauss Society / Internationale Richard
Strauss Gesellschaft   IRSG

International Rostrum of Young Performers   IRYP / Tribune
internationale des jeunes interprètes   IRP

International Society for Contemporary Music   ISCM / Société
internationale pour la musique contemporaine   SIMC /
Internationale Gesellschaft für neue Musik   IGNM / Società
internazionale di musica contemporanea   SIMC

International Society for Music Education   ISMC / Société
internationale pour l'éducation musicale   SIEM

International Society for Music in Medicine   ISMM / Internationale
Gesellschaft für Musik in der Medizin   IGMM

International Society for Organ History and Preservation   ISOHP

International Society for Uruguayan Music   ISUM / Sociedad
Uruguaya de Música Contemporánea   SUMC

International Society of Bassists   ISB

International Society of Bassists. *Newsletter* (jl.)   ISB

International Society of Folk Harpers and Craftsmen   ISFHC

International Society of Organ Builders   ISO

International Society of Performing Arts Administrators   ISPAA

International Society of Violin and Bow Makers   ISVBM

International Songwriters' Association   ISA

International Steel Guitar Convention   ISGC

International Trombone Association   ITA

International Trombone Association. *Journal* (jl.)   ITA J, J ITA

International Trombone Association. *Newsletter* (jl.)   IT, ITA N,

News ITA

International Trumpet Guild ITG

International Trumpet Guild. *Journal* (jl.) IT, ITG, ITG J, J ITG

International Trumpet Guild. *Newsletter* (jl.) ITG N, News ITG

International Viola Research Society IVRS

International Viola Society IVS / Internationale Viola Gesellschaft IVG

International Western Music Association IWMA

Internationale des organisations culturelles ouvrières IDOCO

Internationale Fasch-Gesellschaft *see* International Fasch Society

Internationale Gesellschaft für Musik in der Medizin *see* International Society for Music in Medicine

Internationale Gesellschaft für Musikwissenschaft *see* International Musicological Society

Internationale Gesellschaft für Musikwissenschaft. *Mitteilungen* (jl.; later *Acta musicologica*) Acta, AM

Internationale Gesellschaft für neue Musik *see* International Society for Contemporary Music

Internationale Gustav Mahler Gesellschaft *see* International Gustav Mahler Society

Internationale Heinrich Schütz Gesellschaft *see* International Heinrich Schütz Society

Internationale Hugo Wolf Gesellschaft *see* International Hugo Wolf Society

Internationale Musikbibliothek (publ.) IM

Internationale Musikgesellschaft (jl.) IMG

Internationale Musikgesellschaft. *Beihefte* (jl.) Beih. IMG, BIMG

Internationale Musikgesellschaft. *Kongress* (jl.) KgrIMG

Internationale Musikgesellschaft. *Publikationen* (jl.) PIMG

Internationale Musikgesellschaft. *Sammelbände* (jl.) SBIMG, SIM, SIMG

Internationale Musikgesellschaft. *Zeitschrift* (jl.) ZIM, ZIMG

Internationale Richard Strauss Gesellschaft *see* International Richard Strauss Society

Internationale Stiftung Mozarteum. *Mitteilungen* (jl.)　ISM,
　MittIntStiftungMozarteum

**Internationale Vereinigung der Musikbibliotheken, Musikarchive
　und Musikdokumentationszentren** *see* International Association
　of Music Libraries, Archives, and Documentation Centres

Internationale Viola Gesellschaft *see* International Viola Society

Internationales Musikzentrum *see* International Music Centre

Internationales Repertorium der Musikikonographie *see*
　Répertoire International d'Iconographie Musicale

Introduction à la paléographie musicale (Gregoire Suñol)　IPM

Introit / Introitus　Int., Intr.

Introit verse　intv

Inversion　I

Inversion of a duration series　DI

Inversion of a note (pitch) series　NI

Inverted cancrizans of a duration series　DIC

Inverted 12-tone row that begins on the first pitch of the orig. row
　IO

Invitatorium / invitatory (chant)　inv, invitat.

Irish Folk Music Studies (jl.)　IrishFolkMStud

Israel Music Foundation　IMF

Israel Music Institute　IMI

Israel Music Publications　IMP

Istituto di Studi Verdiani. *Bollettino* (jl.)　BollIstStudVerdiani

Istituto italiano per la storia della musica　IISM

Istituto italiano per la storia della musica. *Pubblicazione*　PIISM

Istituzioni e monumenti dell'arte musicale italiana　IMAMI, Imi,
　Ist. e Mon.

Istoriya russkoy muziki v notnikh obraztsakh (S. L. Ginzburg)　IRMO

Ivrea. Biblioteca capitolare. Codex 115,　Iv

Izdatyelstvo "Sovyetskii kompositor" *see* Soviet Composer
　Publishers

J & W Chester (publ.)　Ch

J. Curwen and Sons (publ.)   Cu

Jacopo da Bologna. *Works* (W. Thomas Marrocco)   MaJ

Jacquot, Jean, ed. *La luth et sa musique*   LSM

Jacquot, Jean, ed. *Musique instrumentale de la Renaissance*   MIR

Jahrbuch der Komischen Oper (jl.)   JbKomischenOper

Jahrbuch der Musikbibliothek Peters (jl.; later, *Deutsches Jahrbuch der Musikwissenschaft*)   JbMP, JbP, JMP, PJB

Jahrbuch für Volksliedforschung (jl.)   Jahrb Volks, JbfVf, JbfVldf, JbVolksliedf

Jahrbücher für musikalische Wissenschaft (jl.)   JMW

Jan, Karl von. *Musici scriptores graeci*   JanM

Japan Contemporary Music Association   JCMA

Jazz (Hellerup, Denmark) (jl.)   J-H

Jazz (Sydney) (jl.)   J-S

Jazz Arts Society   JAS

Jazz at the Philharmonic   JATP

Jazz, Blues & Co. (jl.)   J B Co.

Jazz Composers Orchestra Association   JCOA

Jazz Echo (jl.)   J Echo

Jazz Educators' Journal (jl.; earlier, *NAJE Educator, Jazz Educators' Journal*)   ED J, NAJ

Jazz Forum (German ed.)   JF-D

Jazz Forum (Int'l. ed.)   JF-I

Jazz Freak (jl.)   J Freak

Jazz Hot, Le (jl.)   J Hot

Jazz Index   JI

Jazz Interactions   JI

Jazz International (jl.)   JI

Jazz Journal International (jl.)   Jazz J Int, JJI

Jazz Magazine (Northport, NY) (jl.)   Jazz Mag (US)

Jazz Magazine (jl.)   JZ

Jazz Magazine (Paris) (jl.)   J Mag, Jazz Mag

Jazz Nu (jl.)   J Nu

Jazz Podium (jl.)   JP

Jazz Report (jl.)   J Rep, Jazz Rept

Jazz Research (jl.)   *see Jazzforschung*

Jazz Spotlite News (jl.)   J Spot

Jazz Times (jl.)   J Times

Jazz World Society   JWS

Jazzforschung (jl.)   JazzF / *Jazz Research*, J Res

Jazzfreund, Der (jl.)   Jfreund

Jazznytt (jl.)   Jnytt

Jenaer Handschrift (medieval ms.)   J

Jeunesse et orgue (jl.)   Jeunesse

Jeunesses Musicales de Suisse   JMS

Jeunesses Musicales of Hungary   JMH

Jeunesses Musicales of Israel   JMI

Jewish Music Alliance   JMA

Jewish Music Council   JMC

Jewish Music Forum   JMF

John Edwards Memorial Foundation   JEMF

John Edwards Memorial Foundation. *Quarterly* (jl.)   JEMF Q,
   JEMF Quart

Joseph Haydn: Thematisches Werkverzeichnis (Anthony van
   Hoboken)   H., Hob.

Journal of Band Research (jl.)   JB, J Band Res, JBandResearch

Journal of Church Music (jl.)   JC, J Church Mus, JChurchM

Journal of Jazz Studies (jl.)   JJ, J Jazz Stud, J Jazz Studies, Jo St

Journal of Music Theory (jl.)   JM, JMT, JMTh, JM Theory, J Mus
   Theory, J Music Thr

Journal of Music Therapy (jl.)   JMTherapy, J Music Ther, J Mus
   Therapy, JT

Journal of Musicological Research (jl.; earlier, *Music and Man*)   J
   Music Res

Journal of Renaissance and Baroque Music (jl.; later, *Musica
   Disciplina*)   JRBM, MD

Journal of Research in Music Education (jl.) JRM, JRMEA,
JRMEd, J Res Mus Ed, J Res Music, JResearchMEducation, JRME

Journal of Research in Singing (jl.) JRS

Jubilate Jub.

Juilliard News Bulletin (jl.) JN

Juilliard Review Annual (jl.) JU

Juventude Musical Portuguesa *see* Portuguese Musical Youth

Juventudes Musicales de España JME

Kallmeyer, Georg, Verlag (publ.) GKV

Kamien, Roger, ed. *The Norton Scores* NS

Kammermusik (G=chamber music) KaM.

Kantate (G=cantata) Kant.

Kapellmeister Kpm.

Keeping Up With Orff-Schulwerk in the Classroom (jl.) KE

Keyboard kbd.

Keyboard (jl.; earlier, *Contemporary Keyboard*) CK, Cont. Key.,
Cont. Keybd.

Keyboard Classics (jl.) KC

Keyboard glockenspiel Glsp. (Kbd.)

Keyboard intabulation intab

Keyboard Teachers Association International KTAI

Kinderchor (G=children's chorus) K. Chor

Kirchenchor, Der (jl.) Kirchor

Kirchenmusik (G=church music) KM

Kirchenmusikalisches Jahrbuch (jl.) KJ, KJb, KMJ, Km Jb, KMJB

Kirchenmusikalische Nachrichten (jl.) KmNachrichten

Kirchenmusiker, Der (jl.) Kir Mus, Km.

Kirkpatrick (before a number, identification assigned by Ralph
Kirkpatrick to D. Scarlatti's sonatas) K.

Kistner & Siegel (publ.) K&S

Klank en Weerklank (jl.) Klank

Klarinette (G=clarinet) Kl, Klar.

Klassisch (G=classical)   klass.

Klavier (G=piano)   Kl.

Klavierauszug (G=piano reduction; vocal score)   Kl. A., Kl-A., Kla.

Kleine Flöte (G=piccolo)   kl. Fl.

Kleine Trommel (G=side drum)   kl. Tr.

Knabenchor (G=boys' chorus)   KbCh, Kn. Chor

Koch, Heinrich Christoph. *Musikalisches Lexikon*   KochL

Köchel-Verzeichnis (i.e., L. von Köchel's chronol. list of Mozart's works)   K., K.V.

Kodex (G=codex)   Kod.

Kölner Beiträge zur Musikforschung (jl.)   KBMf

Kommission für Musikforschung der Österreichischen Akademie der Wissenschaften *see* Commission for Music Research of the Austrian Academy of Sciences

Komponiert (G=composed)   komp.

Komponist (G=composer)   Komp.

Komposition   Kompos.

Konservatorium (G=conservatory)   Kons.

Kontrabass (G=contrabass, double bass)   Kb.

Kontrafagott (G=contrabassoon)   Kfag.

Kontrafaktur (G=contrafactum)   Kf.

Kontrapunkt (G=counterpoint)   Kp.

Kontrapunktisch (G=contrapuntal)   kp.

Konzert (G=concert)   Konz.

Konzertierend   konz.

Konzertmeister (G=concert master)   KonzM.

Krummel, Don W. *Resources of American Music History*   RAMH

Kurt Weill Foundation for Music   KWFM

Kwartalnik muzyczyny (jl.)   KM, Kwart. Muz.

Kyrie   Ky.

Landini, Francesco. *Works* (L. Ellinwood, ed.)   Ell

Landini, Francesco. *Works* (Leo Schrade, ed.) *(Polyphonic Music of*

the Fourteenth Century) SchL

Landschaftsdenkmale *(Das Erbe deutscher Musik. 2. Reihe)* LD

Lang, Paul Henry, ed. *Contemporary Music in Europe* LBCM

Larousse de la musique LM

LaRue, Jan, ed. *Aspects of Medieval and Renaissance Music* AMRM

Lasso, Orlando di. *Sämtliche Werke* (F.X. Haberl, ed.) LW

Latin American Music Review (jl.) / *Revista de música latino-americana* Lat Am Mus, Lat Am Mus R

Latvian Choir Association of the U.S. LCAUS

Laudes (Chant, Mass) LDS

Laudes (Chant, Matins) LDMT

Laudes (Chant, Office) LDOF

Lauritz Melchior Heldentenor Foundation LMHF

Lavignac, Albert, ed. *Encyclopédie de la musique et dictionnaire du Conservatoire* EC, EMDC, LavE, LavignacE

Leader ldr.

Leading tone l.t.

League of Filipino Composers LFC

League of Music Societies (Yugo.) / Savez muzičkih društava SMD

Left arm LA

Left channel (tape) l.c.

Left hand / *linke Hand* (G) l.h. L.H.

Leggiero (I=lightly) legg°

Leipziger Allgemeine musikalische Zeitung (jl.) AmZ

Leopold Stokowski Society LSS

Leopold Stokowski Society of America LSSA

Lerner, Edward R. *Study Scores of Musical Styles* LSS

Lesbian and Gay Bands of America LGBA

Leschetizky Association LA

Let vibrate l.v.

Letania Apostolica Let Apost

Letania Canonica Let Can

Liber responsorialis pro festis   LR

Liber Usualis missae et officii pro dominicis et festis duplicibus cum cantu gregoriano   LU, Us

Liber Usualis, with introduction and rubrics in English   L, LU

Liber vesperalis juxta ritum Sanctae Ecclesiae Mediolanensis   LVM

Libretto   li, lib., libr.

Libretto proprio (I=own libretto)   libr. pr.

Licentiate of the Bandsman's College of Music   LBCM

Licentiate of the Birmingham School of Music   LBSM

Licentiate of the Guildhall School of Music and Drama   LGSM

Licentiate of the Royal Academy of Music   LRAM

Licentiate of the Royal Schools of Music   LRSM

Licentiate of the Tonic Sol-fa College of Music   LTSC

Licentiate of the Trinity College of Music   LTCL

Lied und Chor (jl.)   LiedChor

Liederbuch (G=song book)   Ldb.

Liederkranz Foundation   LF

Ligatura binaria (nota.)   lib.

Ligatura quaternaria (nota.)   quat.

Ligatura quintenaria (nota.)   quin.

Ligatura ternaria (nota.)   ter.

Ligature, ligated   li

Ligue canadienne de compositeurs   *see*   Canadian League of Composers

Line   li

Links (G=left)   li.

Listener, The (BBC) (jl.)   List

Litaize, Gaston, ed. *L'Organiste liturgique*   OLI

Litany   l., lit.

London Academy of Music and Dramatic Art   LAMDA

London Musical Club   LMC

London Philharmonic Orchestra   LPO

London Symphony Orchestra   LSO

Long lg.

Long-playing record lp

Longa, longae (nota.) L

Longa duplex (nota.) L-dx

Longo (I=numbering system of D. Scarlatti's sonatas devised by Alessandro Longo) L, L.

Lose Blätter der Musikantengilde LB

Low l.

Lowinsky, Edward, ed. *Monuments of Renaissance Music* MRM

Lucca. Archivio di stato. Biblioteca. Ms. 184 Luc

Lucques. Bibliothèque Capitulaire. Codex 601 (Antiphonaire monastique) (facsim.) (*Paleographie musicale, 9*) LA

Lucrări de muzicologie (jl.) LM, Luzrări Muzicol

Ludwig, Friedrich, ed. *Guillaume de Machaut. Musikalische Werke* LuM

Lusingando (I=tenderly) lusing.

Lute / *Laute* (G) / *luth* (F) / *liuto* (I) / *laúd* (Sp) lt., Lt.

Lute Society LS

Lute Society. *Journal* (jl.) LSJ, LuteSocJ

Lute Society of America LSA

Lute Society of America. *Journal* (jl.) J Lute, JLuteSocAmer, LS

Luth et sa musique (Jean Jacquot, ed.) LSM

M. Witmark & Sons (publ.) W

Madrid. Biblioteca Nacional. Ms. 20486 (medieval ms.) Ma

Madrigal madr.

Maelzel metronome M, M.M.

Maggiore (I=major) magg.

Magisterium in Gregorian Chant, Pontifical School of Sacred Music, Rome (Pontificio Istituto di Musica Sacra) MGC

Magnetico magn.

Magnetofono (I) / *Magnetophon* (G) / *magnétophone* (F) / *magnetofón* (Sp) = tape recorder magn.

Magnificat　Mag., Magnif.

Magnun opus musicum　MaO

Magyar Kórus, Budapest　MK

Main droite (F) / *mano destra* (I) / *manu dextra* (L) = right hand　m.d.

Main gauche (F=left hand)　m.g.

Main, mains (F=hand(s))　m.

Maîtres musiciens de la renaissance française (Henri Expert, ed.)　ExpertMMRF

Major　maj.

Malipiero, Gian Francesco, ed. *Monteverdi: Tutte le opere*　MoTO

Mancando (I=growing quieter)　manc.

Mandolin / *Mandoline* (G) / *mandoline* (F) / *mandolino* (I)　mand., Md.

Mandoline see mandolin

Männerchor (G=mens' chorus)　MCh., M. Chor

Mano destra see *Main droite*

Manu dextra see *Main droite*

Manu sinistra (I=left hand)　m.s.

Manual(s)　m., man.

Maple Leaf Club　MLC

Maraca(s)　mar.

Marcato (I=stressed)　marc.

Marche international du disque et de l'édition musicale　MIDEM / International Record and Music Publishing Market　IRMPM

Marcuse, Sybil. *Musical Instruments: A Comprehensive Dictionary*　MaMI

Marimba　mar.

Marks, Edward B. (publ.)　EBM

Marrocco, W. Thomas. *Jacopo da Bologna. Works*　MaJ

Marrocco, W. Thomas. *Oxford Anthology of Medieval Music*　OMM

Master of Church Music　MCM

Master of Music　MM, M.M., Mmus, M.Mus

Master of Music Education　Mus Ed M

Masterpieces of Music Before 1750 (Carl Parrish, ed.)   MM
Masterpieces of Organ Music (Norman Hennefield, ed.)   MOM
Masters of the Keyboard (Willi Apel)   ApelMK
Max-Reger-Institut. *Mitteilungen* (jl.)   MittMaxRegerInst
Maxima (nota.)   Mx
McKee, Peter Music Co. (publ.)   McKee
McLaughlin & Reilly (publ.)   MR
Measure, measures   m, mm.
Mediaeval Musical Manuscripts   MedMM
Mediant   III
Medium difficulty   m
Medium to difficult   M-D
Meet the Composer   MTC
Mehrstimmig (G=polyphonic)   mehrst.
Mélanges de musicologie critique (Pierre Aubry, ed.)   MMC
Melbourne Symphony Orchestra   MSO
Melodiarium hungariae medii aevi: Hymnen und Sequenzen
   (Rajeczky Benjamin)   MHMA
Melodie und Rhythmus (jl.)   MelodieRhythmus
Melodious Accord   MA
Melody   mel.
Melody instrument / mélodie-instrument (F) / Melodie-Instrument (G)
   mel. instr.
Melody Maker (jl.)   Mel M, Mel Maker, MLDMA
Melos/Neue Zeitschrift für Musik (jl.)   Melos/NeueZM
Member of the Royal College of Organists   MRCO
Memory Lane: Dance Band, Vocal, & Jazz Review (jl.)   Memory
Mens en melodie (jl.)   Mens en Mel, MensMelodie
Mercure musical (jl.)   BSIM, MmBullSIM
Mestres de l'escolania de Montserret   MEM
Metronome   met., mm.
Metropolitan Opera   Met.
Metropolitan Opera Guild   MOG

Metropolitan Opera National Council MONC

Mezzo forte, mezzoforte mf, mff

Mezzo piano mp

Mezzo soprano mezzo sop., ms, MS, mso.

Mezzo-Sopran (G=*mezzo soprano*) Mez.

Mezzo voce (I=half voice) m.v., mzv.

Mezzoforte, mezzo forte mf, mff

Microphone mic

Middle m, M

Migne, Jacques-Paul, ed. *Patrologiae cursus completus, series graeca* Migne. Patr. gr., Patr. gr., PG

Migne, Jacques-Paul, ed. *Patrologiae cursus completus, series latina* Migne. Patr. lat., Patr. lat., PL

Military drum mil. d., mil. dr.

Miniature score min. sc.

Minim (nota.) mi

Minima, minimae (nota.) m, min.

Minor / *minore* (I) min.

Minutes min.

Miscellanea musicologica (Adelaide) (jl.) Misc Mus, MiscM-A, MiscMusicol

Miscellanea musicologica (Prague) (jl.) MiscM-C, MiscMusicol, MMA, MMC

Miserationes (chant) MSR

Missale Romanum ex decreto sacrosancti concilii Tridentini restitutum Miss R

Mit Dämpfer (G=with mute, damper pedal) m.D.

Mittel (G=middle) m.

Mittler (G=medium, middle) mittl.

MM: tidskrift for rytmish musik (Copenhagen) MM

Modena. Biblioteca Estense olim lat. 471 (medieval ms.) ModB

Modena. Biblioteca Estense. [alpha] M. 5.24 (olim lat. 568) Mod.

Moderate tempo m

Moderato mod., modto. (I=moderately)

Modern Drummer (jl.) MD, Modern Drum

Modern Jazz Quartet MJQ

Modern Music (jl.) MM, Mod Mus

Modulator mod

Monatshefte für Musikgeschichte (jl.) MfM, MFM, MMg

Mönkemeyer, Helmut, ed. *Musica Instrumentalis* MI

Monophonic mono.

Monteverdi, Claudio. Tutte le opere (Gian Francesco Malipiero, ed.) MoTO

Monthly Musical Record (jl.) MMR, Mo Mus Rec

Montréal Symphony Orchestra (earlier, CSM, Société des Concerts Symphoniques de Montréal) MSO / Orchestre symphonique de Montréal OSM

Monumenta liturgicae (Martin Gerbert) GerbertMon

Monumenta lyrica medii aevi italica MLMI

Monumenta lyrica medii aevi italica. I. Latina MLMAI-L

Monumenta lyrica medii aevi italica. III. Mensurabilia MLMAI-M

Monumenta monodica medii aevi MMMA

Monumenta monodica medii aevi VII: Alleluia-melodien I (Karlheinz Schlager, ed.) MMMA

Monumenta Musicae Belgicae MMB, MMBel, MMBelg

Monumenta Musicae Byzantinae MMB

Monumenta Musicae Byzantinae. Lectionaria MMB-L

Monumenta Musicae Byzantinae. Principale MMB-P

Monumenta Musicae Byzantinae. Subsidia MMB-S

Monumenta Musicae Byzantinae. Transcripta MMB-T

Monumenta Musicae in Polonia MMP

Monumenta Musicae neerlandicae MMN

Monumenta Musicae sacrae (Dom Rene Hesbert, ed.) MMS

Monumenta Musicae Svecicae MMS

Monumenta Polyphoniae Italicae MI

Monumenti di Musica Italiana MMI

Monumentos de la música española MME, MMEsp

Monuments de la musique française au temps de la Renaissance (Henri Expert, ed.) ExpertMMFR, ExpertMonuments, MMFTR

Monuments of Music and Music Literature in Facsimile MMMLF

Monuments of Renaissance Music (Edward Lowinsky, ed.) MRM

Moravian Music Foundation MMF

Moravian Music Foundation. *Bulletin* (jl.) Moravian Mus

Moser, Hans Joachim. *Musiklexikon* MoserL

Motet mot.

Motetto mot.

Motetus mot.

Movement movt., mvt.

Movimento metronomico M.M.

Mozart, Leopold. *Versuch einer gründlichen Violinschule* Mozart Versuch

Mozart, Wolfgang Amadeus. *Neue Ausgabe sämtlicher Werke* NMA

Mozart-Jahrbuch (jl.) MJb, Mozart-Jb

Münchener Veröffentlichungen zur Musikgeschichte MVM

Mundharmonika (G=harmonica) M. Harm-ka

Munich. Bayerische Staatsbibliothek, Clm 14274 (olim Mus. Ms. 3232a) Mn

Munich. Bayerische Staatsbibliothek. Clm 15611 (ms.) Mn2

Musahino Academia Musicae. *Bulletin* (jl.), BulMusashino-AcademiaM

Music (Schools of Music Association) (jl.) Music (SMA)

Music, musician, musical mus.

Music & forskning (jl.) MForskning

Music & Letters (jl.) M&L, ML, MLetters, Mus & Lett, Music Lett, MusL

Music Advisers' National Association MANA

Music and Dance (jl.) Mus & Dance

Music and Entertainment Industry Educators Association MEIEA

Music and Man (jl.; later, *Journal of Musicological Research*) Music Man

Music and Musicians (jl.) MUMUA, Mus & mus, Mus & Mus

Music Clubs Magazine (jl.) MCM, MusClubs Mag

Music Confederation of Belgium MCB / Muziekverbond van België MVB

Music Corporation of America MCA

Music critic, music criticism muscrit

Music Critics' Association of North America MCA

Music Dealer (jl.) Mus Dealer

Music Distributors Association (formerly NAMMW) MDA

Music Editors' Association MEA

Music Education Council MEC

Music Education League MEL

Music Educators' Journal (jl.) MEDJA, MEJ, Mus Ed J, Music Ed Jnl, Music Educ

Music for Brass MUB

Music Forum (jl.) MForum, Mus Forum

Music in Education (jl.) Mus in Ed

Music in the Baroque Era (Manfred Bukofzer) BuMBE

Music in the Middle Ages (Gustave Reese) MMA, ReMMA

Music in the Renaissance (Gustave Reese) MR, ReMR

Music Index MI, MusicI

Music Industries Association of Canada MIAC / Association canadienne des industries de la musique ACIM

Music Industry Conference MIC

Music Industry Council MIC

Music Information Center/Centre MIC

Music Jobbers' Association MJA

Music Journal (jl.) MJ, Mus J, Mus Jl, Music J

Music Leader (jl.) MusLeader

Music Library Association MLA

Music Library Association. *Notes* (jl.) Mus Lib Assn Notes, Notes,

NO

Music Magazine (Ontario) (jl.)   Mus Mag

Music Masters' Association (London)   MMA

Music Ministry (jl.)   MUM, Mus Min

Music Minus One   MMO

Music News (Chicago) (jl.)   Mus News

Music News from Prague (jl.)   Mus News Prague

Music Now (jl.)   MUS

Music OCLC Users' Group (earlier, OCLC Music Users' Group)
   MOUG

Music of Earlier Times (Johannes Wolf, ed.)   MET, WM

Music of the West Magazine (jl.)   Mus West

Music Operators of America   MOA

Music Parade (jl.)   Mus Parade

Music Performance Trust Funds   MPTF

Music Press (publ.)   MP

Music Publishers' Association of the United States   MPA

Music Publishers' Protective Association   MPPA

Music Research Foundation   MRF

Music Review (jl.)   MR, Music Rev, MusR, MusRev

Music Scene (jl.)   MScene, Mus Scene

Music Simulator-Interpreter for Compositional Procedures (comp.
   lang.)   MUSICOMP

Music Supervisors' Journal (jl.)   Mus Superv J

Music Survey (jl.)   Mus Survey

Music Teacher and Piano Student (jl.)   Mus Tcr

Music Teachers' National Association   MTNA

Music Teachers' National Association. *Proceedings* (jl.)   Mus Teach
   Nat Assn Proc

Music: The A.G.O. and R.C.C.O. Magazine   see   American Organist

Music Theory Spectrum (jl.)   MT, Mus Theory Spectrum

Music Today Newsletter (jl.)   Mus Today NL

Music Trade Review (jl.)   Mus Trade Rev

Music Trades (jl.) Mus Trades
Music Trades Association MTA
Musica (Kassel) (jl.) Mus
Musica antiqua Bohemica MAB
Musica antiqua Polonica MAP
Musica Britannica MB, Mus. Brit.
Musica da camera (I=chamber music) mc, MdC
Musica disciplina (jl.) (formerly *Journal of Renaissance and Baroque Music*) MD, Mus Disc
Musica divina (jl.) MD
Musica: Dizionario, La (sotto la direzione di Guido Maria Gatti) LaMusicaD
Musica d'oggi (jl.) Mus d'oggi, Mus Oggi
Musica elettronica viva MEV
Musica: Enciclopedia storica (a cura di A. Basso) La Musica E
Musica hispana MH
Musica Instrumentalis (Helmut Mönkemeyer, ed.) MI
Musica Jazz: Rassegna mensile (jl.) Mus J
Musica Judaica (jl.) MJudaica, Mus Judaica
Musica mechanica organoedi (Jacob Adlung) Adlung Mus. mech. org.
Musica medii aevi MMedii Aevi, MusMA
Musica minima MMinima
Musica nostra et vostra MNEV
Musica sacra (jl.) MSacra, MusSacra
Musica Schallplatte (jl.) M Schallplatte, Mus Schall
Musica università (Pontina, Italy) MUniversità
Musica viva historica MVH
Música y arte (jl.) MArte
Musicae Baccalaureus (L=Bachelor of Music) Mus.B., Mus Bac, Mus Bach
Musicae Doctor (L=Doctor of Music) Mus D, Mus Doc
Musicae magister (L=Master of Music) Mus M

Musicae sacrae ministerium MSacraeMinisterium

Musical director / *Musik Direktor, Musikdirektor* (G) MD, mus dir

Musical America (jl.; later, *High Fidelity/Musical America*) Mus. Am.

Musical Antiquarian Society. *Publications* MAS

Musical Antiquary (jl.) MA

Musical Aptitude Profile MAP

Musical Arena Theatres Association (now MTA) MATA

Musical Association. *Proceedings* (jl.) PMA, Proc Mus Assn, Proc. Mus. Ass., Proc. Mus. Assoc.

Musical Box Society International MBSI, Mus Box

Musical Canada (jl.) MCan

Musical Corporation of America MCA

Musical Courier (jl.) MCour

Musical Denmark (jl.) Mus Denmark

Musical Events (jl.) Mus Events

Musical Information Retrieval (comp. program) MIR

Musical Instrument Digital Interface MIDI

Musical Instruments: A Comprehensive Dictionary (Sybil Marcuse) MaMI

Musical Newsletter (jl.) MUN, Mus News, MNewsl

Musical Opinion (jl.) MO, MOpinion, Mus Op, Mus Opinion

Musical Quarterly (jl.) MQ, Mus Q, Mus Qu, Music Quart

Musical Theatre Association (formerly, MATA) MTA

Musical Theorists in Translation (Luther Dittmer, ed.) MThT

Musical Times (jl.) MT, MTimes, Mus T, Music Times, MusTimes

Musicalisches Lexikon oder Musicalische Bibliothec (Johann Gottfried Walther) WaltherL, WaltherML

Musicanada (jl.) Mcan, Muscan

Musiche rinascimentali siciliane MRS

Musiche vocali strumentali sacre e profane MVSSP

Musici scriptores graeci (Karl von Jan) JanM

Musician, Player and Listener (jl.) MPL, Mus P & L, Musician

Musicians Against Nuclear Arms MANA
Musicians and Singers Association of Singapore MSAS
Musicians Benevolent Fund MBF
Musicians Foundation MF
Musicians United for Safe Energy MUSE
Musicians' Club of America MCA
Musicians' Emergency Fund MEF
Musicians' Union MU
Musiciens amateurs du Canada *see* Canadian Amateur Musicians
Musicologica slovaca (jl.) MusicoSlovaca
Musicological, musicologist, musicology musicol.
Musicological Society of Australia MSA
Musicological Studies (Luther Dittmer, ed.) MS
Musicological Studies and Documents MSD
Musicologie (F=musicology) mie., music.
Musicology Australia (jl.) Musicol [AUS]
Musik alter Meister MAM
Musik des Ostens MOst, MOstens
Musik, Die (jl.) DM, M, Mk
Musik aus früher Zeit für Klavier (Willi Apel) ApMZ
Musik des Mittelalters und der Renaissance (Heinrich Besseler)
    BeMMR
Musik Direktor, Musikdirektor (G) MD
Musik in der Schule (jl.) MSchule, Mus in Schule
Musik in Geschichte und Gegenwart MGG
Musik International-Instrumentenbau-Zeitschrift (jl.) Mus Int
Musik und Altar (jl.) MAltar
Musik und Bildung (jl.) MBildung, Mus u Bild
Musik und Gesellschaft (jl.) MGes, MusG, Mus u Ges
Musik und Gottesdienst (jl.) MGottesdienst, Mus u Gottesd
Musik und Kirche (jl.) (includes *Schallplatte und Kirche*, q.v.) MK,
    MKirche, MuK, Mus u Kir
Musikalische Denkmäler MD, MMD

Musikalische Jugend   MJugend

Musikalisches Lexikon (Heinrich Christoph Koch)   KochL

Musikantengilder, Die (jl.)   MU

Musikbühne (jl.)   MBühne

Musikdirektor (G=music director)   MD

Musikerziehung (jl.)   ME

Musikforschung (G=music research)   Mg

Musikforschung, Die (jl.)   Mf, MF, Musikforsch

Musikforskning (Norwegian=music research)   Mf

Musikgeschichte (G=music history)   Mg.

Musikgeschichte in Beispielen (Hugo Riemann)   RiemannB, Riemann
   Beisp, RiMB

Musikgeschichte in Bildern   MgB

Musikhandel (jl.)   MH

Musikk-Huset (publ.)   MH

Musiklexikon (G=music dictionary)   MLex

Musiklexikon (Hans Joachim Moser)   MoserL

Musiklexikon (Horst Seeger)   SeegerL

Musikrevy (Stockholm) (jl.)   MR

Musiktheorie (G=music theory)   MTh.

Musiktherapie (G=music therapy)   Mtherapie

Musikwerk, Das   Mw

Musikwissenschaft (G=musicology)   Mw.

Musikwissenschaftlich (G=musicological)   mw.

Musikwissenschaftliche Arbeiten (jl.)   MwArb

Musikwissenschaftliche Studienbibliothek (Friedrich Gennrich, ed.)
   MwSb

Musique d'harmonie   mus. d'h.

Musique de chambre (F=chamber music)   mus. de ch.

Musique de tous les temps (rec. lab.)   MTousTemps

Musique en jeu (jl.)   MJeu, Mus Jeu

Musique en Pologne (jl.)   MPologne

Musique et liturgie (jl.)   Mus et Lit

Musique instrumentale de la Renaissance (Jean Jacquot, ed.)   MIR
Musique sacrée (F=sacred music)   mus. sacr.
Musique sacrée catholique (F=Catholic sacred music)   mus. sacr. cath.
Mutual Musicians Foundation   MMF
Muziekverbond van België   *see*   Music Confederation of Belgium
Muzikal'naya entsiklopediya   ME
Muzikološki zbornik (jl.)   Muz Sbornik, MuzikolZbornik, MZ
Muzyka Kwartalnik (jl.)   MuzK
Muzykal'naia žhizn' (jl.)   Mžizn

Nagels Musikarchiv   NagelNM, NMA
NAJE Educator (jl.; later, *Jazz Educators' Journal*)   J Ed J
Nakladni zavod hrvatske (publ.)   NZH
Naouka i Izkoustvo (publ.)   NI
Narrator   narr.
Nastro magnetico (I=magnetic tape)   nm
National Academy of Popular Music   NAPM
National Academy of Songwriters   NAS
National Accordion Organization   NAO
National Association for American Composers and Conductors   NAACC
National Association for Music Education   MENC
National Association for Music Therapy   NAMT
National Association of Accompanists and Coaches   NAAC
National Association of Band Instrument Manufacturers   NABIM
National Association of Choirs   NAC
National Association of College Wind and Percussion Instructors   NACWPI
National Association of College Wind and Percussion Instructors.
    Journal (jl.)   NAC, NACWPI J
National Association of Composers/USA   NAC, NACUSA
National Association of German Musical Instrument Manu-
    facturers / Bundesverband der Deutschen Musikinstrumenten-

Hersteller   BdMH

National Association of Jazz Educators   NAJE

National Association of Music Executives in State Universities
   NAMESCU

National Association of Music Merchants (also International Music
   Products Association)   NAMM

National Association of Musical Merchandise Manufacturers (later,
   GAMA)   NAMMM

National Association of Musical Merchandise Wholesalers (later,
   MDA)   NAMMW

National Association of Negro Musicians   NANM

National Association of Pastoral Musicians   NAPM, NPM

**National Association of Professional Band Instrument Repair
   Technicians**   NAPBIRT

National Association of Record Manufacturers   NARM

National Association of Recording Merchandisers   NARM

National Association of School Music Dealers   NASMD

National Association of Schools of Music   NASM

National Association of Schools of Music. *Proceedings* (jl.)   NASM

National Association of Teachers of Singing   NATS

National Association of Teachers of Singing. *NATS Bulletin* (jl.)
   NAT, NATCA, NATS, NATSBul

National Association of Women in Music   NAWM

National Association of Youth Orchestras   NAYO

National Band Association   NBA

National Black Music Caucus   NBMC

National Catholic Band Association   NCBA

National Catholic Bandmasters' Association   NCBA

National College of Music (London)   NCM

National Council of Music Importers   NCMI

National Council of Music Importers and Exporters   NCMIE

National Council of State Supervisors of Music   NCSSM

National Federation Interscholastic Music Association   NFIMA

National Federation of Cultural Associations for the Promotion of Music / Fédération nationale d'associations culturelles d'expansion musicale FNACEM

National Federation of Music Clubs NFMC

National Federation of Music Societies NFMS

National Flute Association NFA

National Fraternity of Student Musicians NFSM

National Guild of Piano Teachers NGPT

National Jazz Service Organization NJSO

National Music Camp (Interlochen, Mich.) NMC

National Music Council NMC

National Music Council. *Bulletin* (jl.) NMC

National Music Council of Great Britain NMCGB

National Music League NML

National Music Printers and Allied Trades Association NMPATA

National Music Publishers' Association NMPA

National Musicamp Association NMA

National Old-Time Fiddlers' Association NO-TFA

National Opera Association NOA

National Opera Institute NOI

National Operatic and Dramatic Association NODA

National Oratorio Society NOS

National Orchestral Association NOA

National Piano Foundation NPF

National Piano Manufacturers' Association of America NPMA

National Piano Travelers Association NPTA

National School Brass Band Association NSBBA

National School Orchestra Association NSOA

National School Orchestra Association. *Bulletin* (jl.) NSO, NSOA

National Sheet Music Society NSMS

National Society of Student Keyboardists NSSK

National Symphony Orchestra Association NSOA

National Women's Music Festival NWMF

National Youth Orchestra of Great Britain NYO

Natural nat.

Nebenstimme (G=subsidiary voice or part) N

Nederlandse Pianola Vereniging *see* Dutch Pianola Society

Nederlandse Vereniging van Grammofoonplaten *see* Dutch
  Association of Gramophone Records

Neue Bach Ausgabe NBA

Neue Mozart-Ausgabe NMA

Neue Musikzeitung (jl.) Neue MZ, NMZ

Neue Zeitschrift für Musik (jl.) NeueZM, NZ, NZM, NZ Muzik,
  NZfM

Neues Beethoven-Jahrbuch (jl.) NBJb

Neues historisch-biographisches Lexikon der Tonkünstler (Ernst
  Ludwig Gerber) GerberNL, GerberNTL, NTL

New Composers' Federation / Shinko Sakkyoku Renmei SSR

New Grove Dictionary of Music and Musicians NG

New Music Distribution Service NMDS

New Oxford History of Music NOH, NOHM

New Thematic Catalog of the Works of Carl Philipp Emanuel Bach
  (Eugene Helm) H.

New York Philharmonic Orchestra NYPO

New Zealand Society for Music Education NZSME

New Zealand Society for Music Therapy NZSMT

Nineteenth-Century Music (jl.) NC, Nine Cen Mus, Nine Ct Mus,
  19th-c.M.

Noleggio (I=rental) N

Non divisi non div.

Non vibrato nv

Norddeutscher Rundfunk NDR

Nordic Association of Campanology / Nordisk Samfund for
  Campanologi NAC

Nordic Council for Music Conservatoires NCMC / Nordisk
  Konservatorierad NKR

Nordic Music Committee / Nordisk Musikkomite NOMUS

Nordisk Konservatorierad *see* Nordic Council for Music
Conservatoires

Nordisk Musikkomite *see* Nordic Music Committee

Nordisk Samfund for Campanologi *see* Nordic Association of
Campanology

Nordisk Verbane Musik Rad *see* Nordic Council for Railway Music

Nordiska Kor Kommitten NKK

Nordwestdeutscher Rundfunk (later, Westdeutscher Rundfunk)
NDR, NWDR, WDR

Normale (nota.) norm.

Norsk forening for komponister og tekstforfattere NOPA

Norsk Komponistforening *see* Norwegian Society of Composers

Norsk musikerblad (jl.) Norsk Mus

Norsk Musikerforbund / Norwegian Musicians Union NM

Norsk Musikinformasjon *see* Norwegian Music Information Centre

Norsk musiktidsskrift (jl.) NorskMt

Norske Symfoni-Orkestres Landsforbund NASOL

North American Brass Band Association NABBA

North American Guild of Change Ringers, NAGCR

North American Saxophone Alliance NASA

North American Singers Association NASA

Northeastern Sängerbund of America NOSB

Norton Anthology of Western Music NAWM

Norton Scores, The (Roger Kamien, ed.) NS

Norwegian Music Information Center NMIC / Norsk
Musikinformasjon NMI

Norwegian Musicians Union / Norsk Musikerforbund MFO, NM

Norwegian Singers Association of America NSAA

Norwegian Society of Composers / Norsk Komponistforening NKF

Notation not.

Notation der polyphonen Musik, 900-1600 (Willi Apel) ApelN

Notation of Polyphonic Music, 900-1600 (Willi Apel) ApelN, ApN,
ApNPM, NPM

Notazione (I=notation)　notaz.

Note (pitch) series　inversion of a, ni

Note cancrizans (retrograde of a note series)　nc

Note d'archivio per la storia musicale (jl.)　na, NA

Note series (pitch series in orig. version)　ns

Notenbeispiel, -e (G=musical example, -s)　NB

Nouveau style (F=new style)　n. st.

Nouvelle édition pratique (F=new performing edition)　nouv. éd. pr.

Nouvelle nouvelle revue française (jl.)　NNRF

Nouvelle revue française (jl.)　NRF

Novello & Co. (publ.)　N, Nov.

Novello Chorister Series　NCS

Novi styli　n. st.

Numus West (jl.)　Numus

Nunc dimittis　Nunc

Nuova Consonanza　NC

Nuova rivista musicale italiana (jl.)　nRMI, NRMI, Nuov Riv M,
　　　Nuova Riv M, Nuova RM Italiana, NuovaRMItaliana, R Mus Ital

Nutida musik (jl.)　NutidaM, NutidaMus

Obbligato (I) / *obligat* (F) / *Obligat* (G) / *obligado* (Sp)　obbl., obl.

Oberstimme (G=upper part)　Oberst.

Oberwerk (G=upper manual, part)　Oberw., Obw.

Obligado see obbligato

Obligat see obbligato

Oblong (rec. label)　obl.

Oboe　ob.

Oboe d'amore　ob. d'am.

Oboe da caccia　ob. da cac.

Obrecht, Jacob. *Werken* (Johannes Wolf, ed.)　Obr.

Octavo (L=eighth)　8°

Oeuvres choisies (F=selected works)　oeuv. ch.

Oeuvres complètes (F=complete works)　oeuv. compl.

Offertoriale sive versus offertoriorum cantus Gregoriani (Carolus Ott, ed.) OTT

Offertory, *offertorium* of., off., offert.

Offertory verse ofv

Officium hebdomadae sanctae et octavae Paschae OHS

Ohne Dämpfer (G=without mute, damper pedal) o.D.

Ohne Nummer (G=unnumbered) o. Nr.

Old style o.s.

Old Time Music (jl.) OTM

Oliver Ditson (publ.) D

Onderwys Diploma in Musiek, Stellenbosch, South Africa ODMS

Ongaku-geijutsu (jl.) Ongaku-gei

Oper und Konzert (jl.) Oper u Konzert

Opera (pl. of opus; L=works) opp.

Opera buffa op. buf.

Opera Canada (jl.) Opera Can

Opera Journal (jl.) OJ, Opera J

Opera News (jl.) Op, Opera N

Opéra comique op.-com.

Opera seria op. ser.

Optional opt.

Opus (L=work) op.

Opus musicum (Brno, Czech Rep.) (jl.) OM, OpusM, Opus mus

Opus posthumous op. post.

Oratorio, *oratorium* or., Or., orat.

Orbis musicae (jl.) Orbis mus

Orchesterbesetzung (G=orchestral scoring) Orch. Bes.

Orchestra / *orchestra* (I) / *Orchester* (G) / *orchestre* (F) orch.

Orchestra bells (G=Glockenspiel) orch. b.

Orchestra News (jl.) ON

Orchestral orch.

Orchestral Employers' Association OEA

Orchestrated (by) orchd.

Orchestre des jeunes de la Communaute européenne *see* European Community Youth Orchestra

Orff Institut. *Jahrbuch* (jl.)   Jb Orff Inst

Organ / *Orgel* (G) / *orgue* (F) / *organo* (I) / *órgano* (Sp)   org.

Organ Clearing House LLC   OCHLLC

Organ Historical Society   OHS

Organ Historical Trust of Australia   OHTA

Organ Institute of New South Wales. *Proceedings* (jl.)   ProcOrganInstNSW

Organ Literature Foundation   OLF

Organ Yearbook (jl.)   Organ Yb, OrganYB

Organist   orgt

Organiste liturgique (Gaston Litaize, ed.)   OLI

Organists' Review (jl.)   Organists R

Organization of American Kodaly Educators   OAKE

Organo, órgano *see* organ

Organology   organ.

Organum (Max Seiffert, *et al.*)   Orgm.

Organum   Orgm.

Orgel *see* Organ

Orgue *see* Organ

Orgue et liturgie (Norbert Dufourcq, *et al.*)   OL

Original (form of 12-tone row)   o

Orkester Journalen: tidskrift för jazzmusik (jl.)   Ork J

Ornament, ornamentation / *ornement* (F) / *ornamento* (I)   orn.

Österreichische Blasmusik   ÖsterreichBlasm

Österreichische Gesellschaft für Musik   OGM

Österreichische Gesellschaft für Musik. *Beiträge* (jl.)   Beiträge

Österreichische Gesellschaft für Musikwissenschaft *see* Austrian Association for Musicology

Österreichische Gesellschaft für Musikwissenschaft. *Mitteilungen* (jl.)   MittÖsterreichGesMw

Österreichische Musikzeitschrift (jl.)   OeMZ, Ömz, Öster. Musik.

Österreichischer Sängerbund *see* Austrian Choral Society

Ott, Carolus, ed. *Offertoriale sive versus offertoriorum cantus Gregoriani* Ott

Ottava (I=octave) 8a, 8va, ott.

Ottava alta 8va alta

Ottava bassa 8va bassa

Ottavino (I=piccolo flute) ott.

Ottavo (I=octave) 8.

Ouverture (F) / *Ouvertüre* (G) ouv.

Ovation (jl.) OV

Overture ov.

Oxford. Bodleian Library. Can. Pat. lat. 229 (ms.) PadA

Oxford. Bodleian Library. Lat. liturg. d. 5 (ms.) OxfB

Oxford. Bodleian Library. Lat. liturg. d.20 (ms.) WorcO

Oxford Anthology of Medieval Music (W. Thomas Marrocco) OMM

Oxford History of Music OH, OHM

Paléographie musicale Pal m, PalMus, PM

Palestrina, Giovanni Pierluigi da. *Werke* P, PaW

Pan Pipes of Sigma Alpha Iota (jl.) PP

Panorama de la musique et des instruments PanoramaMInstruments

Paris. Bibliothèque de l'Arsenal, ms. 135 ArsA

Paris. Bibliothèque nationale. Codex 903 *(Graduel de Saint-Yrieix)* facsim. (in *Paléographie musicale, 13*) SYG

Paris. Bibliothèque nationale. Lat. 3549 (ms.) St.M2

Parrish, Carl, ed. *Masterpieces of Music Before 1750* MM

Parrish, Carl. *Treasury of Early Music* TEM

Pars (L=part) p.

Part, parts pt., pts.

Partbook ptbk.

Partition (F=score) part.

Partitur (G=score) P., Part.

Partitura (I=score) pt

Partitura tascabile (I=miniature score, pocket score) ptt

Pastoral Music (jl.) PA, Pas mus

Pastoral Music Notebook (jl.) PAN

Patrologiae cursus completus, series graeca (Jacques-Paul Migne, ed.) Migne. Patr. gr., Patr. gr., PG

Patrologiae cursus completus, series latina (Jacques- Paul Migne, ed.) Migne. Patr., Patr. lat., PL

Pauken (G=kettledrums; timpani) Pk., Pkn.

Pausa p

Pedal p, ped.

Pedal Steel Guitar Association PSGA

Pédale (F) péd

Percussion (E, F) / *percusión* (Sp) / *percussione* (I) pc, perc.

Percussionist (jl.) PE

Percussive Arts Society PAS

Percussive Notes (jl.) Perc notes, PN

Perdendosi (I=dying away) perd.

Performance, performed (by) perf.

Performing and Visual Arts Society PAVAS

Performing Rights Organziation of Canada PRO Canada / Société de droits d'exécution du Canada SDE Canada

Performing Rights Society PRS

Perspectives of New Music (jl.) Pers New Mus, Persp N Mus, Perspectives, PNM

Peter McKee Music Co. (publ.) McKee

Peter Warlock Society PWS

Peters Notes PET

Peters, C.F. (publ.) CFP

Petit pt.

Philatelic Music Circle PMC

Philharmonic Phil

Philharmonic Orchestra PO

Pi Kappa Lambda PKL

Pianissimo (I=very soft) pno, pp

Pianississimo (I=extremely soft) ppp

Piano (I=soft) p

Piano, 4-hands / pianoforte 4 mani (I) pf4

Piano, pianoforte (the instrument) pa, pf., pno.

Piano Quarterly (jl.) PianoQ, Piano Quart, PQ

Piano Technician Guild PTG

Piano Technicians' Journal (jl.) PTJ

Piano Trade Suppliers' Association PTSA

Pianoforte pfte

Pianoforte Industries Export Group PIEG

Pianoforte Manufacturers' Association PMA

Pianoforte Manufacturers' Association International PMAI

Pianoforte Publicity Association PPA

Pianoforte Tuners' Association PTA

Piatto, piatti (I=cymbal, cymbals) pto, pti

Piccolo, pic, picc. / *Piccoloflöte* (G) / *piccolo flûte* (F) / *piccolo flauto* (I) pic. fl.

Pierpont Library, Cod. 396 Morg

Pillet, Alfred & H. Carstens. *Bibliographie der Troubadours* (identification number) PC, P-C

Pincherle, Marc. *Antonio Vivaldi et la musique instrumentale. v. 2. Inventaire thématique* P, P.-V.

Pirro, André, ed. *Archives des maîtres de l'orgue des XVIᵉ, XVIIᵉ, et XVIIIᵉ siècles* (Alexandre Guilmant et André Pirro, ed.) Guilmant-Pirro

Pitch class pc

Pizzicato (I=pinched, plucked) pizz.

Plainsong and Medieval Music Society PMMS

Player Piano Group PPG

Plica duplex pli-dx

Plica, plicata (I=ornamental passing tone) pli.

Poco forte, più forte pf

Poema sinfonico   p. sinf.

Point du Jazz, Le (jl.)   Point

Point of inversion   PI

Polish Music (jl.) / *Polnische musik*   Polish mus

Polish Music Centre   PMC / Polskie Centrum Muzyczne   PCM

Polish Music Council / Conseil polonais de la musique   PMC / Polskie Rada Muzyczna   PRM

Polish Music Publishers / Polskie Wydawnictwo Muzyczne   PWM

Polish Singers Alliance of America   PSAA

Polnische musik (jl.)   *see*   Polish Music (jl.)

Polski rocznik muzykologiczny   Pol. Rocznik Muzykol., PRM

Polskie Centrum Muzyczne   *see*   Polish Music Centre

Polskie Wydawnictwo Muzyczne   *see*   Polish Music Publishers

Polskie Wydawnictwo Naukowe   PWN

Polyphonic Music of the Fourteenth Century   PMFC, PMM, PMS

Ponticello (I=on the bridge)   pont.

Popular Music and Society (jl.)   Pop Mus & Soc, Pop Music S

Poradnik muzyczny (jl.)   PoradnikM

Portuguese Association of Music Education   PAME / Associação Portuguesa de Educação Musical   APEM

Portuguese Musical Youth Association / Juventude Musical Portuguesa   JMP

Portuguliae musicae   PM

Posaune (G=trombone)   Pos., Ps.

Positif (F=choir organ)   p, pos.

Positif-récit   p.r.

Position   pos.

Postumo   post.

Poussé (F=upstroke of a bow)   p.

Praelegenda (chant)   PRLG

Praetorius, Michael. *Werke*   PrW

Präpariertes Klavier (G=prepared piano)   präp. Kl.

Preces (chant)   PRCS

Preludio (I=prelude)   prel.

Prescrizioni (I=directions for playing)   prescr.

Prima I^{ma}

Prime (12-tone row in its original form at its original pitch)   p

Primo 1mo, 1°

Princeton Studies in Music   PSM

Principale   princ

Pro gratiarum actione   grat act

Processionale monasticum ad usum congregationis Gallicae   PM

Production Music Library Association   PMLA

Professional Women Singers Association   PWSA

Program, programme   progr.

Psallendi (chant)   PSLD

Psalmi (chant)   PSLM

Psalter / *psautier* (F)   ps.

Psychology of Music (jl.)   PsychologyM

Publications de la musique ancienne polonaise   PMAP

Publications of Medieval Music Manuscripts   PMMM

Publikationen älterer Musik   PäM, PÄM, PAM

Punctus additionis (nota.)   p.a.

Punctus divisionis (nota.)   p.d.

Quaderni della Rassegna musicale (jl.)   Quaderni della RaM

Quadrivium: rivista di filogia e musicologia medievale (jl.)   Quad

Quantz, Johann Joachim. *Versuch einer Anweisung die Flöte traversière zu spielen*   Quantz-Versuch

Quartet   4^{tet}, 4^{tte}, qt., Qt.

Quartette (G=quartets)   Qtte

Quartetto (I=quartet)   quart.

Quatuor (F=quartet)   quat.

Queen's Hall (London)   Q.H.

Quinta pars   5^{a}

Quintet   5^{tet}, 5^{tte}, qnt., Quintett, qnt, Qnt

Quintette (G=quintets)   Qntte
Quintetto (I=quintet)   quint.
Quinto   5.
Quintus (part, voice)   5

Radio Free Jazz (jl.)   RFJ
Radio Orchestra   RO
Radio Symphony Orchestra   RSO
Radiofonico (I)   radiof.
Radiophonique (F)   rad.
Ragtime Society   RS
Rallentando (I=becoming slower)   rall.
Rassegna gregoriana (jl.)   Rass. Greg.
Rassegna musicale Curci (jl.)   Rass mus Curci, RassegnaMCurci
Rassegna musicale, La (jl.)   LRM, RaM, RAM
Ratchet   ratch.
Raynaud, Gaston. *Bibliographie des altfranzösischen Liedes*   R
Real-Lexikon der Musikinstrumente (Curt Sachs)   SachsL, Sachs,
   SaRM
**"Real time machine" combining analog production and digital
   control of sounds, devised by SALvatore MARtirano, Josef
   Sekon, and others**   SAL-MAR
Recent Researches in the Music of the Baroque Era   RRMB,
   RRMBE
*Recent Researches in the Music of the Middle Ages and Early
   Renaissance*   RRMM
Recent Researches in the Music of the Renaissance   RRMR
Recherches sur la musique française classique   Recherches, RMFC
Rechts (G=right)   re.
Récit   r
Récitant   réc.
Recitative   r, recit.
Record Collectors' Club   RCC

Record Research (jl.)   Rec Res, RR

Record Review (jl.)   Rec R

Recorder and Music Magazine (jl.)   Recorder & Mus, RecorderMMagazine

Recording rcdg.

Recording Industry Association of America RIAA

Reduction, reduced red.

Réduction réd., réduit

Reed Organ Society ROS

Reese, Gustave. *Music in the Middle Ages* MMA, ReMMA

Reese, Gustave. *Music in the Renaissance* MR, ReMR

Reichsdenkmale (Das Erbe deutscher Musik, 1. Reihe) RD

Renaissance manuscript studies RMS

Répertoire Internationale d'Iconographie Musicale RIdIM / International Repertory of Musical Iconography / Internationales Repertorium der Musikikonographie

Répertoire populaire de la musique de la Renaissance (Henri Expert, ed.) ExRP

Repertorio rep

Repertorium hymnologicum (Ulysse Chevalier) Chev

Reprise repr.

Research Center for Musical Iconography RCMI

Resources of American Music History (Don W. Krummel) RAMH

Responds (chant) RS

Response r

Responsory / responsorium r, resp.

Responsory, great re

Retail Print Music Dealers Association RPMDA

Retrograde r

Retrograde inversion ri

Reunion of Professional Entertainers ROPE

Revista Brasileira de Música (jl.) Rev. Bras. de Música

Revista de música latinoamericana *see Latin American Music*

Review

Revista musical chilena (jl.)   Rev. Mus. Chilena, RMChilena, R Mus
    Chile

Revolutions per minute   rpm

Revue belge de musicologie / *Belgisch Tijdschrift voor muziek-*
    wetenschap / *Belgian Review of Musicology* (jl.)   RB, R Belge
    Mus, RBelgeMusicol, RBM, RBMie

Revue d'histoire et de critique musicales (jl.; later, *La revue musicale*)
    RHCM, RMC

Revue de musicologie (jl.)   R de Mus, RdM, Rev music, Rev. de
    musicol, RMusicol, RMie, RMl

Revue du chant grégorien (jl.)   RCG, RCGrég

Revue et gazette musicale de Paris (jl.)   RGMP

Revue grégorienne (jl.)   RG

Revue internationale de musique (jl.)   Rev. Internat. Mus., RIM

Revue musicale de Suisse romande (jl.)   RMSuisseRomande, R Mus
    de Suisse Romande

Revue musicale, La (jl.; earlier, *Revue d'histoire et de critique*
    musicales)   ReM, Rev musicale, RM, RMC, R Mus

Revue musicale S.I.M. (jl.)   RSIM

Revue musicale suisse (jl.)   RMS, RMSuisse / *Schweizerische*
    Musikzeitung   SMz, Schw Musikz, Schweiz Mus

Rezitativ (G=recitative)   Rez.

Rhythm of Twelfth-Century Polyphony (William G. Waite)   RTP

Ricordi (publ.)   R, Ric.

Riduzione (I=reduction), ridotto (I=reduced)   rid.

Riemann, Hugo. *Handbuch der Musikgeschichte*   RiemannH,
    Riemann HdM, RiHM

Riemann, Hugo. *Musikgeschichte in Beispielen*   RiemannB, Riemann
    Beisp, RiMB

Riemann Musik Lexikon   RiemannL

Right arm   RA

Right channel (tape)   r.c.

Right hand   r.h.

Rim (of perc. instrument) r

Rimshot r.s.

Rinaldi, Mario. *Catalogo numerico tematico delle composizione di Antonio Vivaldi* R, Rin

Rinforzando (I=suddenly louder) rf., rfz.

Ripieno r, rip.

Rise of Music in the Ancient World (Curt Sachs) RMAW

Ritardando (I=becoming slower) rit.

Ritenuto (I=suddenly and extremely slower) rit.

Rivista italiana di musicologia (jl.) RIM, R Ital Mus, RItalianaMusicol

Rivista musicale italiana (jl.) Riv Mus Italiana, RMI

Rochester Philharmonic Orchestra RPO

Rocznik Chopinowski (jl.) / *Annales Chopin* AnChopin

Royal Academy of Music RAM

Royal Canadian College of Organists RCCO

Royal Choral Association RCA

Royal Choral Society RCS

Royal College of Music R.C.M.

Royal College of Music Magazine (jl.) RCM

Royal College of Organists RCO

Royal Conservatory of Music, Toronto RCMT

Royal Festival Hall, London RFH

Royal Irish Academy of Music RIAM

Royal Liverpool Philharmonic Orchestra RLPO

Royal Manchester College of Music RMCM

Royal Manchester School of Music RMSM

Royal Military School of Music RMSC

Royal Music Association. *Proceedings* Proc. R. Mus. Assoc.

Royal Musical Association RMA

Royal Musical Association. *Proceedings* PMA, PRMA, Proc. R. Mus, Ass., ProcRoyalMAssoc, P Roy Music, RMA

Royal Musical Association. *RMA Research Chronicle* RMARC,

RMA Research, RMAResearchChron
Royal Northern College of Music RNCM
Royal Philharmonic Orchestra RPO
Royal Philharmonic Society RPS
Royal School of Church Music RSCM
Royal Scottish Academy of Music and Drama RSAMD
Royal Scottish National Orchestra (formerly, Scottish National Orchestra) RSNO
Royal Society of Musicians of Great Britain RSM, RSMGB
Ruch muzyczny (jl.) RuchM, Ruch muz
Rural Music Schools Association RMSA
Russkaya muzikal'naya gazeta (jl.) RMG
Ryom, Peter. *Répertoire des oeuvres d'Antonio Vivaldi* / Verzeichnis der Werke Antonio Vivaldis RV

Sachs, Curt. *Handbuch der Musikinstrumentenkunde* SachsH, SachsHdb.
Sachs, Curt. *History of Musical Instruments* SaHMI
Sachs, Curt. *Real-Lexikon der Musikinstrumente* SachsL, Sachs R
Sachs, Curt. *Rise of Music in the Ancient World* RMAW
Sacred Music (jl.) SM
Sacrificia (chant) SCR
Sadler's Wells (London) SW
Samfundet til Udgivelse af Dansk Musik *see* Society for the Publication of Danish Music
Sammelbände für vergleichende Musikwissenschaft SfVMw
Sammelwerk (G=collected works) Swk.
Sammlung musikwissenschaftlicher Abhandlungen / Collection d'études musicologiques SMwAbh
Samrådet for Nordisk Amatørmusik SamNam
San Francisco Opera (jl.) San Fran Opera
Sandpaper blocks sandp. bl.
Sänger- und Musikantenzeitung (jl.) SängerMusikantenZ

Sartori, Claudio. *Bibliografia della musica strumentale italiana stampata* . . . SartoriB

Satzdauer (G=phrase length) SD

Savez kompizitora Jugoslavije *see* Yugoslavian Composers' Association

Savez muzičkih društava *see* League of Music Societies (Yugo.)

Saxophone / *sassofono* (I) sax

Saxophone Journal (jl.) SJ

Schallplatte und Kirche (jl.) (includes *Musik und Kirche*, q.v.) Schallplatte u Kir

Schering, Arnold. *Geschichte der Musik in Bayern* GMB

Schering, Arnold. *Geschichte der Musik in Beispielen* GM, Schering Beisp, SchGMB, ScheringB

Schilling, Gustav. *Encyclopädie der gesammten musikalischen Wissenschaften* SchillingE

Schirmer, E. C. (publ.) ECS

Schirmer, G. (publ.) GS

Schlager, Karlheinz, ed. Alleluia-Melodien I (*Monumenta monodica medii aevi, 7*) MMMA

Schlaginstrumente (G=percussion instruments) Schl. Instr.

Schlagzeug (G=percussion) Schl., Sz.

Schmidl, Carlo. *Dizionario dei musicisti* SchmidlD

Schmidl, Carlo. *Dizionario dei musicisti. Supplement* SchmidlDS

Schmieder, Wolfgang. *Thematisch-systematisches Verzeichnis der musikalischen Werke von J. S. Bach* S.

Schneider, Herbert. *Chronologisch-thematisches Verzeichnis sämtlicher Werke von Jean-Baptiste Lully* LWV

School Musician, Director, and Teacher (jl.) School Mus, SCM, SMDTB

Schools Music Association SMA

Schrade, Leo, ed. *Francesco Landini. Works* (*Polyphonic Music of the Fourteenth Century, v. 4*) SchL

Schubert, Franz. *Werke* SbW

Schuh, Willi, ed. *Dictionnaire des musiciens suisses* DMS /

Schweizer Musiker-Lexikon   SML

Schumann, Robert. *Werke*   SmW

Schütz, Heinrich. *Heinrich Schütz-Werke-Verzeichnis* (Werner Bittinger, ed.)   S.W.V.

Schütz, Heinrich. *Sämtliche Werke*   ScW

Schweizer Musikbuch   SMb

Schweizer Musiker Lexikon (Willi Schuh, ed.)   SML

Schweizer Musikpädagogische Blätter   SMZ

Schweizerische Chorvereinigung   SCV / Union suisse des chorales USC

Schweizerische Musikdenkmäler   SMd

Schweizerische Musikforschende Gesellschaft. *Mitteilungsblatt* (jl.)   MittSchweizMfGes

Schweizerische Musikforschende Gesellschaft. *Publikationen* PSMfG

Schweizerische Musikzeitung (jl.)   *see Revue musicale suisse*

Schweizerische Vereinigung der Musiklehrerinnen und Musiklehrer an den Mittelschulen *see* Swiss Society of Music Teachers in Secondary Schools

Schweizerischer Tonkünstlerverein *see* Swiss Musicians' Association

Schweizerisches Jahrbuch für Musikswissenschaft (jl.)   SJ, SJbMw

Score   sc

Scottish Amateur Music Association   SAMA

Scottish National Orchestra (now, Royal Scottish National Orchestra) RSNO, SNO

Scottish Pipe Band Association   SPBA

Screen Composers of America   SCA

Scriptores ecclesiastici de musica sacra potissimum (Martin Gerbert) GerbertS, GS

Scriptorum de musica medii aevi. Nova series (Charles Edmond Henri Coussemaker)   CousseS, Coussemaker Scr, CS

Second Line (jl.)   Sec

Seconda, secondo 2da, 2do, 2°

Seeger, Horst. *Musiklexikon* SeegerL
Segno (I=sign) s.
Seiffert, Max, *et al. Organum* Orgm.
Selmer's Bandwagon (jl.) SB
Semibreve (nota.) sb
Semibrevis (nota.) s, sbr.
Semifusa (nota.) sf
Semiminum (nota.) sm
Senza interruzione s. int.
Senza sordino (I=without mute) s.s.
Senza tempo s.t.
Senza vibrato s.v.
Septet 7^{tt}
Septima pars 7^{a}
Sequence, seq / *Sequenz* (G) Seq.
Sestetto (I=sextet) sest.
Sesto 6.
Settimo 7.
Sexta pars 6a
Sextet, *sestet* 6^{tet}, 6^{tt}
Sforzato (I=forced) sf, sfz
Sforzato piano sfp, sfz. p.
Sharp sh
Shellac Stack (jl.) shellac
Shinko Sakkyoku Renmei *see* New Composers' Federation
Short responsory sr
Sigma Alpha Iota SAI
Signum congruentiae (nota.) s.c.
Simplex, simplices (nota.) si
Sine perfectione (nota.) sp
Sine proprietate (nota.) spr
Sinfonia, sinfonico sinf.
Sing Out! (jl.) SI

Singende Kirche Sing Kir

Singstimme (G=singing voice) S., Sgst., Singst.

Sinistra (I=left) s., sin.

Sir Thomas Beecham Society TBS

Sistrum sist.

Sizzle cymbal sizz. cym.

Školska Knijiga (Zagreb) (publ.) SK

Sleigh bells sl. bells

Slidewhistle, slide whistle sl. whistle

Sloejd och Ton (jl.) SoT

Slovak Music (jl.) Slovak Mus

Slovenská hudba SH, SlovenskáHud

Słownik muzyków polskich SMP

Smith College Music Archives SCMA

Smorzando (I=fading away) smorz.

Snare drum s.d.

Snares off sn. off

Sociedad Uruguaya de Música Contemporánea *see* International Society for Uruguayan Music

Società internazionale di musica contemporanea *see* International Society for Contemporary Music

Société belge de musicologie *see* Belgian Society of Musicology

Société canadienne de musique folklorique *see* Canadian Society of Folk Music

Société canadienne pour les traditions musicales *see* Canadian Society for Musical Traditions

Société de droits d'exécution du Canada *see* Performing Rights Organization of Canada

Société de musique des universites canadiennes *see* Canadian University Music Society

Société des auteurs, compositeurs et éditeurs de musique SACEM

Société française de musicologie *see* French Society of Musicology

Société française de musicologie. *Publications* *see* French Society of Musicology. *Publications*

Société française de musicologie. *Rapports et communications* see French Society of Musicology. *Rapports et communications*

Société internationale de musique *see also* International Musicological Society

Société internationale de musique. *Bulletin français* (jl.)   BSIM, BullSIM

Société internationale de musique revue   RSIM, SIM

Société Internationale des Bibliothèques et des Musées des Arts du Spectacle *see* International Association of Libraries and Museums of the Performing Arts

Société Internationale Kodály *see* International Kodály Society

Société internationale pour l'éducation musicale *see* International Society for Music Education

Société internationale pour la musique contemporaine *see* International Society for Contemporary Music

Société Johann Sebastian Bach de Belgique. *Bulletin* (jl.) BulSocBachBelgique

Société suisse de musicologie   SSM

Société suisse de pédagogie musicale   SSPM

Society for Asian Music   SAM

Society for Commissioning New Music   SCNM

Society for Electro-Acoustic Music in the United States   SEAMUS

Society for Ethnomusicology   SEM

Society for General Music   SGM

Society for Music Teachers Education   SMTE

Society for Music Theory   SMT

Society for Self-Playing Musical Instruments / Gesellschaft für Selbstspielende Musikinstrumente   GSM

Society for Strings   SS

Society for the Classic Guitar   SCG

Society for the Preservation and Advancement of the Harmonica SPAH

Society for the Preservation and Encouragement of Barber Shop Quartet Singing in America   SPEBSQSA

Society for the Promotion of Indian Music and Culture Amongst Youth SPICMACAY

Society for the Promotion of New Music SPNM

Society for the Publication of American Music SPAM

Society for the Publication of Danish Music SPDM / Samfundet til Udgivelse af Dansk Musik SUDM

Society for Traditional Music STM

Society of Composers, Authors and Music Publishers of Canada SOCAN

Society of Composers, Inc. SCI

Society of European Stage Authors and Composers SESAC

Society of Icelandic Composers SIC / Tonskaldafelag Islands TÍ

Society of Norwegian Authors of Popular Music SNAPM

Society of Slovene Composers SSC / Društvo Slovenskih Skladateljev DSS

Society of Swedish Composers SSC / Föreningen Svenska Tonsättare FST

Society of Women Musicians SWM

Solfège (F) / *solfeggio* (I) solf.

Solo s.

Sonata son.

Sonate per violino di Giuseppe Tartini (Paul Brainard) B.

Songwriter's Review (jl.) Songwriters R, SR

Songwriters and Lyricists Club SLC

Sonic Arts Network SAN

Sonneck Society SS

Sopran (G=soprano) Sp.

Soprano s., sop., sopr.

Soprano leggiero sl

Sordino, sordini (I=mute(s)) sord.

Sostenuto (I=sustained) sost.

Sound, Harmony, Melody, Rhythm, Growth (analytical system set forth by Jan La Rue) SHMRG

Sounding Brass and the Conductor (jl.) Sound Brass

Source Readings in Music History (Oliver Strunk) SR, SRA, SRB, SRC, SSR

South African College of Music SACM

South African Music Encyclopedia SAME

South African Music Teacher (jl.) SAMT, SA Mus Tcr

South African Society of Music Teachers SASMT

Southeastern Composers' League SCL

Southern Appalachian Dulcimer Association SADA

Southern Rag (jl.; later, *fRoots*) South Rag

Sovetskaia muzyka (jl.) SM, Sovet Muz, SovetskajaM, SovM

Soviet Composer Publishers / Izdatyelstvo "Sovyetskii kompositor" SC

Spain. Consejo Superior de Investigaciones Cientificas. Instituto Español de musicologia IEM

Spettatore musicale, Lo (jl.) SpettatoreM

Spiccato (I=rebounding off the string) spic, spicc.

Spitze (G=point) Sp.

Sprecher (G=speaker) Spr.

Squarcialupi Codex **(Florence. Biblioteca Mediceo-Laurenziana. Pal. 87)** Sq.

Stäblein, Bruno, ed. *Hymnen (I): Die mittelalterlichen Hymnenmelodien des Abendlandes* (*Monumenta monodica medii aevi, 1*) ST

Stabspiel Stsp.

Staccato stacc.

Stainer and Bell (publ.) SB

Stanza st.

State Publishers of Literature, Art & Music, Prague / Státni Nakladatelstvi Krásné Literatury, Hudby a Umĕní SNKLHU

Státní Nakladatelstvi Krásné Literatury Hudby a Umĕní *see* State Publishers for Literature, Art & Music, Prague

Steirisches Tonkünstlerbund. *Mitteilungen* (jl.) MittSteirTonkünstlerbundes

Stereo (jl.)   ST

Stereo Review (jl.)   StereoR, Stereo R, STR

Stimmbuch (G=partbook)   Stb.

Stimme (G=separate voice, part); Stimmen (G=voices, parts)   St.

Stimmig, as in 4stg. (G=voiced, e.g., 4-voiced)   stg.

Stimmigen, as in 4stg. (G=voiced, e.g., 4-voiced)   stgn.

Stopped diapason   st. diap.

Storyville (jl.)   story

Streich, -er (G=string, strings)   Str.

Streichorchester (G=string orchestra)   Streichor.

Streichquartett (G=string quartet)   StrQu

Stressed vibrato   sv

String (-s)   str.

String Education Quarterly (jl.)   SEQ

String quartet   str. qt.

String quartet / *Streichquartett* (G)   Strqua

String quintet / *Streichquintett* (G)   Strqui

Stringendo   string.

Strophe   Str.

Strumentale (I=instrumental)   strum.

Strumenti a corda (I=stringed instruments)   corda

Strumenti a fiato (I=wind instruments)   fiati

Strumenti a fiato di legno (I=woodwind instruments)   legni

Strumenti a fiato di ottoni (I=brass instruments)   ottoni

Strumenti a tastiera (I=keyboard instruments)   tasto

Strumenti ad ancia doppia (I=double reed instruments)   ancia d.

Strumenti ad arco (I=bowed stringed instruments)   archi

Strumento (I=instrument)   str.

Strunk, Oliver. *Source Readings in Music History*   SR, SRA, SRB, SRC

Studi musicali (Florence) (jl.)   StudiM

Studia musicologica (Budapest) (jl.)   StMl, Stu Mus, Studia Mus, StudMusicol

Studia musicologica academiae scientiarum hungaricae (jl.) SM

Studia musicologica norvegica (jl.) SMN, Studia Mus Nor, Stud-MusicolNorvegica

Studie Stud.

Studien zur Musikwissenschaft (jl.) SMw, St z M, StM, StMw, STMW, StuMw

Studies in Eastern Chant (jl.) SEC

Studies in Music (London, Ont.) StudM [CND]

Studies in Music (Nedlands, Australia) SMA, Studies Mus, StudM [AUS]

Studii de muzicologie (Bucharest) StudMuzicol

Studii și cercetări de istoria artei (jl.) StudCercetăriIstoriaArtei

Study Scores of Musical Styles (Edward R. Lerner) LSS

Stuttgart. Landesbibliothek. I Asc. 95 (ms.) Stutt

Subdominant (Roman numeral) IV

Subito (I=suddenly) s

Subject s

Submediant (Roman numeral) VI

Subtonic, leading tone (Roman numeral) VII

Süddeutsche Orgelmeister des Barock SOB

Süddeutscher Musikverlag (publ.) SM

Süddeutscher Rundfunk SDR

Sul ponticello (I=on the bridge) pont., pt, s.p.

Sul tasto (I=over the fingerboard) ST, t

Summa musicae medii aevi (Friedrich Gennrich, ed.) SMM, SMMA

Suñol, Gregoire Marie. *Introduction à la paléographie musicale* IPM

Suomen Laulajain ja Soittajain Liitto *see* Finnish Amateur Musicians' Association

Suomen Musiikkioppilaitosten Liitto *see* Association of Finnish Music Schools

Superius s., sup.

Supertonic (Roman numeral) ii

Suspended cymbal   s. cym.

Suvini Zerboni (publ.)   SZ

Suzuki Association of the Americas   SAA

Suzuki World (jl.)   SU

Svensk tidskrift för musikforskning   STMf, Sven Tids M, Svensk Tid, SvenskTMf

Svenska Musikförläggarföreningen   *see* Swedish Music Publishers Association

Svenska Tonsättares Internationella Musikbyrå   *see* Swedish Society of Composers and Publishers

Svenskt musikhistoriskt arkiv. *Bulletin* (jl.)   SvensktMHistoriskt-ArkivBul

Sveriges Orkesterforeningars Riksforbund   *see* Association of Swedish Symphony Orchestras

Swedish Independent Music Producers Organisation   SOM

Swedish Music Publishers Association   SMPA / Svensk Musikförläggare Föreningen   SMFF

Swedish Society for Musicology   SSM

Swedish Society of Composers and Publishers   SSCP / Svenska Tonsättares Internationella Musikbyrå   STIM

Swedish Society of Popular Music Composers   SSPMC / Föreningen Svenska Kompositörer av Populärmusik   SKAP

Sweelinck, Jan P. *Werke*   SwW

Swell organ   sw.

Swingtime: maandblad voor jazz en blues (jl.)   Swingt.

Swiss Association for Music Education   SMPV

Swiss Federation of Choirs   SFC

Swiss Music Council   SMC / Conseil suisse de la musique   CSM

Swiss Musicians' Association   SMA / Association des musiciens suisses   AMS / Schweizerischer Tonkünstlerverein   STV

Swiss Society of Music Teachers in Secondary Schools   SSMT / Schweizerische Vereinigung der Musiklehrerinnen und Musiklehrer an den Mittelschulen   SVMM

Swiss Tuba and Baritone Association   STUBA

Symphony orchestra so
Symphony, symphonic sym.
Symphony Magazine (jl.) Sym mag
Symphony News (jl.) Sym news
Symphony Nova Scotia SNS
Synchronize, synchronization synch.
Synthesizer synth.
System, *Systeme* (G=staff, staves) Syst.

Tablature (E, F) / *Tablatur* (G) Tab.
Tagliapietra, G., ed. *Antologia di musica . . . per pianoforte* TaAM
Tambour (F) / *tamburo* (I) / *tambor* (Sp) = drum, kettledrum tamb.
Tambourine tamb.
Tamburo (I) / tambour (F) / tambor (Sp) = drum, kettledrum, tamb. tm
Tamtam(s) tam. t., t.ts.
Tasteninstrumente (G=keyboard instruments) Tast. Instr.
Tasto (I=keyboard) t.
Tasto solo t.s., T.S., T.s.
Te Deum TeD
Teil, -e (G=part, -s) Tl., Tle.
Telemann-Werke-Verzeichnis T.W.V.
Tempo (jl.) TE
Temple block t.b., temp. bl.
Tempo primo tem. I°
Tempora t
Tempus t
Tenor (E, G) / *ténor* (F) / *tenore* (I) t, ten., tnr.
Tenor drum t.d., ten. dr.
Tenore see tenor
Tenuto (I=sustained) ten.
Tesoro sacro musical TesoroSacroM
Theil (G=part [Teil]) Th.
Thematisch-systematisches Verzeichnis der musikalisches Werke von

J. S. Bach (Wolfgang Schmieder) S.

Thematisches Verzeichnis der Werke von Carl Philipp Emanuel Bach (Alfred Wotquenne) Wq

Theme th.

Théorie musicale théorie de la musique, th. mus.

Thesauri musici TM

Thompson, Gordon V. (publ.) GVT

Threni (chant) TRN

Tief (G=low) t.

Timbales timb.

Timpani (I=kettledrums) timp., tp., tpi.

Tiré (F=downbow) t.

Tom-tom(s) / *tomtom* (Sp) tomt., t.t.

Tonic t.

Tonphysiologie (G=physiology of music) Tonphys.

Tonpsychologie (G=psychology of music) Tonpsych.

Tonskaldafelag Islands *see* Society of Icelandic Composers

Tonus irregularis (church mode) ir

Tonus perigrinus (church mode) tp

Torchi, Luigi, ed. *L'arte musicale in Italia* Torchi

Toronto. Conservatory of Music. *Quarterly Review* (jl.) CQR

Total harmonic distortion (acoustics) thd, THD

Towarzystwo imienia Fryderyka Chopina *see* Frederic Chopin Society

Tôyô ongaku kenkyû (jl.) Tôyô ongaku

Tract / *tractus* tr, tract.

Traditional Irish Singing and Dancing Society / Comhaltas Ceoltóiri Éireann CCE

Traditional Japanese Music Society TJMS

Traditional Music (jl.) Trad mus

Transcontinental Music Publishing Co. (publ.) TMP

Transcription committed to one of a number of rhythmic interpretations (nota.) Rh

Transcription in square note-symbols that are not diplomatic, without rhythmic value (nota.) Sq

Transcription(s) transc, transcc

Transponiere (G=transpose) transpon.

Transponieren (G=to transpose) transpon.

Transpose tr.

Transposed / *transponiert* (G) transp.

Transposed inversion of 12-tone row it, IT

Transposed original form of 12-tone row ot, OT

Transposed retrograde inversion of 12-tone row rit, RIT, rt

Transposition transpos.

Trascrizione trascr.

Tre corde t.c.

Treasury of Early Music (Carl Parrish) TEM

Treble tr.

Tremolo trem.

Tri-M Music Honor Society TRI-M

Triad (jl.) TR

Triangle trg., tri.

Triangle of Mu Phi Epsilon (jl.) Triangle

Tribune de l'orgue (jl.) Tribune orgue

Tribune de Saint-Gervais TG, TribSTG

Tribune internationale des jeunes interprètes *see* International Rostrum of Young Performers

Tribune musical (Buenos Aires) (jl.) Trib mus

Trill tr.

Trio 3°

Tripartite form ABA

Triplum tripl.

Tromba (I=trumpet) tr., trb.

Tromba, -e (I=trumpet, trumpets) Tr., trbe., tromb.

Trombone (E, F, I) / *trombón* (Sp) tb., trb., trbn., trmb., tromb.

Trommel (G=drum) Tr.

Trompete (G) / *trompette* (F) = trumpet   Trp., trp.

Tropus   trope, tr.

Troubadour   tb

Trouvère   tv

Trumpet   trp.

Tuba   ta, tb., tba.

Tubists Universal Brotherhood Association   T.U.B.A.

Tudor Church Music (jl.)   TCM

Tutti   t.

Übertragung (G=transcription)   Ue.

Udruženje kompizotora Bosne i Hercegovine   *see*   Association of Composers of Bosnia and Herzegovina

Udruženje kompizotora Hrvatske   *see*   Association of Croatian Composers

Udruženje kompizotora Makedonije   *see*   Association of Macedonian Composers

Una corda   u.c., U.C.

Unaccompanied   unac, unacc.

Undesignated instrument   I

Unge Tonekunstnerselskab, Det   DUT

Union des compositeurs belges   *see*   Union of Belgian Composers

Union Musical Española   UME

Union musicologique. *Bulletin* (jl.)   Bull., BUM

Union of Belgian Composers   UBC / Union des compositeurs belges UCB / Unie van Belgische Componisten   UBC

Union of Bulgarian Composers   UBC

Union of Lapp Composers / Foreningen Samiske Komponister   FSK

Union of Polish Composers   UPC

Union suisse des chorales   *see*   Schweizerische Chorvereinigung

Unisono (I=unison)   unis.

United in Group Harmony Association   UGHA

U.S. Scottish Fiddling Revival   SFIRE

Universal Edition (publ.)   U, UE
University Accompanists' Licentiate in Music   UALM
University of California Publications in Music   UCPM
University of California Series of Early Music   SEM
University of Pennsylvania Choral Series   UPC
University Performers' Licentiate in Music   UPLM
University Teachers' Licentiate in Music   UTLM
Unterstimme (G=lower part)   Unterst.
Uraufführung (G=first performance)   UA
Urban Federation of Music Therapy   *see*   American Music Therapy
   Association

Vandenhoeck & Rupprecht (publ.)   V & R
Varia (chant)   VAR
Variae preces ex liturgia tum hodierna tum antiqua collectae aut usu
   receptae (chant)   VP
Variant   var.
Variazione (I=variation)   var.
VEB Deutscher Verlag für Musik (publ.)   DVfM, DVFM, DVM
Verband Deutscher Konzertchöre / German Society of Concert
   Choirs   VDKC
Verband Deutscher Schulmusiker   *see*   German Society of School
   Music Educators
Verdi Newsletter (jl.)   VerdiNewsl
Vereniging van Muziekhandelaren en -uitgevens Nederland   *see*
   Association of Music Dealers and Publishers in the Netherlands
Vereniging voor nederlandse muziekgeschiedenis   *see*   Association
   for Dutch Music History
Vereniging voor nederlandse muziekgeschiedenis. *Tijdschrift* (jl.)
   (formerly the Society's *Bouwsteenen*; formerly *Vereniging voor*
   Noord-Nederlands muziekgeschiedenis)   TMw, TV, TVer, TVMN,
   TVerNederlandseMg
Vereniging voor nederlandse muziekgeschiedenis. *Uitgaven* (jl.)
   UVM, UVNM

Vereniging voor Noord-nederlands muziekgeschiedenis. *Tijdschrift* (jl.) TV

Vergleichende Musikforschung (G=comparative musicology) Vgl. Mf.

Verlag Neue Musik (publ.) VNM

Verse of great responsory rev

Verse, *versicle* v

Verses (chant) VR

Versicle vcle

Versione organistica + solo (I=orchestral parts reduced for organ; organ reduction) vo

Versione pianistica + solo (I=orchestral parts reduced for piano; piano reduction) vp

Versuch einer Anweisung die Flöte traversière zu spielen (Johann Joachim Quantz) Quantz-Versuch

Versus (chant) VRS

Verte (F=turn over [the page]) v.

Very fast f, F

Very slow s

Vespers / *vesperae* Vesp.

Vespertini (chant) VPR

Vibraphone / *vibrafono* (I) vb, vib., vibes, vibr.

Vibrations per second vbs

Vibrato vib.

Vibrato lento (I=slow vibrato) v.l.

Vibrato normale (I=normal vibrato) vn

Vibrato rapido (I=rapid vibrato) vr

Victoria, Thomas L. *Opera omnia* ViW

Vie musicale (Canada) (jl.) VieM

Viella vie

Vierstimmig (G=4 pts., 4 voices) vierst.

Vierteljahrsschrift für Musikwissenschaft (jl.) VfMw, VFMW, Vmw, VMW

Villa-Lobos Music Society VLMS
Vinton, John, ed. *Dictionary of Contemporary Music* DCM
Viol (jl.) VI
Viola va.
Viola d'amore viola, vla d'a
Viola da braccio vab
Viola da gamba va da gba, vag
Viola d'Amore Society VDS
Viola d'Amore Society of America VdASA, VDSA
Viola da Gamba Society of America vdgsa, VdGSA
Viola da Gamba Society of America. *Journal* (jl.) vdgsa, VdGSA
Viole vle.
Violin / violon (F) / *violino* (I) / *Violine* (G) / *violín* (Sp) v.
Violin Society of America VSA
Violin Society of America. *Journal* (jl.) JV, J Violin S, J Violin Soc
   Amer, VSA
Violin(s) vio
Violini (I=violins) vni
Violini primi v^1
Violini secondi v^2
Violino vo
Violins vv.
Violon (F=violin) vlon
Violoncelle (F=violoncello) vcelle
Violoncelli celli
Violoncello / *violoncelle* (F) / *violonchelo* (Sp) vc., vcl., vlc.
Violoncello Society VS
Violone vle.
Virtuoso (jl.) VIR
Vivace viv.
Vlaams Muziektijdschrift (jl.) VlaamsMT
Vocal / *vocale* (I) voc.
Voce media (I=middle voice) vm

Voce recitante (I=reciting voice)   vr

Voce sola   v.s.

Voci (I=voices)   v.

Vogel, Emil. *Bibliothek der gedruckten weltlichen Vokalmusik Italiens . . .*   VogelB

Voice: The Magazine of Vocal Music (jl.)   VO, Voice

Voix (F=voice)   v.

Vokal   vok.

Volksmusik   Volksm

Voltage-controlled amplifier   VCA

Voltage-controlled filter   VCF

Voltage-controlled oscillator   VCO

Volti subito (I=turn the page quickly)   v.s.

Vox (L=voice)   v.

Waite, William. *The Rhythm of Twelfth-Century Polyphony*   RTP

Walther, Hans, ed. *Carmina medii aevi posterioris Latina I/I*   CMA

Walther, Johann Gottfried. *Musicalisches Lexikon oder Musicalische Bibliothec*   WaltherL, WaltherML

Wellesley Edition   WE

Wellesley Edition Cantata Index Series   WECIS

Welsh Music (jl.)   WelshM

Welsh National Opera Company   WNOC

Werke ohne Opuszahl (G=works without opus number)   WoO, W.o.O.

Westdeutscher Rundfunk (formerly Nordwestdeutscher Rundfunk)   WDR

Western International Music Co. (publ.)   WIM

Western Music Association   WMA

Willem Mengelberg Society   WMS

Wind chimes   w. chimes

Wind Quarterly (jl.)   WQ

With snare   w.s., w. snare

Wolf, Johannes. *Geschichte der Mensural-Notation von 1250-1460*

GdM, WoG, WolfM, WoGM

Wolf, Johannes. *Handbuch der Notationskunde* HdN, WoH, WoHN, WolfN

Wolf, Johannes, ed. *Music of Earlier Times* MET, WM

Wolf, Johannes, ed. *Obrecht, Jacob.* *Werken* Obr.

Wolfenbüttel. Herzog-August-Bibliothek. Mss (677 (Helms. 628)) (medieval ms.) W^1

Wolfenbüttel. Herzog-August-Bibliothek. Mss (1099 (Helms. 1206)) (medieval ms.) W^2

Wolkenstein-Codes (Innsbruck. Universitätsbibliothek) WoB

Women Band Directors International WBDI

Women's Association for Symphony Orchestras WASO

Wood block(s) w.b.

Woodwind ww

Woodwind quintet ww quin

Woodwind World — Brass and Percussion (jl.; later, *Woodwind, Brass and Percussion*; earlier, *Brass and Percussion*) WBP, Wood World Brass, Woodwind W, WWBDA

Wooldridge, Harry Ellis, ed. *Early English Harmony from the 10th to the 15th Century* EEH

Worcester. Cathedral Library. Additional 68 (ms.) Worc.

Worcester. Cathedral Library. Codex F. 160. facsimile (*Paleographie musicale*, 12) WA

Workers' Music Association WMA

World Federation of International Music Competitions WFIMC / Fédération mondiale des concours internationaux de musique FMCIM

World Folk Music Association WFMA

World Library of Sacred Music WLSM

World of Music WorldM, World Mus, World Music

World of Opera WO

Wotquenne, Alfred. *Catalogue thématique de l'oeuvre de Carl Philipp Emanuel Bach* Wotq.

Wotquenne, Alfred. *Thematisches Verzeichnis der Werke von Carl Philipp Emanuel Bach* Wq

Württembergische Blätter für Kirchenmusik WürttembergBlätterKm

Wychowanie muzyczne w szkole WychowanieMSzkole

Wydawnictwo dawnej muzyki polskiej WDMP

Xilofono (I=xylophone) xil.

Xylophone xyl.

Yearbook for Inter-American Musical Research (jl.), YbInterAmer-MResearch

Young Concert Artists YCA

Young Musicians' Foundation YMF

Yugoslavian Composers' Association / Savez kompozitora Jugoslavije SAKOJ, SKJ

Zanibon, Editore G. EGZ

Zeitschrift für Hausmusik (jl.) Zeit. f. Hausmusik

Zeitschrift für Instrumentenbau (jl.) ZfI, ZfIb, ZI

Zeitschrift für Musik (jl.) Zeit f. Musik, ZfM, ZFM, ZM

Zeitschrift für Musiktheorie (jl.) Z.f.MTH, Zf Mus Theorie, ZfMth, ZMtheorie

Zeitschrift für Musikwissenschaft (jl.) ZfMw, ZFMW, ZMw, ZMW

Zenei Lexikon ZL

Zimmerman, Franklin B. *Henry Purcell: An Analytical Catalogue of His Music* Z.

Zrodla do historii muzyki polskiej ZHMP

Zupfinstrumente (G=plectral instruments) Zupfinstr.

Zweistimmig (G=two-part) zweist.

Zwiazek Kompozytorow Polskich ZKP

Zyklisch (G=cyclic) zykl.

ABOUT THE AUTHOR

Donald L. Hixon (M.A., Music; M.S.L.S., Library and Information Science) is Fine Arts Librarian Emeritus from the University of California, Irvine, where for twenty years he was responsible for collection development and catalog maintenance for music, art, dance, and theater. As bibliographer, indexer, and editor, he has published numerous monographs, chiefly in the area of music bibliography. Hixon also is an independent piano and theory instructor in the Coachella and Temecula Valley regions of Southern California.